"[Tramble's] sure sense of structure, keen knowledge of male behavior and exquisite sense of pacing all contribute to this novel's overall excellence. I read it fast, and I was sorry when the last page appeared."

—*The Washington Post Book World*

"What stands out is Tramble's ability to convincingly write from the perspective of a young black male. There are twists interesting enough to keep readers wondering and reading. . . . *The Dying Ground* is a book overall about family, destiny and how life choices affect the community more than the individual."

—*Black Issues Book Review*

"*The Dying Ground* weaves a complex tale of love and loyalty against a fascinating backdrop of gangster intrigue and mystery."　　　　—*The Clarion-Ledger*

Praise for **THE LAST KING**

"Tramble proves that she is in line to become one of the greats. . . . Tramble is a hell of a writer with an ear for the spoken word. And she can go hard-boiled with the best of them. . . . With *The Last King*, Tramble catapults to the upper echelon of crime noir."

—*People* magazine (four stars)

"Nichelle Tramble's second book about the danger and sad futility of black street life in Oakland is colder and tougher than her first. . . . Tramble knows how to capture a damaged soul in an instant. . . . Tramble's dialogue is pure poetry, as good as anything in her first book."

—*Chicago Tribune*

"In Nichelle D. Tramble's beautifully written *The Last King*, the streets of Oakland seethe with violence so volatile that the pages practically crackle. The book's evocative atmosphere, realistic dialogue and poignant hopelessness make for some powerful reading. . . . Writing this good doesn't come along often."

—*The Kansas City Star*

"Tramble's tale peels back the layers of a community and exposes the vulnerabilities of black men fighting to survive and preparing to die."   —*The Columbus Dispatch*

"Oakland usually is lost in San Francisco's shadow, but in this book, you get such a sense of Oakland. . . . Tramble does for Oakland what Walter Mosely does for Los Angeles, or what Patricia Cornwell did for Richmond."

—*NPR*

"Tramble offers a view of Oakland that doesn't appear enough in contemporary fiction, and she has a fine ear for dialogue."   —*San Francisco Chronicle*

"*The Last King* is a sensual tour de force of sports, solidarity, and homicide."   —*East Bay Express*

"In true Donald Goines fashion, Tramble tells her own story about loyalty and betrayal in the urban streets."

—*Booklist*

"Tramble shapes realistic people, finding the sympathetic aspects of even the most despicable characters. . . . [Her] at-times gritty approach to noir in *The Last King* is evocative of other top-ranking black mystery writers."

—South Florida *Sun Sentinel*

"The East Bay settings are evocative and accurate."

—*Pages*

Other books by Nichelle D. Tramble

The Last King

THE DYING GROUND

A NOVEL

Nichelle D. Tramble

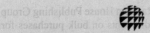

ONE WORLD
BALLANTINE BOOKS • NEW YORK

2006 One World Books Mass Market Edition

Published in the United States by One World Books, an imprint of The Random House Publishing Group, a division of Random House, Inc., New York.

ONE WORLD is a registered trademark and the One World colophon is a trademark of Random House, Inc.

Originally published in trade paperback in the United States by Villard, an imprint of The Random House Publishing Group, a division of Random House, Inc., in 2001.

ISBN 0-345-49482-2

Printed in the United States of America

www.oneworldbooks.net

OPM   9 8 7 6 5 4 3 2 1

To Daddy and Blaik,
angels I knew for a while,

and

Judy Faye Tramble,
my angel here on earth

It was the easiest never to leave home. Ghettos were created to hold their inhabitants inside, but their boundaries were a defense perimeter as well, a secured border within which people felt as if they *belonged*.

—Sylvester Monroe
Brothers

When you will survive if you fight quickly and
perish if you do not,
this is called the dying ground.

—Sun-Tzu
The Art of War

Every time I had a nightmare as a child, my attempts to retell the dream in the midnight hours were always met with the same hushed words: "Wait till morning. If you tell your nightmares before sunup, they might come true."

These words of my grandmother's were always whispered to soothe me, but instead they haunted me for years. It scared me to think I could give birth to the images of death I met in the middle of the night.

I was born in death when my father decided to celebrate my arrival with a lethal drug treat for my mother. A suicidal combination of cocaine and heroin. He survived and she didn't, and I've continued to relive her death ever since. In most of my dreams I follow her, not as the infant I was when she died but as a grown man. She doesn't recognize me when we meet, and that is what frightens me the most.

I've been visited by death every four years since my first days on this earth. I've grown so accustomed to mourning that funerals are rituals to me much like Christmas and Easter.

On my fourth birthday my father followed my mother to the grave. He was a man my family hated even beyond and through his rehabilitation, so I never had the chance to meet him while he was living. Since then we've become acquainted in the middle of the night. His visits are always followed by another death, and I've grown to hate the sight of him.

I dreamt about him just yesterday and I've been holding my breath for what's to come. For the first time in years I tried to tell my grandmother of this fear. All she said was, "Nothing good ever happens at the back of midnight, baby. Don't give those thoughts a reason to live."

But they're already on their way, and this time it's murder.

A murder two hours on the backside of midnight with a single bullet to the head.

CHAPTER 1

"Well, if it ain't little bitty Maceo Albert Bouchaund
Redfield! That name so tall the boy got to walk up under
it and say excuse me every day of his natural-born life."

The crowded barbershop broke into laughter as Cutty
greeted me with a variation of the same put-down he'd
been using for over sixteen years. The fact is that at five
feet five inches I barely reach the first letter of my six-
foot-tall name.

"How short are you exactly, Maceo?" This came from
a balding contemporary of my Grandfather Albert.

"I'm tall as I need to be," I answered.

I eased into the shop, taking note of the old and young
faces waiting in the unusually relentless heat of October.

"And how tall is 'need to be'?" Cutty grinned my way.

Cutty had been my barber since my seventh birthday,
and habit kept me a customer despite the insulting
words. The barbershop was one place in Oakland that
provided shelter if needed and contributed order to an
often chaotic life.

More simply, it was home.

Cutty was as invested in me as a blood relative. Alongside his prized Oakland A's paraphernalia, snapshots of
local celebrities, and barber's license was a photographic
history of my baseball career from Pee Wee League
through high school. Up until the ninth grade, all my

uniforms bore the red-and-white logo of Cutty's salon, Crowning Glory. The pictures were his way of staking a claim before I hit the majors.

"You didn't answer my question. How tall is 'need to be'?"

A waiting customer piped up with his opinion. "I say he's four ten and a half on a good day."

The ensuing laughter reminded me that people often see my height as a flaw. It has been a source of ridicule since I was a young boy, but to me my size is a day-to-day reminder—a reminder to keep life compact and close to the vest. The few times I've reached for the height of others I've been knocked back into place. So I've learned to live as a little man with a big name. And I've learned to smile at the jokes.

"Five foot." Another barber.

And Cutty: "Shit, Maceo ain't seen hide nor hair of five feet." He raised his natural comb to his mouth to think for a moment. "No, I take that back. Maceo was about seven feet tall when he was winning all those championships." And just like that the jokes about my height switched to praise for my baseball career.

I was used to that too.

Cutty picked up a portable fan and held it in front of his face. "Damn, feels like Africa outside."

Oliver, Cutty's partner, rolled his eyes. "What you know about Africa? You barely left Oakland in thirty years!"

"Shit, I know plenty 'bout Africa. I find out all I need to know 'bout Africa every time I go to East Oakland." It was an old joke that never failed to hit its mark.

The bonus October heat had sent everyone out into the streets in pursuit of any company to be had, and the sense of camaraderie and fun among the patrons kept the mood light. Along the curb a few waiting customers sat perched on the hoods of their cars, smoking cigarettes or reading newspapers. A few of the youngstas, unschooled in Cutty's bullet-ridden history, masked shady business deals behind the steady *bump-bump* of rap music.

Crowning Glory, Cutty's shop of thirty years, sat on the Oakland side of San Pablo Avenue, a dirty artery that ran from Oakland's city center all the way through six cities. It was his fifth location since incorporation. Initially his shop had been on Alcatraz Avenue, the Oakland street so named for its clear-day view of the famed Alcatraz Island. It was there, when I was seven, that my granddaddy took me for my first haircut.

When business picked up enough for Cutty to leave Alcatraz, his bad luck began in earnest. His new location on MacArthur and Broadway attracted all the hustlers and Superfly wannabes of the 1970s. Though Cutty hated to compromise his profession, he built his reputation on the mean, slick perms so favored by that generation. And as his reputation grew so did his clientele until finally, inevitably, a crosstown gangster rivalry was played out in his barber chairs.

The first casualty of Crowning Glory was Scott Hathaway, a heroin dealer with control of North, East, and West Oakland. He was slaughtered by an up-and-coming drug dealer named Jordy Prescott.

Legend has it that Hathaway's look of surprise was driven off his face by a bullet through his right eye. A quick nosedive in business confirmed that most people believed Cutty helped set up the flamboyant Hathaway. Only a new location on Shattuck Avenue and a year's worth of time brought people slowly but surely back into his shop.

The next move was caused by a retaliation shooting that occurred three blocks away, but Cutty took no chances. Before moving into the dusty San Pablo storefront, he had the property baptized by a local preacher, he installed church pews instead of seats for the waiting customers, and there hadn't been a murder since. But sometimes, through the ever-ready smile, I suspected that a cutthroat heart beat in the old man's chest. That much bad luck in one place made anybody suspect.

Memories were short, however; the boys dealing on the curb proved it. The eighties had brought a fast and furious new industry into Oakland, the crack trade, and there was evidence of it everywhere you looked.

The circus atmosphere of the drug game seeped into every aspect of urban Black life. Nothing went untouched as newfound wealth allowed men, women, and children to dream of something different. To the older cats, Michael Corleone and the crew of *The Godfather* supplied the props to let them dream in an elegant manner and jump the class barriers of their birth. But the rules and regulations of *The Godfather* became old to the youngstas even before the credits rolled. They had no time for rituals and order, just time enough to shove a big-ass foot through a door and demand the respect only a loaded gun and lots of money could bring.

Scarface was their manifesto.

It was a mess, but more seductive than anything we'd ever seen.

In 1989, the entire Bay Area, San Francisco included, fell under the 415 area code, and under that name a prison gang became a strong independent faction within the penitentiary system, eventually edging out the stronghold of the Black Guerrilla Family and keeping the Los Angeles Crips and Bloods from infiltrating the northern California crime force. The Bay Area was proud of its No Crips, No Bloods policy, but once in a while small pockets of transplanted criminals made their way into the fray, usually by way of family members, more often than not by way of good-looking women.

All that added to the big-man-on-campus swagger of the young men gathered here and there in front of

Cutty's. Fellas who, a mere two years before, never rated second glances now had all the props of true hustlers, and they used every opportunity possible to flaunt them. I rode the wave as a person on the edge of the inner circle, aware all the time that the Wizard was just inside the curtain. Anyone who looked closely knew the center would not hold; the smoke and mirrors would disappear and reveal a body count to equal a homegrown war.

The unseasonable warmth pumped the festivities to a fever pitch, and all I could do was watch. The heat had an entirely different effect on my spirits. While the others laughed and joked and made plans to hit Geoffrey's, Politics, and the End Zone, I waited for what was to come.

The 90-degree temperature just weeks before Halloween threw off my alignment. It felt unnatural to my blood and, coupled with the bad dreams, left me coiled like a snake for the first sign of bad news. It was coming, I just didn't know how or when.

CHAPTER

2

In an attempt to keep cool inside and out, I grabbed a crisp white towel from a broken chair and wiped the sweat pooled on my neck and shoulders. The chair had been broken for as long as I could remember.

Cutty was superstitious to a fault, hailing from the same folklorish state as my grandparents—Louisiana—and he took all minor omens and signs as the gospel. He refused to remove any of the furniture that had been there since he opened for business, and as a result his place looked more like a flea market than a barbershop.

"Man, Cutty, when you gonna fix this chair?" the man next to me asked.

"Soon as you mama come over here with her tool belt."

I winced for the victim. Everything and everybody, no matter how sacred, was fair game. Entering Cutty's meant donning a thick skin and readying a sharp tongue of your own.

Cutty pointed at me when he spotted the towel in my hand. "Boy, what's wrong with you, wiping your greasy face with my clean towels? Grab you some tissue paper."

"I might lose my place in line," I countered.

"That ain't got nothing to do with me," he shot back.

"All right, all right."

"How's the pitching arm?" Cutty continued. "You had some good stats year before last."

"I remember that." A man about my age turned to give me a quick pound of his fist. The gesture was the surest sign of respect Oakland had to offer. "You're the Watch Dog."

I nodded in affirmation, but I was reluctant to resurrect an old past through conversation. Watch Dog is the nickname I received while pitching for the St. Mary's High School baseball team. My habits before each pitch earned me the title and a bit of local notoriety, but it's been at least a year since I've even picked up a ball. An injury plus cowardice saved me the disappointments of being second string on my collegiate team. But since Oakland is such a small town I am constantly reminded of my much-copied pitching style.

During sophomore year I developed the habit that would become my signature on the field. I would study my surroundings down to the last detail before releasing a pitch. While the ball rested in my hand I would take in the batters, the opposing players, my teammates, the fans, the coaches, the vendors, the announcer, and the scouts, and if there happened to be birds and dogs in the park I studied them too. I'd take it all in, then wait for that perfect moment when the air and the elements sang in unison.

Strike!

Every time.

That long prep dismantled a lot of batters and secured me a place on four all-star teams. The waiting, the patience, the timing; those were the keys to my success on the field.

In life I try and apply the same rules. If given the chance I'll chose silence every time, listening instead to what the talkers *don't* say, what they avoid, what their hands, legs, and arms add to the conversation. The body is always closer to the truth than the mouth, and I've come to trust silence the way others avoid it. This practice, like smiling at jokes, has served me well and kept me out of trouble.

"I was at Bishop O'Dowd when you were pitching for St. Mary's. You took the championship from us. Three times." He stuck his hand out. "Lamont Quailes."

"Maceo Redfield."

"I remember. I remember. You use to kick it with my cousin Billy. Y'all was hella tight back in the day. Matter fact, I was with Billy when I saw you last."

I took a closer look at him and smiled. "Monty! Man, wassup? I didn't know you played ball."

"I mostly rode the bench. Too many superstars for me to play, but they wasn't tough enough to face you." He pointed across the room to one of the Little League pictures. "Remember that? They couldn't even touch you way back when."

The picture in question happened to be my favorite, one I kept on a wall at home. In it I'm in the front row of a winning team, game ball at my feet, my two best friends—Jonathan Ford and Billy Crane—on either side. The photo captured a peace that no longer existed among the three of us. The years managed to drive a wedge through our friendship, a gulf further widened by women, an unhealthy rivalry between Billy and Jonathan, and the complexities of time and age. For a couple of years, though, the lines of our friendship were simple and clear. Me, the natural mediator smiling easily in the center, four inches shorter but the definitive link between them both.

Monty gave me another pound and a wider smile, then looked me up and down, noting my Negro League baseball jersey, vintage original from my grandfather's closet.

My stomach clenched for what was to come.

"You still play?" he asked.

"Naw. I was at Cal for a minute but that didn't work out." I didn't want to discuss my injury or the player who relegated me to relief pitcher.

"You know why, don't you?" Cutty intervened to fill in the gaps. "Cal recruited an Asian cat from southern California with an arm that's something else."

The man turned back to me for details but Oliver chose that moment to announce the Daily Double. I was grateful. It was more than just the Asian recruit that kept me from the UC Berkeley team. It was also a rebellious arm, playing fast and loose with tuition money, and a penchant for quitting that I have yet to shake. My athletic scholarship was revoked after I hurt my arm and dropped below the required twelve units—a weak excuse to former fans and a weaker excuse to myself.

"Hey there, Maceo. You think we gonna have us a Bay Bridge Classic?" The Bay Bridge Classic was what the locals had taken to calling the possible 1989 World Series matchup between the Oakland A's and the San Francisco Giants. The competition between the two cities was legendary, held up because the fairy-tale city across the bay viewed Oakland as a ringwormy poor relation.

Oliver chimed in. "Not if they keep playing like they did today. Toronto beat the green and yellow off of 'em. Seven to three. That's a damn shame."

I pulled off my A's cap and waved it in the air. "Just give 'em a minute. They're going to the Series, ain't no doubt about that."

Oliver looked skeptical. "We'll see."

"Shoot, we thought you was gonna pitch your way right into the A's camp," Cutty said. "Vida Blue, Catfish Hunter, Maceo Redfield. Got kinda nice ring to it."

"Don't forget Rollie Fingers." A graying old man walked in the door and entered the conversation like he'd been there from the beginning.

Cutty waved to him. "Them boys had some names, didn't they?"

The old man sat down. "Oakland was the place back then, I'll tell you that. The A's going back to back to back, '72, '73, and '74, while the Raiders ran roughshod over everybody."

To many Oaktown residents the Raiders' departure had marshaled in a decade of decline that refused to let up, but diehard fans kept the faith that one day the silver and black would find their way home and restore the city to its former glory. Even Cutty kept the candle burning with a black poster that shouted Al Davis's famous words of inspiration in flaking silver letters: JUST WIN, BABY!

When the Raiders abandoned ship in 1982, it was like taking a big careless bite from an already rotting apple: a stingy gesture, and a precursor to the upcoming havoc of the Reagan eighties, crack, and the continued decline of inner cities. As factories closed, jobs went south, and blue-collar slid quickly into no-collar, Al Davis showed his ass in Technicolor by mooning a city that was devoutly faithful to the silver-and-black pirate logo. Oakland residents responded in kind to Davis's disrespect. Seemingly overnight, bold billboards and bumper stickers populated the Bay with a simple, heartfelt message: THANKS, AL DAVIS. YOU SON OF A BITCH!

I loved it; it gave me my first real taste of pride in the outlaw style of my hometown.

"Boy, the Raiders had some rednecks, didn't they?" the old man continued, with undisguised pride in his voice. "Tough white boys, just kickin' ass everywhere." He shook his head. "They don't make 'em like that no more."

"Right, right. You got a point, Lester." Cutty smiled. "You still write Davis them hate letters?"

Lester grinned. "Aw, naw, the FBI told me to cut that shit out." I had to belly-laugh and so did half the shop. Cutty laughed the hardest until he remembered the remains of my bloodied carcass.

"Any chance me and your granddaddy gonna see you out on the field before we die?" he asked.

"Shee-it," Oliver interjected. "Dave Stewart ain't giving up his spot for nobody, Black, White, or Puerto Rican. Hear what I'm saying?"

"That's true. Then there's always the added expense of the platform cleats they have to order for Maceo." The laughter wasn't as hearty the third time around, simply because it was time for fresh meat.

Oliver reached for the remote control, and all eyes turned to the television set suspended above the shampoo bowls. In addition to the grooming services of the salon, Cutty also ran what he called a "sporting establishment."

"Show time!" We all watched the television screen as a string of Thoroughbreds stepped onto Bay Meadows racetrack in preparation for the opening race.

"All bets in, gentlemen," Oliver announced, from the front of the shop.

On his cue the gathered men stood up, marked their seats with personal items, and placed crumpled bills inside an empty fish tank.

"Check out that specimen there. Number nine. Pharaoh's Jewels. Have you ever seen horseflesh that pretty?" Oliver gazed in admiration at the favored horse.

"Those ponies ain't got nothing on Maceo's aunties. When I was coming up we called 'em Redbone Redfield Racehorses. Fine, fine, fine, every last one of 'em." Cutty licked his lips in admiration. "Hotbloods!"

The gamblers in the room chuckled at the racetrack term for Thoroughbred horses. I was used to the litany about my hard-living, hard-loving aunties, so I just smiled. The men on the streets knew them as the good-looking, hard-drinking party girls they were, but to me all five of them were my mother, my own mother, the third daughter out of six, having died of a drug overdose the day after my birth.

"Which one is your favorite?" Cutty paused to wait for Oliver's answer.

Oliver considered for a moment. "The double whammy! Them twins, Josephine and Cornelia.

"Here we go!" Oliver's yell cut through the banter. "Devil's Folly!" He pointed toward the screen as a long shot crossed the finish line, a horse with a name to match my sense of doom.

"Who woulda thought." He quickly scanned the list to see the lone name next to that of the winning horse. He looked my way. "Well, I'll be damned. Somebody actually picked that old hag. The purse goes to Maceo . . ."

". . . Albert Bouchaund Redfield the First," Cutty finished. "What's the total?"

Oliver flipped through the crumpled bills. "Ninety dollars . . ."

". . . and a free haircut," I chimed in, "and a jump to the head of this line."

Before he could answer, the doorbell announced a new customer. I was surprised to see my best friend, Holly, stroll through the front door—surprised since he considered Cutty's to be the birthplace of bad luck.

Holly's feminine name masked the wild-hearted boy I'd known since second grade. His real name was Jonathan Ford, but he was nicknamed, thus named according to the streets, for the East Oakland neighborhood where he was raised: Seventy-ninth and Holly, referred to as the Kill Zone even by Oakland's young mayor, technically the 34th District and a plague to the police department.

At the age of seven, Jonathan saw a fleeting image of nearby Berkeley on the local news. He liked the tree-lined streets, the students walking down Telegraph Avenue, and the cleanliness. Simple as that, he decided Berkeley was where he wanted to live.

He walked to East Fourteenth and caught the first bus he saw. Pure luck had it headed to downtown Oakland, the point of exchange for many city routes. The 43 was the first bus to happen along and Jonathan climbed on. He jumped off at a park when he spotted a group of young boys playing bases. At that time Bushrod Park was second home to a ragtag crew of running buddies, led by myself and Billy Crane, my partner in crime since I'd learned to pick my own friends. It was at least a mile shy of the Berkeley border, but Billy and I welcomed him as a new kid in the neighborhood, and he let us believe that story. It was an entire week before we realized he was a stray, but by that time the three of us had melted into a trio. He was newly christened Holly and became a permanent resident in my Dover Street household. My grandparents, able to recognize need when they saw it, welcomed him with open arms.

He became an honorary Redfield so quickly that many

people forgot we weren't brothers, though we looked nothing alike. He lived in a long, lean frame and had the sharp, wolfy features of his own uncles. Even way back then he favored the simplicity of two colors, black or beige, and he mastered the art of girls years before I could even stumble through introductions.

In a flat-out foot race regarding women I came in dead last to Holly and Billy, but that meant nothing until it meant everything, and Billy drifted away little by little while Holly remained family.

He was included and loved by my granddaddy until he was seen, at the age of seventeen, with a telltale wad of money in his hand. My word-stingy grandfather didn't preach or yell. He simply looked at the roll of hundreds and said, "Looks like you got enough money to live on your own." Holly moved out that night, too sensible to take it personally.

Holly's foray into the drug game came after Billy's and escalated once he moved out, but it never affected my love or loyalty to him. He chose his path, and I chose mine. And as he graduated through the ranks of his chosen profession, I entered my first year at UC Berkeley. We continued to navigate each other's worlds with the confidence and ease of best friends who were really brothers. There was no place he couldn't go with me, and I knew he believed the same.

As Holly entered Cutty's, he lifted his chin in the silent Oakland greeting. I returned the salute and registered the shell-shocked look in his eye that years of friendship helped me recognize.

He looked at me across the crowded shop. "Man, Maceo." His voice broke. "Billy's dead, man. Somebody killed Billy Crane last night."

"Where's Flea?" I asked, not hearing the panic in my words.

CHAPTER 3

The year 1989 was already shaping into a paranoid's wet dream. Some doomsayers claimed that the world was racing toward its conclusion by way of Tiananmen Square, the Alaskan oil spill, AIDS, George Bush, Manuel Noriega, Howard Beach, and, in some corners, New Kids on the Block. But for me it was simply hearing Holly say that Billy was dead.

Billy had stopped being family long ago, at least by the strict definitions of friendship, but we were still related through the streets and memories, through people we loved and hated and a community smaller than either of us ever realized.

Billy was a drug dealer by trade but much more than those two words could describe. He strictly adhered to an honor-among-thieves code that had faded fast in the gangsta rap eighties. The creed "Vengeance is mine" had nothing to do with Billy or his way of doing business.

His legend was born when he was robbed after a drug deal with a new customer named Clarence Mann, a frowning, serious-minded dealer from San Francisco's notorious Hunters Point. Mann gave Billy forty thousand dollars toward a purchase of cocaine. Billy left to pick up the product, promising to return within twenty minutes.

On his way back to the meeting place, Billy was accosted at a stoplight by four hooded men. He was not harmed, but they got away with Billy's money and an equal amount of narcotic. The obvious suspect was Mann, but Billy never voiced that thought. And while the unwritten rule of the street excused Billy the debt, he paid Mann's forty thousand dollars out of his own money.

His reputation was made by that one act. There wasn't a dealer in the Bay who would gain a thing by double-crossing the old schooler. The resulting enemies would run too deep to ever make a profit.

So, now, news of Billy's death telegraphed the very real possibility of a street war; the deafening silence in the shop legitimized the fact. We all knew the town would divide into camps, either for or against the killers, and the vast drug territory that fell under Billy's jurisdiction was up for grabs the moment steel met flesh.

I tried to walk toward Holly, but I couldn't move. The news froze me in place. The doomsayers could scream all they wanted about an apocalypse, but closer to home the chaos of 1989 manifested itself to me in Billy's murder. It also propelled Oakland into the big time. With his death we shot past our own personal best of 146 killings. In a year not yet over, Billy was the tie-breaker that guaranteed us the same notoriety as New York, Miami, and D.C.

Monty stepped in front of me, blocking my view of the door. "What happened? What you mean, he's dead?"

"Just what was said. Somebody blew the mother-fucker's brains out."

I couldn't see the door, but I immediately recognized the voice.

Orlando "Smokey" Baines stood behind Holly, grinning and savoring the news of Billy's demise. He looked like a coal mountain, six five, a solid three hundred and twenty pounds constantly stuffed into green tailored suits, sloe-eyed, with gold hoops in each ear and the canines missing on either side of his mouth.

He wore his size well after years of high school and college football, but his career had been cut short at blond blue-eyed Arizona State after too much hand-to-hand combat with women a third his size. Rumors persisted that he still hadn't mastered that nasty habit. In short, Smokey was a goon, and there were few people who welcomed his company on this or that side of the grave.

It was a crime to hear of Billy's death in his presence.

Smokey inched forward and blocked out all the customers gathered at the door, clamoring for any news Holly had to offer.

"I heard the same thang myself." Smokey ran his hand over his goatee, barely suppressing the grin at his lips. He made a pistol with his diamond-clad right hand. "Pow!"

I saw Monty shaking in agony. Fury raced through his body, but it would take every man in the shop to save him from Smokey if he decided to make a stupid move.

"Man, shut the fuck up." Holly turned to Smokey with pure anger replacing the white in his eyes. Holly's odds, one on one, were about as bad as Monty's, but Holly had always loved the edge and the charge of danger.

"Oh, you wanna get bad, huh? Act all upset. You should be upset. You was the one talking all that ying-yang about hooking Billy up with Mexicans." Smokey paused effectively, then grinned. "What? Didn't think I knew?"

Holly's stance was still aggressive but Smokey's knowledge of his business plans had taken the air out of his menace. Smokey's words were true. Holly had been the first to approach Billy about moving toward Mexico, but their styles and beliefs, and Billy's refusal to take the backseat, had killed the deal at its inception. No one knew that but us—or so we had thought.

"Man, what happened?" Monty's voice was a plea.

Smokey spit at his feet. "Yeah, tell this whining bitch something before I knock him out."

"Why you bringing all that drama in here? Speaking ill of the dead." Cutty gripped a natural comb in both hands.

"Old man, please," Smokey responded.

"Old man nothing! This is my place of business!"

Smokey laughed at him and took measure around the room. Very few people met his eye. He smirked. "Oh, it's like that, huh? Just like that." He snapped a finger. "Billy a kingpin, up there with Felix Mitchell, Nicky Barnes, and all them. Don't work for me, but y'all can spread your ass cheeks if you want to.

"Billy was steadily shutting people down. He had every corner of this town sewed up. Couldn't nobody make a move or get near his connection, but now y'all gonna sit here and make him a hero.

"I ain't gonna front now and act like he was my ace. Didn't like him yesterday. Don't like him today."

"Now ain't the time, Smokey." Monty tried edging toward the door. Smokey stopped him with a hand on his shoulder.

"Your boy thought he was better than people." He tried to mimic Billy's sleepy speech pattern and his strict work ethic. "Won't sell to pregnant women, won't come off no rock to get my dick sucked, ain't selling to people wit' kids in the car. All that. Bullshit. He was selling cocaine. Crack! He wadn't no better than the next nigga."

Before Smokey finished his speech, Monty had muscled his way blindly out the front door.

"Where's Flea? Is Flea dead?" My own voice sounded like it belonged to someone else.

"I ain't heard nothing about Flea." Holly flicked his

eyes toward Smokey in warning but I couldn't stop myself.

"Nothing?" I asked again.

"Oh, that's right. You had a jones for Billy's girl." Smokey threw his head back and laughed.

Holly ignored the disrespect. "All I know, Billy was at a stoplight on Alcatraz and College. Somebody shot him in the head. They found him slumped over the steering wheel. He had his pistol, money, and gold on 'im—everything."

"Then it wasn't a jack?"

Holly shook his head as patrons rushed from the shop, shocked by the news, feeling the old tentacles of Cutty's curse.

Cutty spoke up as his shop bled customers. "What you talkin' 'bout, youngblood? Where you hear this?"

"Just heard it."

I grabbed my cap, forgetting my winnings and everything else as I rushed toward the door.

"I gotta find Flea."

CHAPTER

4

Felicia Bennett, affectionately called Flea by all who knew her, was a close friend and the love of my short life. She arrived at Cal my sophomore year, and I hadn't been the same since. The first time I saw her I was gathered with a group of friends from the baseball team. Despite my sporadic appearances in the dugout, I had made good friends among the players.

A few of us were perched on the steps in front of Sproul Hall checking out the incoming freshmen and hoping to see her. News of Felicia's arrival from Los Angeles had spread through the male community like wildfire. I had been told about her so many times I knew every detail of her physical appearance before we even met. Despite that, I was not prepared for the flesh and blood.

I had my head down reading the sports page when a hush fell over our group. I looked up just as she passed and that was all I needed. Before the others could gauge the here and there of Felicia Bennett, I knew her. I knew her 'cause I'd been waiting on her since my first hour of puberty.

When I glanced up she looked my way, winked one time, and kept striding. I looked behind me, so did my boys, and just that quick she slipped past us all. We broke out laughing, each and every one of us. The laugh was spontaneous; it felt good, and it let us all know—she spoke directly to our egos—that despite the package she was all right. She didn't take herself too seriously. Once we knew that, she broke about seven hearts all at once.

She was in my first class, African-American Literature, filled to the gills with a racially mixed bag of students. She came in late, after the seats were chosen, and ten men cursed themselves for not having one to offer. I was not one of them. She slid into a chair beside me and placed a stick of gum on my open book. She popped hers in big loud ghetto smacks and pulled a notebook from her bag. I unwrapped the gum and slid it into my mouth just as the professor entered the room.

Harry Livingston, a burly Black man and former proballer with a penchant for the written word, was a larger-than-life campus figure. His sound bites peppered the local news like weather reports, while his *Oakland Tribune* and *Daily Cal* editorials covered everything from tuition to the exploitation of Black athletes. His devotion to his students, his community, and his race were legendary.

As Livingston made his introductions I watched Felicia from the corner of my eye. There was no getting around her beauty. At five feet ten inches she stood about five inches taller than me, with shoulder-length jet-black hair, parted in the middle and cut to precision. She was deep brown more than she was dark, and her eyebrows turned down toward her nose, which gave her a sexy, devilish appearance. She had small features, almost pointy, but that didn't do justice to how delicate she looked. She had a faint mustache that in all the time I knew her she never bothered to destroy.

She was wearing navy plaid shorts, a white sleeveless sweater, and navy boat shoes with white laces. She stretched her long legs out in front of her, kicking off her shoes in the middle of Livingston's lecture. Her toenails were painted a bright red, and on both feet her second toe rested on the big one. It looked like her toes were poised to snap to a beat, and I liked her casual acceptance of what others might have viewed as a flaw.

She wore a gold bracelet on her ankle and an upside-down question mark tattooed just below it. I couldn't think of a single thing to add, and neither could God.

Once the lecture was over, I followed her out of the classroom. "What's your name?" I asked her.

She stretched before answering, emphasizing the height difference even further.

"Felicia." There was a California desert twang to her voice, unique to Los Angeles Blacks. She popped her gum. "You can call me Flea."

"Wassup, Flea?" I smiled but it wasn't derogatory. Her name fit.

"My brother Reggie couldn't pronounce Felicia when I was a baby. It came out Flea, and that's what it's been ever since."

"I'm Maceo Redfield."

"Dang!" She let a giggle escape. The name disarmed her, just as it disarmed most people. Like I said before, it's bigger than me. She sized me up, and I knew, since I'd seen my aunties do it, that she was trying to figure out if I was "home" or not. If I made that category I was destined to get the familiar "dang"s and "ain't"s and all the other "ing" words with the g dropped. I smiled, hoping she would drop the g's for the rest of my life. She did for a while. But even when the easy friendship moved into something deeper I never expected to keep her.

Felicia Bennett was too close to everything I wanted.

CHAPTER

5

Billy: dead. Felicia: missing.

None of the words made sense together, but the doom I'd expected announced itself. I felt iron in my mouth, like I'd gargled with pennies, a taste like blood, a bitter taste that always followed bad news. I grabbed another one of Cutty's towels and covered my eyes to keep myself from reeling.

"What, is this fool about to cry?" Smokey sneered.

In a quick flick of my pitching arm I responded to Smokey's disrespectful mouth by snapping the towel. The whip reflex sizzled in the air and stopped dangerously close to his left eye. The gesture was quick, thoughtless, and fueled by anger mixed with grief. Smokey's grinning theatrics had broken through my usual calm.

All hell broke loose.

Behind me I could hear the scrape of chairs and a scattering of feet as customers broke for the back room. A few even braved a sprint for the door.

In a swiftness that belied his size, Smokey charged forward with every intention of snapping my neck.

Holly met his speed. He moved in front and smashed Smokey in the throat, doubling him over as he gasped for air. Before Smokey could reach around to grab the gun in his waistband, Holly snatched the towel from my hand and removed it. I could feel the heat and energy radiating from his body. There was no mistaking the gleam in his eye at the prospect of violence, at the idea of silencing Smokey once and for all.

Holly unleashed a devilish smile, moving like a prizefighter. Smokey rose up and managed enough saliva to spit at Holly's feet. He would take a bullet before being punked into submission.

Holly leveled the towel-covered gun at Smokey. Anger. Chaos. Fear. Holly still thought fast enough to eliminate the possibility of fingerprints.

He waved the gun close to Smokey's right eye. "I'ma keep this."

"One shot's all you get, nigga," Smokey answered.

"All I need."

The cock of another gun silenced them both.

Cutty stood within kissing distance of Smokey, the barrel of his gun resting calmly at Smokey's temple. The jovial old man was nowhere in sight. He had been replaced by the cutthroat who had survived numerous gangsta regimes.

"Back on up and outta here." Cutty hit a floor alarm,

wired right to a security team, with the toe of his shoe. "Back up and don't ever bring ya' silly ass back in my shop."

Smokey held his hands in the air. "It's cool, old man, it's cool."

His eyes said anything but. They were plastered to Holly's face, marking time until one of us paid. I'd set in motion what Holly was willing to play to the end.

Smokey turned to me. "I always thought you was a punk; maybe some first-class pussy made you a man. Or maybe it got you hiding on street corners droppin' bullets in your old ace."

I ventured a response. "Or maybe you making all this noise 'cause you got something to hide. Your hands stand up to a powder test?"

He turned to Holly. "Tell your monkey to make sure he wants to play in this game."

"Cutty asked you to step," Holly responded.

Cutty hit the floor buzzer a second time. "And when the police come I'ma tell them exactly what happened, my way, show 'em the shop videotape if I have to, just in case you thinkin' about doing something stupid."

Smokey looked to Holly. "Now ain't the time . . . but it's coming."

"You know where to find me."

"Territory up for grabs. Winner take all." Smokey's words were a challenge, and everyone in earshot knew it. "Could that be the reason?" His mouth, as usual, placed us on the far side of danger. In the open air he added me and Holly to a suspect list that would travel from mouth to mouth.

I could hear the accusations swirling around me as people formed opinions and chose sides.

"Naw, Maceo," they would say. "You serious? Patna too square for that, but, you know, the man had it bad for Billy's girl.

"Shit, and Holly, Holly been a gangsta from way back and Billy made it hard for brothers to make a move without his permission." A disgusted shake of the head would follow. "Money and women always get in the way of big business."

I knew Holly heard the same rumblings in his own head. He spit at Smokey's feet. "Get at me, nigga."

"If you don't get got first."

CHAPTER

6

Smokey backed out, looking everyone carefully in the eye. I watched silently and noted who among the gathered men met Smokey's gaze. Holly waited until Smokey climbed into his white tricked-out Jaguar convertible before dropping the gun and towel into a paper bag shoved behind a mirror. Patrons eased around us, making their way out, already forming their own versions of our encounter.

Cutty sighed heavily. "Y'all need to clear on out of here."

Holly left without uttering a word. I hesitated before Cutty. I didn't know what to say, but he said it all. "I'm too old to move my business again." He dropped into a chair and looked around his vacant shop. Behind him in a faded photograph, the three of us—me, Holly, and Billy, dressed to conquer Little League—smiled into our futures.

* * *

"Smokey, that stupid motherfucker. He kicked this shit off sooner than necessary. There's enough folks out there willing to believe I did my boy." Holly looked out at the smoldering pavement.

I remained silent, my foot pressed to the floor as I gunned down San Pablo to Ashby Avenue in the city of Berkeley. I barely saw red, yellow, or green lights as I tried to pull down images of Billy or Felicia. None came. My mind wouldn't run the old movies through my wall of pain.

I was also troubled that I'd stepped over the line in a moment of anger. Despite my friendship with Holly and my insider's knowledge of the business, I'd managed for twenty-three years to stay free and clear behind the guise of baseball and family.

"Slow down, man," Holly warned.

Holly rode at my side as I raced my Dan Gurney special Cougar through a yellow stoplight. The car was my pride and joy, complete with a steering wheel that tilted to the side when I opened the driver door and original plates. It was black cherry, with gold Zenith wire rims and Vogue tires. The car cost $15,000, my entire four-year college tuition. I'd spent it in one shot, thinking in the back of my mind that my grandfather would cough up the money I needed for school after a long-winded lecture.

I was wrong.

He simply looked at the car, told me to hand-wash it with soft rags and get a job. My mouth dropped open in shock, but even then I respected the old man for being so hard-core.

That little break in enrollment came right on time. It was the same semester I learned about Stuart Tagami, a Japanese-American recruit from southern California's Mater Dei High School. At the sound of his name, the wind told me he had the power to unseat me. I eliminated the possibility before it happened. I quit.

I told my coach I wanted to concentrate on school, give baseball a rest for a year, and spend more time with my family. My heart told me the truth. I simply didn't have the balls to go up against Tagami.

Holly clutched the door handle as I hit the corner on two wheels. "Damn, man, you even know where the fuck you going?"

"I gotta find Flea."

"Nig, you know how many people looking for that girl? Billy's boys think she set him up."

I realized then he knew more than he'd revealed in the barbershop. Even in dire straits Holly thought with an ice-cold mind.

"How'd you know?"

"Word's already out. They're gonna kill her."

"Flea wouldn't set Billy up."

"Right now people are too mad to remember that. And the police found her purse in the passenger seat with one of her tennis shoes. She was in the car when Billy got shot. The passenger door was wide-open. She must've run."

"Are the police looking for her too?"

"Them fools don't know what they looking for. OPD and the Berkeley police stood on the corner fighting over his body. 'Parently he got shot right on the border and both cities was trying to claim him. Rookie shit."

"Who got it?"

"Oakland, but Berkeley was mad as hell 'cause it's a front-page murder. If you ask me I think they both gonna work it."

"How you know all that?"

Holly shrugged to indicate he'd plucked the information out of thin air. "Just heard it."

"But you haven't heard where Flea could've went."

"Nope."

I banged on the steering wheel. "Aw, man, Flea. Where you at, baby?"

"Why you trippin' that hard off that girl? She ain't been wit' you in months, and you still . . ." He shook his head. A frown punctuated his words.

I knew that whatever answer I gave him, I could never make him understand. I had ventured out and allowed myself to love Felicia, a girl I'd never expected to keep. Holly, on the other hand, found women as easily replaceable as clothes. "Replaceable" wasn't a word I could apply to Felicia. I didn't expect, even with the benefit of two lifetimes, to find anyone who could even come close to her.

"You think you gonna get her back if you find her?"

"I just wanna find her, man."

"Who you talking to? You ain't workin' this hard just to get a little handshake."

"Leave it alone." Holly's habitual cynicism was not the remedy for my problems. He never permitted himself the bright side of things, while I continually hoped the bright side would make sense of all the darkness.

I wheeled the car through a slightly yellow light and turned onto Chabot. An unmarked police car blocked the end of the street. Holly put his hand on the door when he spotted it. "Let me out at the corner. I'll catch you later."

I rolled to a stop and turned to him. "You know, Billy came to see me a couple months ago." For some reason I didn't tell him there had been another visit after that.

Holly looked surprised.

"It was right after he made Flea quit her job at the Nickel and Dime." My grandfather had given Felicia a part-time job as a cocktail waitress in his bar. Billy hadn't liked so many players, potential enemies, having such easy access to her, so he'd pulled the plug on her job immediately.

He never came right out and included me in the equation, but the unsaid spoke loud and clear. Despite Felicia's commitment and love for Billy, there was no getting around the connection she and I had between us. Only once after we'd broken up had it strayed into something more, a lonely night between us both, me missing her, her missing Billy. We didn't speak of it after it happened, and I never mentioned it to Holly, but Felicia saw it in my eyes whenever she looked at me.

Holly jumped out of the car. "I'll catch up with you later." He pointed at me. "Don't forget the package under the seat." I'd forgotten that Smokey's gun was stashed in the car.

"You think she coulda killed Billy?" I asked.

"Do you?"

"Flea ain't like that."

"But you don't know what she was into."

"I know her."

"All you know, nigga, is that she left you."

There was no response to that so I moved to safer ground: the confrontation with Smokey. Since childhood Holly was used to playing my savior. Once my athletic ability made me a local star, Holly and Billy took to protecting me from fights. "Gotta save the pitching arm" became the code phrase for getting me out of trouble, and without a second thought, or Billy for backup, Holly fell into his old routine.

"Man, I'm sorry about that shit back there," I offered.

"Don't trip, it's all part of being a hustler. It was gonna go down anyway."

Holly rarely apologized for the life he led, and he did not live in regret. He nodded, chin up to let me know we were cool, then continued, "And it ain't like I didn't know the rules."

CHAPTER

7

With Holly's words ringing in my ear I waited until he disappeared into the shopper traffic on College Avenue before continuing down the street. Flea's Victorian apartment house was at the end of the block, slightly detached from the others. I pulled up in front and looked to the attic window that served as her bedroom. She'd lived there since I'd known her, bypassing the dorms and their inherent lack of privacy. I killed the engine and waited, hopefully, for the flutter of curtains that would mean she was home. None came.

I pushed open the outside door and climbed the three flights of stairs to her top-floor apartment. The door was slightly ajar, so instinct made me avoid the squeaky board to the left. Through the sliver of space I could see a slick blue sport coat, shiny enough to indicate it belonged to law enforcement. I recognized the voice of Phillip Noone.

Noone had spent a good portion of his twenties in relentless pursuit of my Aunt Desiree. Desiree, the second oldest, was the least forgiving of her suitors' mistakes, and Noone had been the butt of many family jokes. He became a fixture in the front room of my grandparents' house, rising eagerly whenever one of them entered the room. Desiree would keep him cooling his heels for hours but he'd sit ramrod straight, feet pointed forward, until she made an entrance. His slow torture finally came to an end when Desiree abruptly relocated to New Orleans. I hadn't missed Noone's patronizing presence for a second.

"So, you're saying, Miss Fowler, that you haven't heard from your roommate since yesterday?"

Regina shook her head and wiped away tears. "Not since she left for class. She has classes all day on Fridays, and next week is midterms. But we usually talk a couple of times during the day."

"Were there any messages on the machine?"

"No."

"Has she been acting strange lately?"

"What do you mean?"

"Has she exhibited any unusual behavior?"

"She's just herself. She's just Flea."

"Okay." He took a deep breath to emphasize his impatience. "Are you sure about that?"

"Yes. She was fine."

"Had she been fighting with Billy?"

"They didn't really fight."

"How long were they together?"

"About a year and a half."

"And they didn't fight? Come on now, all couples fight."

"Not them. Flea likes to laugh and Billy"—her voice caught—"Billy was too low-key for that. That wasn't his style. They liked being together too much."

"Let's get this straight. This couple, one of whom was a known drug dealer—"

I knocked on the door and let myself inside. Noone looked truly surprised to see me. He was standing over Regina, who sat stiffly on the edge of the couch. He stood to his full height once I entered the apartment and locked his rictus smile in place. His left eye crinkled in the displeasure I recognized from the past.

Whenever I saw Noone I was always struck by the oddity

of his features. He had the thin lips usually assigned to blond stockbrokers. They had no give, little mirth, and lacked the volume usually paired with the wide nose and the kink at his temples. The mismatched mouth gave him the appearance of an incomplete plaster of Paris, the work of a thoughtless child who'd stopped mid-project to complete a more interesting task. Noone tried unsuccessfully to hide the mishap with a salt-and-pepper mustache and goatee but it didn't work. The pink-rimmed lips announced their inadequacies whenever he chose to speak.

"Maceo."

"Noone."

He looked at Regina. "You two know each other?"

"Maceo's a friend of Flea. She . . ." She paused and looked my way.

I finished the sentence for Regina. "Flea was my girlfriend for a minute."

"Is that right?" He turned from Regina and motioned me forward. "Why don't you have a seat?"

"I'm cool standing here." I kept my place near the open door.

"How's your aunt?"

"Which one?"

His eyes crinkled further. "Desiree."

"Fine from the way she tells it. She's still in N'Awlins." I pronounced it in the manner of my grandparents.

"That right? I never understood why she'd move to such a backward-ass state. Excuse my language, Miss Fowler."

Regina turned to me. "Mace, you seen Flea?"

I shook my head. Noone resumed the questions. "So, you haven't heard from Miss Bennett either?"

"Not in a couple of days."

"I see. You said you were dating for a while?"

"Yes."

"And you still keep in touch?"

"We're friends."

"And her new boyfriend, Billy Crane, didn't have a problem with that?"

"No reason to. Flea and I were just friends."

"Did you have a problem with that? With being just friends?"

The phone rang and Regina ran for it, startling us both. She snatched up the receiver on the second ring. "Hello, Flea?... Oh. No, she ain't here.... Yeah, I heard. No one's seen her. Look, let me call you back." She hung up the phone as a new batch of tears streamed down her face.

Noone closed his notebook and started for the door. He placed a card on the coffee table. "If either of you hear anything, give me a call." Noone nodded toward me. "Tell your aunt I said hello."

"A'ight." I mangled the word, recalling Noone's dislike of slang. The devil on my shoulder also made me remember his hatred of nicknames. "I'll tell her Half Past said hello."

He stopped in his tracks, the old nickname—bestowed by Desiree—causing his shoulders to clinch. Both of us shared the memory of Desiree's sneer of a greeting: "If it ain't old Half Past Noone."

"You remember that, huh?"

I nodded. He held my eye.

"Well, give her my best anyway." He disappeared out the door. Regina and I listened to the heavy tread of his boots on the stairs. She dropped into a chair by the window and watched him get into his car. She was crying softly, her head turned away in true grief. Both of us knew that the longer Flea stayed gone, slim was the chance of us ever seeing her again.

I watched Regina from across the room, trying to allow her a little privacy but staying close by. While her shoulders shook I noted for the hundredth time that

Regina was actually prettier than Flea. She just didn't have the same oomph, as my gra'mère called it, that something special that made a woman more than just a pretty face.

The biting Brooklyn sassiness that Regina parceled out to everyone else was absent when she dealt with Flea. They were soul mates, closer than sisters and fast friends from the moment they met. Flea always joked that Regina's Puerto Rican father and Bajan mother made her Black twice. The joke never failed to get a laugh out of Regina.

Regina initially disapproved of Flea's involvement with Billy, having lost her older brother to the cruelties of the New York City crack trade. Though she never stopped fearing for her friend she knew, like everyone who came in contact with them, that they were meant for each other. I knew it better than anyone.

When Flea first met Billy, she and I had been making our way through a damn near chaste relationship until my greediness caused their paths to cross.

About a week after making love to her for the first time, I took her with me to Cutty's to get a haircut and show her off. Crowning Glory wasn't the place for a woman, but I knew I'd get a year's worth of bragging rights off one visit.

I chose Saturday, a busy Saturday. When we arrived a silence fell over the shop, and I heard a few guttural heartfelt "damn"s. Flea, her long legs kissing the sky, wore a navy plaid tennis skirt, a crisp white shirt tied loosely at the waist, and a silver anklet with a butterfly charm I'd given her.

We took a seat in the last pew and the conversation returned to a low hum. I couldn't count all the sly glances thrown her way.

Billy walked in five minutes later. I nodded to him while Flea fiddled with the clasp on her anklet. She didn't see him at first, and when I replay it in my mind I wish that I'd never brought her there that day.

When she did look up at Billy, she shot straight up out of her seat. I reached out to grab the hem of her skirt but she dodged me with a flick of her hips. She stepped to the outside of the pew and looked right at Billy, daring him to believe he could do anything but look back. He stared her down. The rest of us watched, mesmerized by the electricity.

Billy looked my way and raised one eyebrow, slightly.

Cutty, in a wrenching act of kindness, said softly, "You might as well step on out the way, youngblood."

I looked at the two of them and knew he was right. There was nothing I could do. She was gone. I was already out of the picture. Out of the corner of my eye I saw a few heads drop in respectful acknowledgment of my loss.

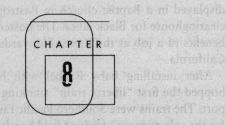

CHAPTER

8

Ghost town.

The nickname for West Oakland didn't come without its own truths. On every block there were remnants of the area's past life as "Harlem West." Seventh Street still housed the buildings of the Creole Club, the Swing Club, Harvey's Rex Club, and the world-famous Slim Jenkins's Place.

Harold "Slim" Jenkins was a Louisiana boy, like my granddaddy, who opened a club that would become the

West Coast anchor for Black entertainment and racially mixed crowds. Duke Ellington, Cab Calloway, Dinah Washington, and even Count Basie made stops in West Oakland, but those days were long gone. Once-prosperous Seventh Street was now like every other skid row across the country, the last stop on a train going nowhere. Despite the frayed edges, many old-timers refused to leave their homes and abandon what had saved them from the Jim Crow South. For most of Oakland's Black population, the rural South was a not-too-distant memory. They had deep roots in either Louisiana, Arkansas, or Texas.

My family was no exception. In 1940, the effects of the Depression were still being felt when smooth-talking recruiters set up shop in Southern churches, filling the minds, ears, and hearts of dust-covered congregations with dreams of the West Coast and endless California sunshine.

My grandfather still has the recruitment poster he saw displayed in a Baptist church in Bastrop, Louisiana, a clearinghouse for Black labor. The poster trumpeted the benefits of a job at the Kaiser Shipyards in Richmond, California.

After installing baby Rachel with his parents, he hopped the first "liberty train" smoking out of Shreveport. The trains were Southern Pacific railcars chartered for the sole purpose of taking field hands to a new plantation on the Pacific, a waterfront shipyard gearing up for another war.

He disembarked in West Oakland and watched in amazement as Blacks, Mexicans, Italians, Scots, Chinese, and Portuguese moved freely around one another on the sidewalks. He wandered the streets taking in the mom-and-pop shops that advertised "down home" meals, noted the men dressed from head to toe in tailored suits, and the shiny women they carried on their arms.

He stopped long enough to spot a sturdy-looking Black man in coveralls and a Kaiser baseball cap looking intently at a racing form. He tapped him on the shoulder. "Excuse me, sir." He pointed to the baseball cap. "I'm suppose to report there tomorrow, sunrise."

The man interrupted his speech, "If it ain't there then it's Moore Dry Dock or one of the canneries." He made a wide gesture to take in bustling Seventh Street. "Somehow or other, every one of these men tied to one a them places." He extended a hand. "Sherman Johnson."

Daddy Al took the strong hand in his, and a lifelong friendship was born. The two men would forge a bond that sometimes excluded the wives they adored and fostered a history of secret-keeping.

As I approached the A-frame house of Sherman's widow, Gloria Johnson, I spotted the two-tone Cadillac Uncle Sherman loved more than his life. Daddy Al had driven it, tears streaming down his face, through the streets of Ghost Town the day Sherman dropped from a heart attack. I often wondered how many of our family secrets went with him.

Sherman had been dead for over five years but Mrs. Johnson refused to get rid of the car that sat dead in the driveway. She even refused Daddy Al's offers to have it cleaned and tuned for her use. "That ain't necessary" was all she would say, so the car sat year after year with a desperate plea etched on the glass of the back window: WASH MY ASS!

"Mrs. Johnson, you home?" I stood on the porch knocking on the screen door. I could hear the television buzzing loudly inside but there was no sign of the old woman.

"Caesar? Hey, boy, you in there?" I called into the house. I could see the back end of the ancient hound that lived with Mrs. Johnson. He turned and growled without much enthusiasm.

"Hush up all that noise. You don't pay rent here."

I wasn't sure if she meant me or Caesar so I lowered my voice. "Mrs. Johnson, it's me, Maceo. Albert's grandson. I'm at the front door."

She appeared then, wizened and brown like a coconut with her hair pulled atop her head in a silver-and-white bun. The three-bedroom house she called home was one of several properties owned by my grandparents. Daddy Al had a total of fifteen rentals throughout Oakland and two in Berkeley. Most of his tenants were older people, friends from Louisiana and Arkansas or coworkers from his days as foreman at the Del Monte Cannery after he left Kaiser.

Mrs. Johnson lived in the house for a mere forty dollars a month, a price she insisted was too low and Daddy Al thought was way too high. Mrs. Johnson and Daddy Al had a ritual about the rent that they performed without fail. Every month on the first Daddy Al would arrive to collect Mrs. Johnson's rent. She'd invite him inside to chat a little while about Gra'mère, the aunties, my slow progress through school, and my grandfather's furniture-building hobby.

After their catch-up talk she'd give him a bag of her garden vegetables to take home to Gra'mère. Then she'd let him get as far as the door before she'd say, "Don't forget that envelope on the table."

And there it would be, a sealed envelope with two crisp twenty-dollar bills inside and *Albert Redfield* scrawled across the front. Daddy Al would pick up the money, slide it into his coat pocket, and head straight to the bank, where he'd deposit it back into her account.

The house had been her home for over forty years and now she lived there alone, except for Caesar. At one time her oldest son, Numiel, and his wife, Donna, rented the basement apartment, but they'd long since moved back to Louisiana so that Numiel could work as the caretaker of Red Fields, the Redfield family home in northern Louisiana.

"I have the TV up loud so I can hear it out in the garden. I don't like to miss Bob Barker if I can help it." She opened the screen door and motioned me inside the house. "Hot enough for you?"

Caesar sniffed around my feet, and I bent down to pet him. He was about as old as Mrs. Johnson but he hadn't held up as good. His coat was tatty in places and his back legs barely held him upright.

Mrs. Johnson's kitchen was decorated in a green-and-yellow scheme to pay homage to the A's. A woman after my own heart. Her refrigerator was covered with A's memorabilia, season tickets, and programs.

"What you think my boys gonna do to them Giants, Maceo?"

"Put 'em to bed."

She smiled. "That's what I'm talking about. Yes, indeed."

I followed Mrs. Johnson out to the vegetable and flower garden she'd made famous throughout the Bay Area. She did a brisk day-to-day business with the commuters from the West Oakland BART station. Her little stand, where she sold bagged vegetables and bunches of flowers, was a fixture at the edge of the lot.

On Sundays she opened her backyard and basement to weekend shoppers, which was the reason I was there. On more than one occasion Flea helped at her sales booth.

I took a seat on the bottom step and watched her move through the garden.

"Did you taste the okra I sent to your grandmother?"

I waited until the BART train passed before answering. "She used it in her gumbo last weekend."

"How'd it taste?"

"It made the gumbo better."

"Hmph." She kept moving. "I tasted a little of that

gumbo. If you ask me, Antonia uses too many spices."
She tossed a bruised tomato into a wooden barrel. "I
mash them bruised ones up and put them back in the
soil."

"Is that right?"

"That's what makes my product fresher. I have customers coming all the way from Orinda and Marin now.
Rich white ladies in big cars always trying to give me
they old clothes. I tell 'em, just pay me my money. I didn't
ask you for all that."

I picked up an old copy of *The Oakland Tribune* discarded on the stairs. The headline consisted of a number:
146. Since the first murder of 1989 the *Tribune* had kept
a gruesome tally, its sensationalized headlines heralding
Oakland's escalating murder rate.

"Mrs. Johnson, has Felicia been here to see you?"

She disappeared behind a tree, and something in her
pause let me know she'd seen my friend.

"She usually helps me out on Sunday afternoons. Last
week she and that boy of hers came by here and took me
to a picture show. Something silly with that Eddie Mur-
phy boy in it." She chuckled to herself.

"Have you seen her since?"

The thud of rotten tomatoes hitting the bottom of the
barrel filled the air.

"Mrs. Johnson?"

"You remember my husband Sherman, Maceo?"

I was caught off guard by the question. "Of course I
remember Uncle Sherman."

"He was a good man, my Sherman. He wasn't the
kind of man you got in trouble behind. He wasn't handsome enough for that." She paused. "But Felicia's boy he
was handsome. Strong. Just the kind of man I went back-
wards around corners to avoid.

"You know your grandmother's sister got herself in
trouble behind some man, too. Back in the forties when

we first came out here. Celestine." She shook her head. "She was fast, but she didn't deserve what she got."

The murder of my great-aunt, Celestine Bouchaund, Gra'mère's sister, still sat on the police books as unsolved. Her death was rarely talked about in our family, but every couple of years the press would resurrect the story. Her murder was to Oakland what the Black Dahlia murder was to Los Angeles, and it plagued Gra'mère like a salted wound. Except for the odd times it made the paper, no one ever mentioned Celestine aloud.

The one time I'd asked Daddy Al about it he'd placed his finger across his lips to silence me. Then he'd whispered, "Black justice, Southern style." I took it to mean that, like most unsolved crimes in the Black community, the people closest to the victim knew the perpetrator and had handled the payback themselves. Quiet. Swift. No police.

"Pretty and slick were two things I never trusted in a man, but Celestine got her head turned just like Felicia did. I'm not saying her fella was all bad, but most people ain't got lives long enough for the life he wanted to lead.

"When Billy first started coming around here with Felicia, he didn't think I remembered him from when y'all was little, but even my boy, Numiel, knew him. I remembered him well. The four a y'all spent that summer together at Red Fields in Claiborne Parish."

My mind had avoided images of that summer since Holly walked into Cutty's. The last year the three of us could still be considered a trio, Daddy Al caught wind of the troubles that could pull us away from ourselves and each other. Too many of his friends had lost their boys to the streets, nothing new, but it looked more treacherous each year.

Daddy Al and his cronies still lived as if they'd never left Louisiana, as if an entire city hadn't grown up around them and choked the weeds of their country mores and traditions. The remedies they offered against modern temptations did not take root against the urban ills of their new environment, but their preference for "back home," a home many of them had left behind nearly fifty years before, still took precedent.

Before I could stifle images of Daddy Al's solution to our budding manhood, a picture of Billy and Holly hitting my fastballs into the sweet-potato fields nearly strangled me into tears.

I stood up and shook my body the way I did on the field after a missed play or a nagging injury. "Have you seen her, Mrs. Johnson?"

"Why you asking all these questions, Maceo?"

" 'Cause I need to know she's okay."

Her face clouded in anger. "She ain't okay. She saw that boy's brains get blown out."

"So you've spoken to her?"

"Lord Jesus. Get on out of here, boy, before I have to hurt you. I promised that girl I wouldn't talk about nothing with nobody, hear me? Nobody."

"Felicia is my friend."

"Then respect her wishes. She'll be all right after a while, and that's all I'm going to say."

"I understand. I'm sorry I bothered you."

"You ain't bothered me. I'd tell you if you did."

I stood up. "Do you need me to do anything before I go?"

"Can you move those bags of soil over there? Back them up against the fence until I can get to 'em."

I moved the bags and waited for the inevitable. "Oh," she said, "and take Caesar around the corner for me."

I smiled to myself, knowing that Caesar wouldn't make it past two houses before I'd have to carry him. Outside I moved at his pace, which meant one step every twenty breaths. Finally, the two of us just stood and watched the cars exit and enter the BART station.

"Come on, Caesar." I picked him up and walked back to the house. Mrs. Johnson met us on the porch.

"He suckers you every time."

I placed Caesar near the front door and moved away. In an uncharacteristic move Mrs. Johnson came forward and squeezed my hand.

I squeezed back. "Just tell her if she needs me—"

She closed the door before I could finish the sentence.

CHAPTER

9

Searching for Felicia, looking for clues that would lead to Billy's murderer, served to keep my grief at bay. I felt heartache and despair at the inside of my eyelids and nipping at the heels of my feet. The search was also an extension of the neighborhood back-and-forth I'd done as a little boy for mothers and fathers looking for their kids.

"Maceo? You seen Gary? He was suppose to be back here over an hour ago." The words were always posed as a question, but they really meant "Find my kid." And off I'd go after whoever was missing. In Gary's case I knew, from whispers on the street, that he was spending most of his free time in the company of Mr. Donovan, a shellacked and reclusive man who lived three blocks away. The kids knew, long before the adults, that Mr. Donovan was the first in a long line of older men who'd succeed in turning Gary out.

"Maceo?" Another voice, this time female, this time with more worry than the last call. "Maceo, Karen said she was spending the night with your Aunt Cissy and she ain't made it home yet. She there?"

Karen was nowhere near Dover Street, and her mother knew it just as I did, but she'd rather have my eyes see the results of her worry, so I would go find her daughter and spare her what we both already knew. Anybody who'd seen Patrick Selig, a two-time tenth grader, hanging around the junior high five lunch periods in a row knew Karen was hot on his heels.

And so it went until I became a crossroads of information for the lost and found, the secret-keeper of the well hidden and the ones on their way to being lost.

Information on Felicia's whereabouts and the how and whys of her disappearance would come to me in due time, but I felt a need to keep moving toward my own conclusion. I wanted to learn for myself the answers to Billy's death.

Once I left Mrs. Johnson's I turned onto Market Street, then into an alley in search of Holly. He lived close to Mrs. Johnson in a ramshackle lean-to in the back of a warehouse. The warehouse itself was occupied by a group of hippie artists who maintained a love/hate relationship with Holly. The result was that he didn't ask about their activities and they didn't ask about his.

I circled the surrounding blocks looking for his car. He never parked in front of his own home. He was cautious to the point of paranoia, but it served him well.

While Billy had moved into the more traditional avenues of the drug game, Holly found his niche as a specialist, a cooker: the man to call if you needed drugs cut into multiples for the biggest profit. In leaner times, dealers would learn to do it themselves or teach an underling, but in the free-flowing eighties only true hustlers at the top of their game could afford Holly's prices and expertise. It became a symbol of prosperity to have your drugs cut by him.

In addition to buying his chemistry services, you also bought his discretion and a patna to ride on enemies after a single phone call. His profit margin ran so high Holly never saw a day of hand-to-hand sales, and he'd become accustomed to flying first-class with his doctor's bag of tools in his lap to service clientele as far away as D.C.

Holly's success was mythmaking at its finest. There were many rumors, each more elaborate than the next, but they basically meant the same thing. Holly was a genius. Holly was a magician. Holly was worth every fucking penny of his fee: a cool one thousand per unit of cocaine.

His secret: multiplication.

With the impossible-to-obtain procaine, a medicinal anesthetic under lock and key in all hospitals, he was able to up product one hundred percent and still produce excellent results.

It was simple. A dealer brought him fifty units; Holly gave him back a hundred with the purity to power a space shuttle and collected $50,000 for his trouble. Where he got the procaine was a detail he'd take to the grave.

A self-taught ghetto chemist, Holly enrolled without fail every semester under the name Roberto Marley in any chemistry course offered through UC's extension program. He astonished his professors with his knowledge and continually refused all job offers. The mythology of Holly took on a life of its own with each criminal success he experienced.

It all started or ended with John Claire, depending on how you viewed the facts. Either way it added fuel to the fire. John Claire was Holly's personal whipping boy while we were in middle school together. He died mysteriously, with only Holly present, and no one had ever been sure it wasn't Holly's kill. He maintained, vehemently, that

Claire simply suffered a fatal seizure and hit his head when he fell. Many people believed that the events happened in the opposite order. They believed that the open gash that exposed the grayish matter beneath Claire's skull came first, after a hit by Holly, and the seizure came second.

What initiated the doubt was Holly's relationship to Claire. Holly could not abide his presence. He was not normally a bully by nature, but he used John Claire to exorcise all the demons in his own life. The schoolyard battles between meek defenseless Claire and the ferocious Holly were as common as the Chef's Surprise in our school lunch.

On the day of the incident, Holly was alone with Claire behind the gymnasium while the rest of us were in class. Holly had kept Claire behind to "talk" to him, "talk" being a euphemism for a beating.

It was October, I remember because of the decorations. I noticed Holly's empty seat when we sat down for social studies, and almost immediately afterward a woman's anxious wail pierced the classroom. It was Mrs. Ashefani, Holly's favorite teacher, a bohemian Black student from San Francisco State University.

We all rushed to the window, our teacher included, to see Holly pressed silently against the wall while Mrs. Ashefani screamed at a horror we could not see. The principal rushed out to calm her, and his hand immediately went to his mouth as he dropped to his knees and called out for an ambulance.

Ten minutes later we all watched as John Claire was wheeled away with bright red blood caked in the nappy hair behind his ear. More of it pooled in the corners of his mouth like pink drool. Holly was led away in cuffs, none of us sure of his role in Claire's condition.

He was released that afternoon for lack of evidence, and he defended himself to me only once.

"He just shook and fell, Maceo. He hit the steps. That's it." I took his word on the surface, but a small doubt remained. Billy, on the other hand, thought Holly was telling an outright lie. He remembered a little more clearly, as did many others, the systematic way Holly tortured Claire simply for being weak. His silence about the issue, after that first week, only compounded his mystique, but the whispers and doubts dogged him from the schoolyard into adulthood.

And now that adult, with possibly one kill to his name, was richer than Croesus, though he lived like a pauper, stacking his money for the rainy day guaranteed to come. He was always open to one more big score, another way to add to his Midas pile. And it was that greed that led him back to Billy.

A job cutting for some Mexicans out of San Jose gave him a pipeline to a windfall he couldn't ignore. The Mexicans were looking to move into the East Bay market and needed a trustworthy connection. Holly knew just the person.

Billy.

Besides, the middleman fee would guarantee early retirement, and a score big enough to impress Billy. Despite being self-assured and self-sufficient, the competitive side of Holly burned to beat Billy at his own game. He suggested a partnership, but Billy wouldn't agree to terms that favored Holly. The deal died within twenty-four hours, the Mexicans went underground, and Holly was left with a stinging, bitter taste at the sound of Billy's name.

I thought about this as I searched the streets for his rusted-out blue Nova.

Three blocks from my starting point I found it in the driveway of an abandoned house. I doubled back to his cottage. In the three years Holly lived there he'd done nothing to make it livable. The grounds were concrete, the warehouse itself an industrial gray. A cracked clay wheel stood between the two properties, as well as an old stone oven that was home to a feline family.

The lean-to itself was a peeling white structure that I called the bat cave. Inside, it was spare and clean: spit-shined wood floors, heavy drapes, a twin mattress on a wooden frame, a big-screen television, and a first-rate collection of bootleg kung fu tapes. At a separate storage facility he kept two thousand comic books in custom-made boxes. He refused to pay utilities, frugal to the end, so he heated his rooms with the fireplace. He used a counterfeit cell phone, bricks as they were called in the Bay because of their cumbersome size. The electricity was provided by long cords from the warehouse.

His roommates, two pit bulls named Krueger and Carlos, waited patiently on the porch. They barked to let Holly know he had a visitor. I'd known them since they were puppies, yet they never displayed even the slightest sign of welcome.

Before I could call out, Holly hastily exited his front door. He fastened the buckle of his belt and closed the door firmly behind him. I was surprised.

"Did I catch you at a bad time?" I knew there was a girl behind the door.

He looked back at his house. "It's cool. What's up?"

"I just came from Mrs. Johnson's house. Flea's been over there to see her."

"Man, you still on that?"

"I got to find her. If Billy's boys don't kill her, the police gonna have her hemmed up behind this."

"Maceo—"

I held up a hand. "Remember Noone?"

"That square-ass cop?"

"Yeah. He's working the case. Fool's a detective now."

Holly shook his head, recalling several unpleasant run-ins. "You spoke to him?"

"He was trying to intimidate Regina when I got to the house."

A noise from inside the cottage startled us both. Holly looked back quickly and pulled the door even tighter.

"Why you out here?" I asked.

"I heard you honk." Both of us knew I hadn't honked, so I held his gaze for a moment. He was the first to look away. I stepped off the porch.

He made a motion to come with me. "You need me to ride somewhere?"

"I was gonna run up to Telegraph."

"Okay. Give me a minute and I'll meet you at the car."

I turned to go but couldn't resist a last dig. I lifted my chin toward his closed door. "She cute?"

He flinched slightly before answering. "Don't even trip."

CHAPTER

10

Half an hour later I maneuvered the Cougar up Berkeley's Telegraph Avenue while Holly rode shotgun. Given the choice, Holly always picked me to drive. His license had been suspended for over a year and even when he had it, legally, the harassment he suffered from local cops barely made it worthwhile. My role as chauffeur meant we saw each other at least once a day. I was used to his "Ride me up the street" requests—up the street meaning anything from a mere two blocks away to longer rides to San Jose or even Los Angeles.

On the busy avenue the usual menagerie of homeless people, street kids, and students filled the sidewalks not taken up by vendors. Halfway down the block we spotted a group of guys standing in front of Rasputin Records.

"There's Black Jeff." Holly nodded toward a dreadlocked youth balancing on his skateboard. His ratty clothes hid that he was one of the most successful skateboarders on the West Coast and one of the only Blacks in the sport. He had flipped the race card by registering for all his events as Black Jeff, the derogatory name his competitors used when discussing him. His use of it earned him a bit of respectful notoriety and forced them to say it to his face.

Whenever he was in town, Black Jeff made the sidewalk in front of Rasputin's his home. At his side was his usual misfit crew: Mike Crowley, a neighborhood kid who conversed in obscure rap lyrics, and Off-Beat, a White kid with a predilection for Black culture. Holly grimaced when he saw Off-Beat.

"Man, I can't stand that trick."

"Easy, player, the man just confused." I rolled to a stop at the curb and waited for Black Jeff to approach the car.

"Wassup?" I leaned across the passenger seat to give him a pound.

"You, baby." He returned the pound and extended his hand to Holly. Holly shook back. He liked Jeff and had even financed a skateboard event or two when Jeff was down on his luck. "Man, y'all hear about Billy Crane? That was some cold shit. He was cool people."

"What'd you hear?" Holly asked.

"I heard he was on College with his girl and somebody smoked him." He looked at me, suddenly remembering my connection to Flea. "You know his boys are looking for her?"

"I heard."

"I don't believe she had anything to do with it, but Charlie and them mad as hell." Charlie Carl was Billy's stepbrother and a wild card. He and Flea had never gotten along. Charlie resented Billy's commitment to a "broad," as he put it, and Flea never tolerated his lack of respect. I heard from her more than once that she and Charlie had exchanged harsh words.

"You seen Charlie?"

"Last I heard he was roaming the streets trying to find a way to get himself killed. I wouldn't fuck with him tonight if I was you." Jeff backed away from the car as Mike Crowley approached.

"You'll shiver, you'll shake / Your back might break / But do it anyway / To see what you can take."

"Spoonie Gee," Holly answered. He was a veteran at Crowley's rap game and was rarely stumped by obscure lyrics. Crowley's favorite pastime was greeting people with words he never expected anyone to recognize. The more underground the artist, the better. And if you failed to identify the rapper he simply refused to speak with you. No second chances.

"My boy is up on ol' Spoonie." Crowley sounded impressed.

"Spoonie Gee and the Treacherous Three. I knew about him before you, baby. You heard about Crane?" Holly asked.

"That was fucked up. Billy was straight."

We sat in silence for a minute and considered the truth of the statement. "I heard his girl got in the cut." Crowley nodded toward me.

"Ain't nobody seen her."

"She knew the drill. Saw that gun and got ghost. Heard she left her shoe in the car and everything."

"Charlie been looking for her?"

"Charlie looking for anybody. Stay away from that fool." He tapped his head. "He ain't right. You know

Billy had started to cut him loose 'cause Charlie was acting too wild."

This was news to me—and Holly too, judging from his expression.

"Since when?" he asked.

"Since Charlie fucked with those white boys." I remembered then that Charlie had started dealing in strict-as-hell Marin County, bringing heat into Billy's quiet territory. "Soon as white boys start muddying the pool, Feds ain't too far behind."

"And they'll snitch in a minute." Holly had a hard and fast rule against teaming up with white boys.

"You know that's right," Crowley agreed.

"Billy and Charlie weren't cool anymore?" I asked.

"I wouldn't say that. You know Billy didn't like static. He just kind of shut down for a while and let Charlie go on his own."

"Think we can find Charlie at the Caribe tonight?"

"Probably. You know his ancient ass can't give up that dead spot." Any club that played anything other than rap was useless to Crowley, and Caribe was all island music.

"This murder don't make no sense when you think about it. Who would take Billy out like that?" Crowley seemed as confused as we were. "There's always Smokey, but he's a chump deep down."

"He woulda had to have somebody wit' him that Billy trusted." I could tell from his words that Holly somehow suspected Felicia.

"That brother was sweet!" Crowley continued. " 'Member back in the day he went through that party in Richmond and tore things up?" Billy had a fierce reputation as a street fighter, and the Richmond party lived on as his best bout. "He was slaying people left and right. Went in there to get his boy Charlie out. Shit, I can't believe the man is gone."

"I hear ya. Chaos on the streets. Sign of the times."

"Holly, baby, niggas gone crazy in the eight-nine, losing they minds. You know I got three—not one, but three—kids in my class named Corleone. First name. And one Montana, and you know damn well they ghetto-ass parents didn't mean the state. Corleone! Now . . . what . . . the . . . fuck . . . is . . . that?"

Crowley ran an after-school program at Bushrod Park. The neighborhood had grown used to seeing him lead his motley crew of kids through the streets like the Pied Piper.

"And you two fucking wit' Smokey. That fool worse than Charlie 'cause he think he got something to prove."

"We handlin' it." Holly stopped the direction of the conversation.

Crowley motioned backward over his shoulder. "You know Off-Beat was slangin' rock for Billy?"

Off-Beat looked toward us eagerly but Holly grimaced.

"I hate that clown. What was Billy fuckin' with him for?"

"He ain't all bad. Just took the Beastie Boys too serious."

"You think he knows anything useful?"

Crowley shrugged. "He might."

"Check it out and let me know."

Crowley caught my eye. "You better watch out for your girl, Maceo. People, 'specially Charlie, talkin' big shit about findin' her."

"I hear ya." I popped the ignition.

Crowley started to back away from the car. "Somebody need to call her brothers to get her the fuck up out of Oakland."

Felicia's older brothers, members of Los Angeles's infamous Eight Tray Gangsta Crips, had made an unforgettable impression on Oakland when they visited the city. Flea and I were kickin' it when Reggie and Crim—short for Criminal—came out to see her. Reggie had been shot more than once and lived to retaliate each time. He was loud, fearless, and quick with a gun. The younger brother was quiet, given to very few words, and a notorious street fighter. He too had been shot, but knives were his weapon of choice. Before their arrival Flea had tried to explain that her brothers were ghetto stars in their South Central neighborhood. She told me this but I was not prepared for them when I met them.

The two of us were sitting on the steps in front of Dwinelle Hall when a distinctive whistle lit up the campus. The sound caused people to look up in curiosity. Flea, in the middle of a conversation, heard the sound and jumped to her feet. Then she let go with a whistle of her own. A whistle came back, and their fierce call-and-response stopped several students in their tracks.

Finally, two men came into view, both loaded down with the blue wardrobe of L.A. Crips. The taller one, who I found out later was Reggie, had a swinging style to his walk. One arm swung loosely, almost in slow motion, back and forth across his body while he favored his left leg in a cool-as-hell skip. The other arm held up pants sagging so low they defied gravity. His jeans were unwashed Levi's, with copper buttons instead of zippers and copper stitching to match. He had sharp creases down the front of his pants and a crisp white T-shirt. His tennis shoes were blinding-white K-Swiss and his hair was braided in tight cornrows. A scar on the left side of his mouth gave him a permanent grimace. He wore gold hoops in both ears, and a toothpick dangled from his lip.

At his side was Crim, the quiet brother who made more than a few people uneasy as he passed. Both of them spoke in death and murder even in silence, but in Crim it breathed on its own. Crim was dressed like Reggie but with a blue T-shirt instead of white. Crim also wore a short Afro, more functional than stylish, and silver hoops. They both had the same dark skin as Flea. In Reggie you saw a handsome devilish face beneath the gangster, but Crim was a sight to behold. The man was ugly bordering on monstrous, with rock-hard arms and a short neck to match. Inbred pit bull was the first thing that came to my mind.

While the rest of us watched, Felicia flew down the stairs and grabbed both of them in an embrace. After they finished hugging she turned and motioned me forward.

"Maceo, these are my brothers." Surprise crossed my face but I recovered quickly and offered a hand. They both ignored it.

"Wassup?" I asked.

Reggie nodded and looked me up and down. I allowed the scrutiny, knowing how older brothers can be. I was also no fool. I knew immediately that the brothers had a fight-to-the-death pack mentality that could be unleashed at the slightest provocation.

"This is Reggie. And this is Crim." She swatted Crim on his crossed arms. "What y'all doing here? Aunt Venus know you came?"

"Naw, we just rode out this morning. Wanted to see our baby sister and shit." Reggie managed a semblance of a smile.

"How long y'all staying?"

"As long as these white people can stand us." Reggie directed his words at two frat boys who'd strolled a little too close. They jumped away as he leaned toward them. Once they were a sufficient distance away, Reggie turned back to Flea. "Let's go eat."

"All right. Maceo, you wanna come?" All of us knew there was no point in my joining them.

"I have to study. I'll call you later."

Flea leaned over to give me a kiss. Her brothers stared. By way of an exit Reggie simply said, "Check you out, square padna." I noticed the *d* he used in "padna," another difference between the Bay Area and Los Angeles. We preferred to come down hard on the *t*—"patna"— but I chose not to point that out to either one of the Bennett boys.

I watched the three of them walk away, Flea between her brothers. For the entire week they were there I stayed as far away from Flea as possible. Trouble was just waiting on that family. It came less than twenty-four hours later when they started a mini-riot at San Francisco's End Zone nightclub. The End Zone, so notoriously violent that it displayed handwritten signs that read LADIES PLEASE INFORM SECURITY IF YOU'RE BEING HARASSED OR MANHANDLED, was not equipped for what they unleashed.

The details of the evening were sketchy, but everyone agreed that the fight ended bad for everybody but Reggie and Crim. The same thing was repeated at Geoffrey's, the Caribe, and Silk's. By the time they left northern California there were very few people who wanted to see them return.

Holly shook his head in response to Crowley's suggestion. "Don't nobody need to call them niggas out here." His one encounter with them had left him spooked for over a week.

After their visit I had been grateful that my squareness saved me from their wrath. The fact that I fell into the athlete category spared me their violence more than any sort of loyalty to their sister. If the mood had struck them I could have just as easily fallen victim to their crimes, though I was too far on the other side to even consider. But Holly they recognized as one of their own, which left him with a rare sense of fear.

"I'm just saying"—Crowley stepped back from the car—"somebody got to look out for Flea and nobody, not even Charlie, will fuck with her brothers. Peace." He rejoined Black Jeff and Off-Beat as Holly and I drove away.

Silence accompanied us as I headed back to West Oakland. Holly finally broke it with a few reluctant words. "Crowley's right. If you wanna help your girl, you gonna have to get her brothers out here."

CHAPTER

11

After dropping Holly at home I headed over to Bushrod Park. I was due to pick up my Little Brother, Scottie Timmons, from Little League practice, murder or not. An impassioned sermon by Harry Livingston had convinced me to become involved with Oakland's Big Brother organization, and Scottie was the result.

"Maceo!" Scottie yelled when he spotted me.

"What's up, waterhead?" I noticed Livingston at the end of the bleachers sitting with his daughter, Lisa. He was so busy stuffing his face with a hot dog he didn't notice my arrival. I tapped him on the shoulder. "Pig'll kill you if the white man don't get you first." I took a seat as his lips twitched into a laugh.

"Now what kind of nonsense is that?"

I pointed at the hot dog. "Pork will do you wrong, my brother."

He laughed and nodded toward the field. "The boys

are looking good this year. Maybe we can finally put a hurting on Richmond."

"Maybe. What about the big boys? A's or Giants?"

"Neither one. I'm a Kansas City man myself."

I placed my hand across my heart. "You killing me, you know that. Up until this moment I had respect for you."

"And now you don't?"

"Not a bit." I paused. "You heard about Billy Crane?"

"This morning. Any word from Felicia?"

"I haven't heard from her. If she saw anything she's probably laying low for a while."

"Any clues?"

"No. Billy was only into dealing—"

He held up his hand. "*Only* into dealing? Do you *know* how that sounds?"

"I meant—"

"You meant that you've accepted this genocide without question if you can even put those words together in a sentence. And don't think it ain't genocide, this shit about to wipe out an entire race!"

"Billy was straight, man."

"His straight was about as crooked as Lombard Street."

"All right, all right, I surrender." I'd do anything to avoid one of Livingston's long-winded sermons. But I could tell he was reluctant to let me off the hook.

"Everybody makes choices, Maceo. You may not pull the trigger, but if you have knowledge of the crime you're just as guilty."

"Let's not get into all that."

"Why not? Where else you got to go?"

"Right now, my only concern is finding Felicia and making sure she's all right."

"What do the police think?"

"Those idiots . . ."

"Y'all youngstas pick some curious enemies. Drug dealers should be your enemies. I ain't saying the police are knights in shining armor, but y'all accept criminals without question."

I stood to go. "I'm not in school this semester, remember. I get to skip your lectures."

"Okay, then, let's talk about that! Why aren't you in school? I looked your grades up. They're decent. You got some other kind of trouble?"

"Life. I'm just taking a break."

"Break, huh? You'll break right to the graveyard if you don't watch out." He paused. "Just like your friend Billy."

He dissolved into a foul mood, me not far behind him as Scottie ran up the bleachers.

I gave him a pound. "You ready to head on home?"

I shook hands with Livingston and followed Scottie out to my car. Scottie was a stray much like Holly had been, with a harassed young mother as his only parent. I'd had more than one encounter with Miss Chantal, so I avoided her like the plague. Scottie and I had a ritual that helped me to accomplish that. I would drop him on the corner and watch him run to his house. Once he was safely inside he'd turn the bathroom light on and off three times: our signal. Then I'd hit my gas pedal before Chantal came out onto the porch.

Once, when I first met Scottie, I pulled an overnight with Chantal that I regretted the moment it began. The one time I felt sorry for her was the one time I woke up in her bed.

In the car Scottie shuffled through the cassettes scattered on the floor.

"Can I play this?" He was waving an NWA tape.

"NWA! Your mama lets you listen to them?"

"Shoot, my mama the one bought it for me."

"You need to be jockin' Kid n' Play." He grimaced. "Or the Fresh Prince."

"They ain't saying nothing."

I had to agree, but I still thought NWA and a seven-year-old should stay as far away from each other as possible. "How 'bout this?" I handed him LL Cool J's latest. "You think he's a sucker too?"

He grabbed the cassette. "He's cool." He popped in the tape, turned it up loud, looked at me, and grinned. "That's my song right there."

We rode in silence for a moment, listening to the music and watching the theater of the Oakland streets.

"Maceo, why don't you play baseball anymore?"

His question nearly made me miss a turn. I turned down the radio. "What made you ask that?"

He shrugged. "I don't know. My mama and her friend was talking about it yesterday."

"What your mother know about baseball?" I tried leading him off the trail.

"I taught her a little bit of stuff, but her friend knows more than me. She said they use to call you the Watcher."

I corrected him. "The Watch Dog."

"What's that mean?"

"Just a nickname. I used to take a long time before each pitch so people started calling me that."

"Dang, you was the pitcher! Jason Stevens pitches on our team. He's hella raw. He can throw a fastball the *coach* can't even hit."

"Yeah?"

"Yep." He paused for a moment. "I want to throw like that. You wanna teach me?"

"I thought you was shortstop."

"I can do both."

"Is that right?"

"Yep, so I figured you could show me some of your tricks."

"You want me to give away my superpowers?"

Scottie laughed. "My mama's friend said you use to watch them put the white lines on the field before the game."

I was shocked by this tidbit I'd forgotten. Once before a game I'd arrived early enough to find the grounds-keeper putting the lines on the field. I sat in the dugout alone and watched him go about his job. He was an old cat, probably years past the retirement age, but he took his job seriously. He was slow and methodical, and I found I pitched better whenever he handled the field.

"Your mama's friend a Fed? Why she know so much about me?"

"She went to school wit' you."

"What's her name?"

"Patrice Hall."

"Uh, nasty Patrice?" Scottie's head whipped around so fast I knew I'd made a mistake. Sometimes when we got deep in conversation I would forget he was a little boy.

"Why you call her that?"

"I was just kidding. You know I like to mess with you sometimes." He looked skeptical but didn't press the issue.

Patrice Hall was the perfect friend for Chantal, but I'd never say that to Scottie. She was two years behind me in school and an avid fan of baseball players. Unlike the majority of my teammates, I'd resisted the fruit off that tree.

Scottie tapped me on the leg and pointed to an ambulance parked haphazardly at the curb in front of his home. A group of neighbors had gathered on the sidewalk, rubbernecking and hoping for snatches of conversation that might include remnants of the truth.

Scottie's apartment building was a horseshoe-shaped two-story complex called Bay Manor Villas, or the BMVs, which in local lingo translated to Baby's Mama Village because of all the single mothers that lived inside. The courtyard consisted of burnt-out grass and a jungle gym that had seen too many unsupervised children. Daddy Al, the latest owner, replaced the structure every four months and instructed the kids and parents to take better care, but the words didn't seem to stick.

"There's my mama." Scottie leaned his head out the window and beamed at the woman scowling in my direction. Chantal stood at the head of the gathered crowd, arms folded across her chest, braids piled on top of her head. She had the look of a wolf that had just caught its prey. Me.

I followed Scottie out of the car. "Maceo, Maceo, Maceo, what I gotta do to catch up with you?" She asked the question in a taunting singsongy voice.

I nodded toward the ambulance. "What's up?"

"One a these crackheads going into labor. I hope they

take the baby right there at the hospital and give it half a chance."

"Chantal, man, that's cold-blooded."

"Nah, uh-uh, her not having her tubes tied is cold-blooded."

"Did you call the ambulance?" Chantal was the unofficial apartment manager of the complex, a polite way of saying she monitored all the comings and goings, breakups and makeups, of the inhabitants. After meeting Scottie and hearing about his old neighborhood, Daddy Al rented a first-floor apartment to Chantal. He never regretted a good deed but he grew to regret her weekly reports on who was doing what, who might be trying to move out in the middle of the night, and who wasn't paying rent but just had a big-screen TV delivered. Both he and Gra'mère had become used to tenant phone calls complaining about Chantal's guerrilla tactics.

"Yeah, I called; you know she ain't got no phone. Knocked on my door, hemming and hawing and holding on to that little scrawny belly." She looked toward the paramedics as they made their way down from the second floor. "Oh, and here come Miss Thang."

Chantal's eyes were focused on a woman walking behind the paramedics and spitting out information with an authority that didn't match her surroundings. Miss Thang was dressed in a nylon jogging suit stretched to the limits by a generous figure. She had a short boyish haircut, high cheekbones, and slanted Asian eyes. I watched as she held the patient's hand until she was lifted into the ambulance.

The crowd started to disperse once the ambulance turned the corner and the sirens faded away. I continued to stare as the woman bent down to tie her shoelaces and look at her watch.

"What you lookin' at?"

Scottie giggled as his mother busted me out with her nosy question.

"Man, why you so mean? You're just evil, Chantal."

"Whatever." She turned to the jogger. "Where you on your way to?"

"I came to see if Scottie wanted to run the lake with me." Scottie perked up at the mention of his name.

"Scottie got homework, dinner, chores—"

"We won't be gone long. I thought we could run, then stop for some ice cream."

"Ya thought wrong. I don't know how they do it where you from, but you cain't just stop by unannounced and expect peoples to drop they plans."

She held up her hands. "You're right, Chantal." Her voice was polite but impatient. "Next time I'll call when I want to spend time with my family."

"Oh, now we family."

"We always been family."

Chantal guffawed loudly into the air. "Yeah, right."

The woman's eyes flickered over me in one dismissive gesture. I saw immediately that her gaze placed me on the far side of drug dealer. I looked no different from the boyfriends and exes that snuck in and out of the complex at all hours of the night. Her assumption bothered me and so did the possibility that she had placed Chantal and me together. I moved toward my car.

"Where you going? I ain't finished talking to you," Chantal snapped.

"Well, I'm finished taking your abuse."

"I ain't even said nothing. I thought you was a tough guy, hanging around with ballers, hustlers. Ain't some a Holly's cool rubbed off on you?"

I ignored her and spoke to Scottie. "Next time, little man."

"Don't forget about what I asked you."

My mind was a blank. "What was that?"

"Pitching. Teaching me how to pitch."

I hesitated. "We'll talk about it."

The jogger stepped up to Chantal's side. She stood with her hands on her hips, an anger I couldn't claim right behind her eyes. "Don't you want to give him a straight answer?"

Chantal looked amused. "Relax, girl, that ain't his daddy." Bewilderment crossed the jogger's face. Chantal smiled at me. "I been trying to explain to sister-girl that Scottie's father ain't a factor, but she don't hear me when I talk."

She looked at me. "Sorry, I just thought—"

"Don't worry about it." I caught her eye over the roof of the car. "I'm Maceo Redfield."

She held up a hand and gave a small wave. "Alixe Hunter."

Scottie grabbed her hand. "This my Auntie Alixe. My mama's sister from Japan."

"Which explains why she wants to go jogging close to sundown." Chantal continued her biting commentary. "Everybody else locked in the house, and she wanna go run the streets looking for trouble."

"The lake is well lit," Alixe countered.

"The bushes ain't, and somebody'll drag your ass in there so quick."

"Thanks for worrying about me." She looked at me. "So, how do you know my nephew?"

"The Big Brother program. Me and waterhead been hooked up for about a year."

She wrapped her arms around Scottie and kissed him on the head. "Nice kid, huh?"

I smiled at Scottie. "Sometimes."

Scottie scowled. "I ain't a troublemaker."

"Of course you're not." She kissed him again. "You can jog with me another time. Okay?"

"Call first." Chantal couldn't resist a last jab.

"I'ma get out of here too." I had visions of intercepting the jogger on the next block.

"There you go again, running off. Should I make an appointment to sit down and talk to you? 'Cause you know you never said why you don't call."

"I don't think that's a good idea, with me being Scottie's Big Brother and all. I don't want things to get messy with him."

"You wasn't worried about all that when I met you at the club. You was kinda glad when you crawled in my bed." Luckily, Alixe was distracted by Scottie.

" 'Crawled' being the operative word."

"Don't talk shit." She moved closer while I backed away. "What? You afraid of me now?"

"I was afraid of you then."

"Trick." But there was a little more humor in her voice.

Alixe watched us with interest.

"I'll catch y'all later."

"Wait. You hear about Billy Crane?"

"Yeah. Holly told me this morning."

"He was cool people. Too bad. Didn't you kick it with his girlfriend for a minute?"

"She was a friend of mine."

"So, you the shooter? You know, clear the way for yourself?"

I slid into the front seat. "You's a cold piece of work, Chantal."

She shrugged her shoulders while I locked eyes with her sister. I got nothing back. In the rearview I caught sight of them both and almost laughed aloud. Side by side the two women represented the light and dark sides of my desire. Chantal, easy access and not at all what I wanted, while her sister physically represented everything I'd ever dreamed about—beauty, body to die for—just like Felicia.

CHAPTER

13

"Granddaddy, you in there?" I pushed open the garage door and found Daddy Al dozing in his favorite chair. A blues station played on the radio while my Doberman, Clio, reclined at his feet.

The garage space had been made over into a wood-shop and was Daddy Al's domain. The woodshop was adjacent to the main house, a three-story structure that at various times had housed the aunties, relatives, and stray friends. My own house, a two-story place I called "the cottage," sat at the back end of the property, with my front door facing the back door of the main house and the entrance to the woodshop. I'd lived there since my fifteenth birthday, and the setup allowed for easy monitoring of my comings and goings by my grand-parents.

Inside the woodshop, on Daddy Al's worktable was a headboard for my Aunt Cissy's bedroom. I fingered the wood, lingering on a small detail: a trademark pineapple, a West Indian symbol of fertility that he included on all his bedroom pieces.

I closed the door behind me and motioned Clio for-ward. She came over to receive her customary pat and re-turned to her place at his side. She was my dog, but she preferred Daddy Al's company.

I walked around the table and sat in an unfinished chair across the room. I had a clear view of Daddy Al from my position, and through the window I could see Gra'mère's silhouette as she moved around the kitchen. The two of them had been married for over forty years and in that time they had raised six girls, me and Holly, and countless friends of their daughters.

Gra'mère was godmother to at least one hundred babies in the San Francisco Bay Area. After relocating to Oakland from Louisiana, she opened the Celestine Home for Young Ladies, named for her murdered sister. What started as a small operation grew to encompass three Victorians bought dirt cheap in the heart of West Oakland. Many of the lost girls, who fled small Southern towns for the West Coast, made their first stop on Seventh Avenue and their last stop at the Celestine Home.

Gra'mère, along with Mrs. Johnson and other members of the Eastern Stars, a philanthropic club for Black women, taught hygiene, child rearing, cooking, sewing, and etiquette. Most of the girls arrived on their doorstep pregnant or with a baby in tow, but by the time they left they had learned basic skills to help in their survival. A few went on to become teachers and nurses; almost all made one of the founders godmother to their children.

By the time she retired, Gra'mère had seen over six hundred girls flow through the doors. The city of Oakland honored her with a lifetime achievement award for her work at Celestine. That she saved many lost girls from ruin was small consolation for not being able to save her own sister. So even in retirement her work as savior continued. She would never and could never turn away a stray.

"What's bothering you, Maceo?" Daddy Al asked from his chair, his eyes closed in thought.

"You awake, huh? Is that how you fool burglars?"

He patted Clio's head. "You know burglars ain't coming nowhere near here." I nodded in agreement. Clio had scared off more than one person who'd wandered into our backyard. "Ain't you suppose to be at the bar?"

"I'm heading up there after dinner."

"Move your chair over here closer to me. I'ma get back to work." He stood and turned on the light above the worktable. "I'm trying to finish this piece to give to Celestine for Christmas." Celestine was Cissy's given name and the only one Granddaddy used. "She's wanted this bed ever since she saw one at the homeplace in Louisiana."

"That's all she talked about when she got back."

"And there ain't no way Antonia's letting the original leave her mother's house."

I took a seat where he indicated. Clio, sensing my mood, actually joined me.

"I heard about Billy." Daddy Al continued to shave the wood of the headboard. His knowledge of my grief didn't surprise me. He and Holly talked on the phone at least twice a day. "I'm sorry about him and about Felicia."

"She disappeared."

"She'll turn up. Too much blood was spilled." He continued to shave. "You know, back in Louisiana people used to believe that if you buried somebody face down with eggs in the palm of their hands it would drive their murderer out into the open."

"Did the family do that with Gra'mère's sister?"

He stopped working and looked directly at me. "There wasn't a need for that."

I gave him a wry smile. "Black justice, Southern style."

He resumed work. "Sometimes that's all you have. And all you need." I looked at my grandfather's strong dark hands, his fingers the size of Andouille sausages, knowing he'd used them once to kill a man. Even at the age of seventy-one, Daddy Al possessed the vitality of a man half his age. He'd spent his entire life working and had a solid rock-hard body to prove it. In youth he'd stood a powerful six foot, with dark serious eyes and a head always covered with a work hat, or a dapper Borsalino in his off-hours.

"You believe in murder?"

He stopped and looked at me. "Cutty called over here and told me about you and Holly at the shop. Don't do nothing silly behind that girl, hear?"

I dropped my head, feeling the sting of tears for the first time that day. In the silence of the workroom I knew he was searching for a story to help me through my pain.

"You know your Aunt Rachel ain't your grandmother's blood daughter." I nodded at the age-old information, wondering how that was relevant to my situation with Felicia.

Any visitor to our home knew the difference because Rachel called Gra'mère Miss Antonia while the other daughters simply called her Momma. Miss Antonia is the name Daddy Al used when he first met Gra'mère. He dropped the formality once they were married, choosing to call her Lady Belle instead, but Rachel kept the old name alive.

"Rachel's mother was my first wife, Elizabeth. She wasn't pretty like Lady Belle, but she didn't have as easy a life either. Her mother ran away when she was a little girl and her father, Papa Cray—that's what we called him in the parish—raised her by himself.

"I knew Elizabeth my entire life but I never thought much about her. She was quiet and shy because of a lame leg, but she was sweet." He began to chop a new piece of wood with steady, even blows.

"Papa Cray was probably one of the cruelest men I ever met. Just full of hatred. His father, the sheriff, was white, and he didn't acknowledge Cray in public, but

Cray was able to get away with a whole lot of shit 'cause of his daddy.

"One night when I was seventeen years old I took a walk to cut cypress knees."

He paused, and when he continued his voice had dropped a notch.

"While I was cutting I heard this pitiful sound. I thought an animal was wounded, so I walked to the edge of the creek, and I saw that man doing things to that child." He stopped to wipe sweat from his forehead.

The story chilled me to the bone so I offered him a reprieve. "You don't have to tell me—"

"I went over there the very next morning and asked for Elizabeth's hand. We had never talked a word about it, but she stood by my side while I spoke to her father. Papa Cray laughed at us both and said, 'Sure you can marry her, but it don't mean nothing.' We were married the very next day and she moved in with me, Mama, and Daddy.

"I didn't love her then like a husband loves a wife, but I grew to. And she loved me for saving her life. I promised her every night before we slept that I would protect her. And I did. She never went anywhere on the property without a guardian.

"When she got pregnant I think that was the happiest I ever saw her. Rachel was born in May, and Elizabeth loved that little girl with a fierceness. Papa Cray disappeared around that time so we all relaxed a little bit.

"Then one day Daddy and me went to see about some horses and Mama went to midwife. Elizabeth stayed home with Rachel."

I saw Daddy Al's eyes glisten from the memory but I made no move to stop him. Like I've said before, I was born to violence and these stories were part of my legacy.

"When we got back that night the house was dark and

I knew something was wrong. Me and Daddy ran into the woods and found Elizabeth unconscious under a tree. Papa Cray had raped her and cut her up real bad. Rachel was sitting right next to her mother, quiet as a tomb and covered in blood. When I picked her up she started screaming. I had to carry them both just so Rachel could feel her mother.

"I laid Elizabeth on our bed and we cried all night, like children. The doctor came to patch her up—the white doctor, so I knew the sheriff had sent him. I waited until sunrise and then I went to find Cray."

He paused and looked toward Gra'mère's silhouette in the kitchen window.

"He was sitting at his kitchen table like he'd been waiting on me. I killed him with my own hands and then I set the house on fire. I wanted Elizabeth to see the blaze from our bedroom window."

I shook off a chill as Daddy Al reached for his pipe. I watched as he tapped the pipe to rotate the tobacco. Somehow I knew his tale of long-ago violence was a bad omen for Felicia.

"I left the parish that night and went to Rayville, over near the Mississippi border. I let a year pass, enough time for the sheriff to cool down, and then I went home in the middle of the night. My father told me the sheriff had died the week before. I ran upstairs and Rachel came right into my arms, though she hadn't seen me for a year. Elizabeth was in a chair by the window, and she didn't move when she saw me.

"When Cray attacked her he destroyed something inside of her. She wasted away the year I was gone."

He took a puff on his pipe.

"She hung herself from shame after I got back, and I've believed in murder ever since."

CHAPTER

14

Eight o'clock at night, and the heat still held everyone in check. With my grandfather's words ringing in my ear I rode the three blocks to the Nickel and Dime with the windows down, hoping the slight breeze would bring some relief. I had the evening shift at the bar, and hoped it would keep my mind off of Billy and Flea.

I waved to neighbors gathered on their porches and children as they tumbled through lawn sprinklers. The sidewalks were packed, the streetlights casting an eerie yellow glow over the busy scene.

The bar was walking distance from the house but I drove whenever I had the closing shift. More often than not, locking up meant driving home a regular who'd had a little too much to drink.

The Nickel and Dime was a neighborhood bar with an attached restaurant operated by my twin aunts, Josephine and Cornelia. Daddy Al had owned the place since 1950. The majority of the patrons were Southern natives and graduates of the canneries and shipyards. But on the weekends we got a large number of younger people looking to drink cheap before hitting the nightclubs. I worked about twenty hours a week for pocket change, and since my rent was free I was rarely strapped for cash.

Otis Payne, the security guard, sat on a stool at the front entrance. He was dressed in a grimy T-shirt, his uniform top folded neatly beneath his wide butt. His gun was holstered at his belt, barely covering a hole in his T-shirt.

"Hot enough for you, Maceo?"

"It's not hot enough for you, I guess. Daddy Al gonna be steaming if sees you out here like that."

Otis waved me off. "I got it covered. SueSue over at y'all house. She gonna call when Albert leave coming up here."

"That's your plan?"

He nodded.

"You know if SueSue get ahold of some food she'll forget all about you."

His eyes widened at the thought of his wife's legendary appetite. He reached for his shirt. "It ain't right, me sitting out here in this furnace when y'all got air-conditioning inside."

"I'll have Vicki bring you out some water."

I was halfway through the door before I heard him mutter, "Put something in it besides ice cubes."

Inside, the oval bar in the center of the room was packed three deep with regulars and a mixed bag of weekenders, all thirsty, clothes damp with sweat. The dance floor and the surrounding area were almost empty of people. I could see the two cocktail waitresses, Vicki and Pam, working double-time to cover the tables and booths at the edges of the dance floor.

The room was dark, the only light coming from the candles shining dimly inside water glasses. The cracked red Naugahyde of the booths had faded to a dull burnt orange. In the far corner, the house band, heavy on the blues, adjusted mikes and checked equipment. They weren't due to play until nine, but they always arrived early for an hour of free drinks.

I slid my bat under the bar and ducked under the opening. I'd barely adjusted my baseball cap before three orders were shouted in my face. Paulie Mourning, the other bartender, winked and kept on pouring.

Easter Lilly, a neighborhood working girl who only did business Monday through Friday, sat at the end of the bar with two glasses of top-shelf brandy. I knew from our many late-night conversations that she was a "suffering alcoholic." She suffered for every day she couldn't end with a bottle of brandy, but she'd been sober for three years and change. She had her own form of AA, Saturday night at the Nickel and Dime, smelling the fumes of the best brandy we had and watching the surface of the liquor for messages. So far the messages had kept her from picking up either glass.

Behind her the three wise men sat at a table near the stage. Potter, Tully, and Soup Can were well into their eighties and entrenched in their roles as elder statesmen. They held court in the dark space seven days a week, offering opinions on every subject under the sun, especially my wrongdoings.

"Quittin' time." Paulie handed me the key to the cash register.

"Wassup, man?"

"My feet, soon as I get home." He reached for his hat stashed under the bar. "People been in here all day 'cause we got air-conditioning. It's hot as hell out there, and the sun ain't even up no more. I been pouring all day, trying to keep tempers down, but somebody'll get they ass kicked 'fore too long."

"Anything else?"

"Everybody paid up here at the bar. Sandy called in sick, but Vicki and Pam covering the floor pretty good, band due to go on at nine, and Easter Lilly got both her drinks." He shook his head. "And just like every other week she won't touch neither one."

"It's her world, man."

He ducked under the counter and headed for the door.

"Oh, Maceo, sorry to hear about your boy. People been talking about it all day."

"Thanks, Paulie."

"See ya Monday."

"See ya."

Across the room Soup Can waved his empty glass in the air. I motioned for Vicki, a waitress in the bar for over twenty-five years. She was in her fifties but held her own in the short black skirt and white tuxedo vest. Her heels were always a good inch or two taller than any of the younger women's.

I poured a glass of scotch and slid it across the bar. "This for Soup Can?" She scooped it onto her tray. "You gonna have to drive him tonight, Maceo. This is his sixth drink, and he didn't eat none of the dinner your aunties sent over. How you anyway, baby?"

"I'm fine. Thanks for the warning."

"We heard about Felicia." Vicki had trained Felicia during her short stint as a cocktail waitress. "Any news?"

"Nothing yet."

"Well, don't give up."

"Beertender!"

I responded to that call and the next until the band struck up and the crowd moved away to the dance floor.

The Nickel and Dime wasn't a family place. The decor was haphazard—dark, worn in most places—but it had the feel of a good house party. The bar had served the neighborhood so long that most of the regulars referred to it as Daddy's Place, the name his children used among themselves.

As soon as any of us became old enough to work, Daddy Al gave us a task. Everyone started off filling salt and pepper shakers, folding napkins, and wiping off ta-bles and counters. It ended for Phine and Nelia in ownership of the adjacent restaurant and for me as a part-time bartender.

The band was into their second set when I saw Holly stroll in the back door. He looked around to note who was seated where and which exits were open. I motioned him over and placed a bottled water on the counter. Holly rarely touched alcohol. He wasn't a fan of anything that dulled his senses or reflexes.

"Anybody been in yet?"

I knew he meant anybody that would translate to friend or foe. "Not yet."

"Give it time. I just hope Smokey don't end up wit' too many big guns on his side."

"You think he coulda did it?"

"Fo' sure." He cracked open the water bottle. "Daddy Al here yet?"

"Naw, he should be here by midnight just to check things over."

"Otis out there damned near butt naked."

"He got his shirt off again?"

"Shirt off, T-shirt off." He shivered. "Flesh everywhere."

"Wassup, Holly?" Holly turned to find Chantal at his elbow.

"Wassup, monster mouth?"

Chantal giggled, a sound I would never pair with her. Holly was the only one I knew who took the bark and bite out of her. Far as I knew he hadn't dabbled in Chantal's goodies, but she made it obvious they were there for the asking.

Behind her her sister stood with a scowl that encompassed the whole room and me in particular. "Chantal," she said.

Holly reacted to the voice and the sight of Alixe by looking her boldly up and down. She had changed from the jogging suit I saw earlier into a pair of loose-fitting jeans that did nothing to disguise her figure and a white T-shirt that barely grazed the top of her waistband.

"What?" Chantal turned around to face her sister. "I'm trying to bond wit' you and shit, but we just got here and you already got attitude."

"I thought you meant a movie or something."

"Relax. Maceo, you remember Alixe?"

"Yeah, wassup?"

She didn't bother to respond.

Chantal shook her head. "No manners."

"What can I get y'all?"

"On the house?" Chantal asked.

Holly reached in his pocket for a roll of bills. "I got it."

"That's not necessary." Alixe looked pointedly at the money and then edged her way up to the counter. He stepped back, a retort already forming on his lips.

I shook my head to fend him off. "I can take care of it. Chantal, what do you want?"

"Give me a Rolling Rock," she answered.

Alixe looked at me. "A beer for my sister and I'll have a ginger ale."

"You're not drinking?"

"I'm on duty tomorrow."

"Duty for what? You a cop?" Holly looked boldly in Alixe's face.

"Does it matter?"

"Wouldn'ta asked if it didn't." For whatever reason, Holly and Alixe had taken an immediate dislike to each other.

"On duty at the hospital. I'm a nurse."

"Is that right?" Holly laughed. "I definitely had you figured for a cop."

She ignored him, grabbed her drink, and headed for a table across the room.

Holly grinned at Chantal once she left. "She ain't got your charm."

She smiled back. "That's what I been saying."

I moved away to fill a request, leaving Chantal and Holly to their own horrors. I kept my eye on Alixe and witnessed her swatting men away like flies. She caught my gaze once or twice without invite.

In the mirror above the bar I saw Holly move away from the light and direct Chantal to her table. I followed his gaze to the entrance where Clarence Mann stood, flanked on both sides by the two Samoans he never left home without. They were menacing from sheer size, Boo Yaa Tribe braids adding drama to their already imposing presence.

Holly casually sipped his water while his free hand rested behind his back. It was wrapped around the gun he kept in his waistband.

Clarence scanned the room until he spotted Holly. They locked eyes, each regarding the other, trying to gauge where their opponent fell in the pecking order. Clarence waited a moment and then lifted his chin. Holly returned the gesture, and we all relaxed.

Across the dance floor I saw Chantal join Alixe at her table. Both seemed fascinated by the undercurrent of violence rippling through the room.

Clarence, or rather the Samoans, cleared a space at the bar.

"What can I get ya?" I asked.

He nodded to Holly. "You drinkin'?"

Holly held up his water. "I'm cool."

"All right then. Let me get a shot of Hennessy." He turned to the Samoans. They looked at each other, then back at Clarence. "And two Manhattans. One dry. One sweet."

How he knew all that skipped past me, but I mixed the drinks while Clarence made his intentions known.

"What's the word, man? I got some news today"—he dropped his head and shook it over an empty glass left by another patron—"that fucked me up and could mean a war."

"It already jumped off," Holly answered.

"Who kicked it?"

"Smokey Baines. You know 'im?"

"Loud-mouth motherfucker, like to put his hands on women?"

Holly nodded.

"Think he did it?"

"He making a lot of noise if he didn't."

I slid the drinks across the bar.

"He accuse you?" Clarence asked.

"First thang."

Clarence downed his drink. "Here we go then." Behind him the Samoans smiled. Big smiles. "We ridin' together, man?"

That time Holly smiled.

"Day or night, nigga. I'm riding."

Within the hour the unholy alliance forged between Clarence and Holly grew to include Emmet Landry and Malcolm Rose, two players with equal clout. Each came with their own force and their own motives. Everyone else fell to Smokey, by default or otherwise.

Around midnight I walked outside for a little fresh air and to shake off the stiffness and dread that had settled into my joints.

I leaned back against the brick wall, then noticed a red ember glowing in a dark corner. I couldn't see the person but I smelled the pungent odor of a recently struck match.

"Hey, now, you can't smoke rock around here."

My warning was greeted with a soft tingle of a laugh. Alixe stepped from the shadows and held her cigarette up to the light. "What about these? Cigarettes okay?"

"Oh, hey, Alixe, sorry about that. Sometimes—"

"Don't worry about it." She used the heel of her shoe to grind the spent match into the driveway. "Did you come out here to smoke too?"

"Me? No, I don't smoke."

"That's right, you're the athlete."

I couldn't help the pride that filled my chest. "You've been checking up on me?"

"I asked a few questions after you left this afternoon. I wanted to know who Scottie spends so much time with."

"Really? I thought there might be a more interesting reason."

Before she could answer I heard the creak of the swinging doors behind me. Then footsteps headed in our direction, right into the attraction I saw building between Alixe and myself.

"I was wondering where you went off to. I thought you might have left me." Chantal took a seat on the hood of a car parked in front of her sister.

"I just came out here for some fresh air." Chantal's presence drained the humor and light from Alixe.

Chantal looked at me. "Can you believe that, Maceo? Miss Medical School smokes like a chimney."

"Well, you know"—I tried to keep Alixe on my side—"sometimes habits are hard to break."

"Whatever." Chantal waved her hand in the air and swung her braids around. "I'll be glad when this heat goes. This is ridiculous. Earthquake weather."

I knew what she meant. Californians distrusted weird weather patterns. Whether it was true or not, we all believed that heat waves, thunderstorms, and hail all meant an earthquake was coming.

"So, what brought y'all here tonight?" I directed the question to Alixe, who'd grown quiet.

She shrugged. "Your guess is as good as mine. I thought my sister wanted to hang out but maybe she just needed a ride."

"Now, why you say that?" Chantal actually managed to sound hurt by the accusation.

Alixe lit a second cigarette and shrugged when she saw me eye the pack. "What do you mean, why? We haven't exchanged two words since we got here."

"We're at a club!"

"So?"

"So? Sister-girl, it's obvious you ain't had a girlfriend in your life."

The words fell like bricks in the open air. In the silence I knew that even Chantal realized she'd exposed a wound. She tried to cover but the arrow had been shot. "I mean, 'cause girlfriends show up together, then, you know, spread their wings for the fellas."

Alixe remained silent, the quick drags she took from her cigarette a direct indication of her anger.

"We show up together and everything, but if there are cute dudes around why we need to talk to each other? We can talk at home or in the car."

"Is that how it goes?"

Chantal's anger peaked. "That's how it goes here."

"Thanks for letting me know"—she paused for a minute—"sis."

Chantal stood up. "See, that right there. That's exactly why me and you ain't never gonna be family! We too different, and you want to make me remember it every minute."

She walked off before Alixe could respond. I drank my water and waited for an explanation. I'd known Chantal for over a year and she had never mentioned a sister, and Scottie hadn't ever mentioned an aunt. It seemed that both women were new to the boundaries of family.

"You sure you don't want a cigarette?" Alixe held the pack out to me. "Misery loves company and everything."

"Don't need a new habit."

"Well, I can't seem to break mine, but I make really good promises to myself to quit."

I laughed. "And you mean it when you say it, don't you?"

"Oh, I'm so sincere."

"And it gets easier every time you lie, doesn't it?"

"Every time."

We shared a smile. "So, what happened right there?" I motioned toward the doors Chantal had slammed through.

"A little difficulty bonding."

"That's all?"

"That's the sum of it. We've only known each other three months, and ..."

"And it's not what you expected."

She let out a sigh. "On so many levels. Can you believe I actually invited her to travel in Europe with me last summer?" She responded to my questioning look. "This was before we met. When it was just phone conversations."

"She didn't go?"

"Do you think either one of us would still be alive? No, she didn't go. She had the sense to say no. But she invited me to come live out here after I got back, and *I* didn't have the sense to say no."

"You picked up, just like that, and moved here from Japan."

"I left Japan a long time ago." I waited for her to elaborate but she didn't.

"You like Europe?"

"Loved it."

"What'd you love?"

"The anonymity."

"I meant which country, but that'll work."

We laughed together easily, our voices mixing with the passing traffic and the sounds of the music from the bar.

"Holland." She lifted her shirt. "I got a belly-button ring in Amsterdam."

I tried to hide my surprise at seeing a jeweled hoop in the center of her stomach.

"Shit, did that hurt?"

"What is it guys tell you when you lose your virginity? Only for a minute, baby."

"I didn't hear that."

"But did you say it?"

I held up my hands. "I plead the Fifth."

"I bet." She laughed. "You ever been to Europe?"

"Naw."

"You should go."

I shook my head. "I'm not too big on being the only Black person in a crowd."

"Don't let that stop you. You'd be surprised where we show up." She said it with the admiration of someone who'd been raised in a racially sterile environment. Chantal's wounding comment about her lack of friends probably feasted from the same wound. "You should go whenever you get the chance."

"So Holland was your favorite, then anonymity."

"Something like that."

"You don't feel anonymous in Oakland?"

"I don't feel anything in Oakland."

I put my hand over my heart. "How can you not feel Oaktown, baby?"

"It's easy if you have the view I have." I knew she referred to the carnage of Highland hospital.

"Have you traveled a lot?"

She nodded. "My father is military. I grew up with my mother in Okinawa, but I'd visit him two or three times a year, wherever he was stationed."

"Okinawa, huh?"

She nodded.

"Not a lot of Black folks?"

She gave a short, harsh laugh. "Just me. Or at least that's how it felt." I could tell from her eyes the words held a host of bitter memories. "What about you? You ever leave Oakland?"

"Oh, I been known to go over to San Francisco once in a while."

"Seriously, Maceo."

"A little. Here and there. Mostly Louisiana, two or three times a year. Australia once with my baseball team, West Indies with some family. Nothing alone"—I pushed her with my elbow—"or anonymous."

"Always with a crowd?"

"Always."

She turned and looked me dead in the eye, guessing something that must have lived right there on the surface. "But you still feel alone, don't you?" She held up a hand. "You don't have to answer. I can recognize it a mile away."

The doors swung open behind us and Holly, followed by Emmet, Malcolm, Clarence, and the Samoans, spilled from the bar. They stumbled out, drunk on kinship. The laughter in their words was heavy with their own heroics, the retold stories of spectacular drug deals, enemies beat down, and police outsmarted. I watched them for a moment, feeling the aloneness Alixe had just mentioned. There was a part of Holly that despite our friendship I could not or would not touch.

He saw us in the corner and ambled over. He grabbed the water from my hand and drained the bottle. "Wassup, man? We heading out. You wanna ride?"

"Gotta close up."

He eyed Alixe with a greedy gaze. "What about you, Miss Lady? You wanna ride?"

She blew smoke just short of his face and didn't bother to answer. The easiness and laughter that had been present while we talked disappeared the moment Holly arrived. It didn't have to be explained; the pure dislike between them was chemical.

Holly grinned and gunned up to taunt her but I shook my head.

He raised an eyebrow in question but let it go when I grabbed the water bottle back. He nodded toward Alixe and said, in reference to her, "You're on a rookie mission with this one, Maceo."

He whispered it, a stage whisper that Alixe couldn't decipher, but she felt the animosity and aimed back.

"You look familiar," she said to him, taking another long drag. "You ever been treated at Highland? We get a lot of gunshot victims there."

"Can't fuck with the witch doctors at County Hospital."

"Witch doctor." She looked at me. "The second time I heard that tonight. I guess Oakland is smaller than I thought. You sure you've never been there?"

"Positive. Maybe I just got that kind of face."

She studied him a little too long for comfort. Holly shifted uneasily. A story with Holly as the villain hovered just behind her eyes. "It'll come to me." There was absolutely no surrender in her face. I had a premonition of one day having to choose between the two of them.

He backed away from her. "Don't hurt yourself." He said to me, "Later, nigga." I watched as he climbed into Emmet's BMW. It screeched out of the parking lot with Clarence's Mercedes and Malcolm's Audi close behind.

"You're a mystery man, Maceo."

"How you figure that?"

"You're different from them even if you hate to admit it. I can see it, and I just met you."

"Alixe . . ."

She ignored me and continued. "Holly, on the other hand, is Oakland and everything I've grown to hate about it since I got here. And Oakland is him. But you, Maceo, you're something else."

"You gathered all that from a two-minute conversation?"

She snorted. "Doesn't take much more than that."

"A nurse *and* a mind reader?"

"You have to be sometimes. You want me to tell you what else I think?"

"No."

"You hate the difference, even though it makes you who you are. It would be easier just to be like everybody else."

I backed away. Her words made me feel claustrophobic. "I gotta get back inside."

She looked at me, surprised that I didn't welcome her reading of me. "Something about you just doesn't jibe with the surroundings."

She studied me for a minute, trying to weigh her next words.

"Or with Holly." She paused. "But you'll probably fight that fact until it kills you." She walked toward an army-green postal Jeep parked on the street. "What time are you off?" she tossed back over her shoulder.

I couldn't find my voice.

She continued anyway. "Maybe I'll come back at closing." She climbed in the Jeep and lit another cigarette. "Tell my sister I'll wait in the car."

CHAPTER

15

By two o'clock the bar was closed tight as a drum and I was ready to call it an evening. I hadn't expected the night to end without violence, but somehow we had managed to muddle through.

I was dead on my feet as I turned on the alarm system, but I propped Soup Can up against my side. His bones were made of liquor, so he was no help in keeping himself upright. He mumbled, hiccuped, and laughed at the end of his inaudible sentences.

As I helped him into the car I looked up at the apartments that bordered the parking lot. The locksmith on the first floor was dark but above the shop an exposed bulb in a brightly painted kitchen revealed Easter Lilly in a moment of repose. I hadn't seen her leave the bar, but I remembered pouring her two still-full brandy glasses down the drain.

Daddy Al didn't usually allow working girls on the property, but Lilly was the exception. She used her apartment to handle clients, and her bedroom had an unobstructed view of the Nickel and Dime. On two occasions she'd called the police, in the middle of turning tricks, to report a robbery in progress. Each time she'd saved the bar from losing money.

Above us Lilly swayed beneath the exposed bulb, the yellow walls a sad backdrop. She held a sequined red dress out in front of her while she looked for spots and snagged seams. I knew the dress. She pulled it out every Saturday for Sunday morning services. She liked to sit front and center in her bright outfit.

As she'd told me more than once, "I wear the same dress, same color, every week. You see, I'm a truthful person and that dress tells the truth to anybody who'll listen." Gra'mère had tried on several occasions to pull Lilly in off the streets, but she stayed put. My guess was that turning tricks was penance for an unnamed infraction.

I smiled up at her from the passenger side of the car but she was oblivious to me as she swayed to music I couldn't hear.

Soup Can's rheumy eyes followed mine to the window. "That's some kind of dress," I said.

He sobered up long enough to answer. "That's some kind of woman." He tipped an imaginary hat and spilled into the car.

I watched Lilly a moment longer as she moved seductively with the dress pressed against her chest, the arms stretched out like a partner in a tango, but stopped my vigil when she turned off the overhead light.

I got Soup Can buckled into the car and closed the passenger-side door. I was backing away when out of the corner of my eye I noticed a black sedan idling on the corner.

I remembered Smokey's gun still crammed beneath the seat but there was no way to reach it. I'd have to navigate a locked car, a drunk, and my own fear—fear that a gun in my hand would be the final bridge to the other side.

I fumbled with my keys, dropped them, and bent down to pick them up. I noticed then that the lights of the car were off, which obscured the license plate, but I could hear the low hum of the engine. Trouble.

I made a split-second decision and rolled under my car. A shot that sounded like a roller-coaster whiz of hot compressed air shattered the rearview mirror on the passenger side, the mirror where I'd stood a moment before. Another shot, again nearly silent, obliterated the E at the end of NICKEL AND DIME.

I scrambled like a crab, then rolled, until I had cleared the width of the car and made it to the garbage Dumpster backed against the fence. I could hear my heart in my ears, the steady *thump-thump* of blood rushing through my body, and felt the sting of rising bile in my throat. Sweat poured from my forehead and obscured my vision.

I rolled over garbage, discarded condoms, broken bottles, and weeks of sour liquids that made rivers in the ground beneath me.

"Fuck!" I whispered when I realized Soup Can was left exposed. I doubted that the shattered glass had woken him from his drunken slumber.

My view was blocked by garbage and the tires of the Cougar but I was sure I heard footsteps. I edged back toward the tight space between the Dumpster and the fence, aware that—if I made it—up and over was the only course of action, then an outright sprint.

"He ain't here. Musta jumped the fence," I heard someone say.

I didn't recognize the voice but my instincts were right. Trouble.

The response to my would-be killer came from across the street, muffled; I couldn't make out the words.

"I looked under the car. He ain't here."

"What the hell?" The voice in close proximity to the car had finally awakened Soup Can. "Maceo? Hey, you, what you doing? Get on away from this car!"

My heart raced. Soup Can's voice was no longer sloppy with drink. It had the definite clarity of terror.

"Shut the fuck up, old man."

"Get away from this car!" I heard a scuffle, then saw Soup Can's feet as he was dragged across the lot. "Hey!"

"Motherfucker." I saw a foot connect with the old man's ribs. He curled into a ball to protect himself. I stayed put. "Getting in the way. What's wrong with you?"

What came next was the sickening sound of the man's gun hitting the side of Soup Can's head. Overhead I saw Lilly's light come on. The attacker saw it too because he straightened up, delivered one last kick to Soup Can, and ran back the way he came.

"Let's go! Let's go!" the gunman yelled.

The shout from across the street was clearer, definitely in command, but I couldn't be sure who it belonged to. I heard Lilly's window rattle open and then water splashed down, lots of water, scalding-hot water, enough to send the river of condoms rolling toward my eyes and mouth. I stayed put, regardless.

I gave up my hiding spot once I heard the unmistakable screech of tires. I rolled out and sprang to my feet just as Lilly came down from her apartment. Soup Can lay in a tight ball on the ground. The side of his face was wet and sticky with blood and vomit.

"Maceo, where'd you come from?" Lilly pulled her sash tight to cover the nakedness beneath. She tore the sleeve from her robe and held it to the open gash on Soup Can's cheek. He was unconscious.

"I rolled under the Dumpster after they fired the first shot."

"They was out here shooting! I didn't hear anything."

"Musta had a silencer. I didn't hear it either until the mirror shattered."

"I was just getting in the tub when I heard voices. I had some hot water on the stove, for my bath, and when I saw that man out here I tossed it out. I might have missed." She shrugged. "I might have got 'im."

"Thanks, Lil." I wanted to smile but my muscles, even the facial ones, were locked down in fear. I could taste the salt of my own sweat. I hoped my knees weren't visibly shaking.

Soup Can mumbled as he started to resurface.

Lilly pursed her lips. "How they gonna beat an old man like that?"

Soup Can opened his eyes. "No good reason."

I held his hand as sirens sounded in the distance.

The sirens brought the neighbors out in various stages of undress, and it was only minutes before the North Oakland grapevine pulled Daddy Al from his bed. I saw him storm toward where I stood in the watery stew around the Dumpster.

"What happened?" he asked me.

"We're trying to figure that out, sir." The patrol officer stepped in between Daddy Al and me. "May I ask your name?"

"Albert Redfield. This here is my grandson. What happened, Maceo?"

I shrugged. "I was putting Soup in the car."

"Soup? Is that the gentleman there?"

We looked toward Soup Can, who looked depleted and old under the glare of the streetlamp.

"Yes. He had too much to drink, and I was going to drive him home."

"You work here?"

"I'm the bartender."

"You hurt?" Daddy Al stepped around the officer and put a soft hand on my shoulder.

"I'm fine. Just some cuts and scrapes when I rolled under the car." Behind Daddy Al I saw the wide headlights of Alixe's Jeep swerve into the parking lot. Just what I needed.

"Did you see your assailants?"

"No. They were parked across the street, lights off, motor running. I couldn't see the license plate."

"Dark car, motor running. Sounds like a hit," the officer added.

I didn't bother to confirm the obvious.

"Was there any trouble in the bar tonight?"

I shook my head. "None."

"What happened after you noticed the car?"

"I rolled under the Cougar and kept rolling till I was under the Dumpster."

The officer looked surprised that I'd had the sense to keep myself alive. "Then what happened?"

"I couldn't see anything else but I heard someone talking."

"That bastard hit me wit' a gun, kicked my body like I was a dog!" Soup Can straightened up enough to be mad. "Had on a mask."

"A mask?" The officer moved toward Soup Can, thought better of it, and went to his car and called for another officer.

Alixe approached tentatively with a small bag in her hand.

"You okay, Maceo?" The concern in her voice seemed genuine.

"I'm fine."

"Let me clean you up."

"What you doing back here?"

She opened the bag and inched her hands into a pair of gloves. "I told you I might come back. I dropped Chantal off a couple minutes ago. She talked me into going to another bar."

I motioned toward Daddy Al. "Alixe, this is my grandfather, Albert Redfield."

"Hello, young lady. You a doctor?"

She smiled. "Nurse. My sister lives in your apartment complex, by the way. Chantal Hunter."

"Chantal? Is that right?"

"Yes. She's told me about your family and how nice you've been to her."

I watched as Alixe charmed Daddy Al into submission with her politeness. While they talked I saw Clarence's Mercedes slow down at the stoplight. I watched as the car inched past, Holly's face visible in the backseat. I didn't expect them to stop, not with the police in attendance, but I knew Holly would be waiting for me at the cottage.

I nodded his way to let him know I understood; then the car sped off.

CHAPTER

16

We were held for over an hour as the attending officer and his backup questioned us in detail. Alixe stayed around, sitting quietly in her Jeep, looking at her watch only once. Easter Lilly invited Soup Can to sleep on her couch, sparing me the trouble of driving him home.

I was grateful.

Once we were released, I refused the hospital but accepted a quick once-over from Alixe. The Cougar was unharmed, save for the rearview mirror, as was I, save for a few cuts, but I was nervous, scared, about what the attempt meant. It wasn't a stretch to realize it was directly related to my confrontation with Smokey. Alixe followed Daddy Al and me back to the Dover Street house.

"This have anything to do with the trouble at Cutty's?"

"I don't know. Could have been a robbery attempt."

Daddy Al looked skeptical. "Guess you figure I don't know trouble when I see it."

"I'm not sure what was going on. Could be Smokey. Could be related to Billy."

"Billy? How?"

"Smokey fingered me and Holly at the shop."

Daddy Al raised an eyebrow. "You and Holly? How he figure that?"

"Well, Holly because he and Billy were in the same business."

"And you?"

"Because of . . ."

"Felicia." He shook his head. "Maybe you need to go out to Louisiana till all this blows over."

I turned into the driveway. "You can't send me to Louisiana like you sending me to my room."

"I can do what I please. You talking to a grown man."

"I'm a grown man too."

"Not if you can't keep your ass out of trouble."

"I can handle this."

"By getting shot?"

"Daddy Al, you can't fix everything for me. You cannot decide how I live my life."

"Is that what you think?"

Alixe chose that moment to knock on the window. Her Jeep idled in front of us.

"Can we talk about this in the morning?" I jumped out of the car before he could respond. He waited a moment, then walked into the house without another word to me.

"He upset?" Alixe asked.

"Just a little bit."

"I don't blame him. Nice place, this Oakland."

"It's not Holland, but it has good and bad just like everyplace else."

"Good?" She looked doubtful.

"Yeah, good. I just got shot at and I can still see it."

"Those are what's called rose-colored glasses."

"Daddy Al thinks it's stupidity."

"Well . . ."

"Don't say it."

She laughed. "Really, Maceo. Don't you want to see the world? See something different?"

"Don't you want to drop it?"

"What about the violence?"

"There's violence everywhere."

"True, but Oakland's trying to set new records."

My fatigue and exasperation finally got the best of me. "Alixe, look, you already made up your mind. What's the point of this conversation?"

"I'm sorry. I know you're tired. You want company? Want me to sit with you?"

I looked pointedly at my watch. It was almost four A.M. "Don't you work tomorrow?"

"Actually I do. I just don't want you to be alone."

"I'll be fine. I'll be 'sleep in about five minutes."

"Then I'll get some rest too."

She leaned forward and kissed my forehead. She let her hand linger on my cheek. I wanted her to come inside. I wanted nothing more, but I knew Holly was there.

"I'm listed, you know. If you want to give me a call."

"I'll do that."

"Be safe."

"Always."

I waited until she was inside the Jeep before I started to talk. "Lake Merritt. The Oakland A's. The Warriors. En Vogue. Paramount Theatre. Tony Toni Toné. Joaquin Miller Park. Jack London Square. The weather."

She laughed. "What are you rambling about?"

"Oakland. Those are the things I like about it."

"I got something too."

"What?"

"You." She blew me a kiss and drove off into the night.

Holly was there just as I expected, pacing the front porch of the cottage. I could see Daddy Al watching us both from his bedroom window.

"What happened?"

"Follow me inside. Daddy Al ready to bust heads." Holly looked toward the window, then shamefully looked down.

Once we cleared the threshold I turned on the air conditioner. It was still hot despite the early morning hour. I was surprised to find Clio sprawled across the couch. I walked into the kitchen and pulled two sodas from the refrigerator. There was a note from Gra'mère pasted on the door: *Macaroni and cheese. Meat loaf. Lemon cake.*

"You hungry?" I shoved the cellophaned plate across the counter to him.

"Naw, nigga. What happened? I saw Five-Oh all over the bar."

"Somebody took a shot at me."

"When?"

"As I was leaving."

"Smokey?"

"Don't know, but that's my guess."

"Damn. I shouldn't'a left you there. I'm slippin'. We just left you there wide-open."

"Relax." The irritation I felt with Daddy Al bubbled to the surface. "I can handle myself."

"Don't act hard. You wouldn't leave *me* uncovered, would you? That's all I meant. Did you see anybody?"

I relayed the events to him, with a few details I'd kept from the police. To implicate Smokey would eventually send the trail right back to Holly.

"Maceo, man, you gotta lay low on this."

"I'll lay low when I find Flea. I owe it to her." I looked him in the eye. "We owe it to Billy."

He looked away.

"You in or out?" I asked him.

"I ain't gonna leave you wide-open."

"That's not what I asked you."

He paused for a moment. Holly had long ago stopped feeling connected to Billy, but this went beyond that.

"In or out?" I repeated.

"Fuck me. What about you? The schoolboy route won't work on this mission, *hear-what-I'm-saying?* Can *you* hang, Maceo?"

I didn't answer. I didn't know at that moment where the question would take me, but I did know I wanted to find Felicia. Teaming with Holly would sometimes mean doing things his way. It would also mean I couldn't fence-sit and use athletics as an excuse. I wouldn't be able to classify the journey as an accident, someplace I arrived because the wind sent me there. This road, one way or another, would lead me to myself, good or bad.

Holly let me consider as long as I needed. Then he asked, "Is your girl that important to you?"

"You in or out?" I asked again, and extended my hand.

"In, nigga." He sighed and gave me a pound to seal it. That was all I wanted to hear.

CHAPTER

17

When the last Ice Age ended, the great glaciers that covered the earth melted and disappeared so fast that the
oceans overflowed. Those oceans flowed into rivers, and
the rivers carved a gorge at the Golden Gate and birthed
the San Francisco Bay. Thousands of years later that
gorge was a playground on one scorcher of a Sunday.

The heat wave continued in full force, clearing the sky
to Alcatraz and San Quentin prison and out to Mount
Tamalpais in Marin. I cruised along Highway 80 with a
clear view of both bridges and the white sails bobbing in
the water.

"Jump off here," Holly directed. "Swing by Flea's
house."

I took the Ashby Avenue exit and followed the streets
up to College Avenue.

As we pulled up in front of the Victorian house we
heard the sound of shattering glass. Seconds later, Regina's scream launched us out of the car.

Holly was ahead of me as we raced up the stairs. Both
of us knew that Charlie was the cause of everything going
wrong in the apartment.

"Where the fuck she at?" Charlie's voice boomed
through the open door.

We rushed inside to find the doors of Flea's black armoire kicked in. The television screen had also been
shattered by what looked like a man's foot.

"Charlie!" Holly bellowed out the name but stayed close to the door.

Charlie, like Billy and Holly, was an outlaw, but I had less of an affinity for him. Charlie was driven purely by emotion, a trait I found hard to admire. If he was mad he lived in that anger; if he was happy he manhandled those around him to feel the same elation. He ran black or white, never gray. Charlie was muscle without an ounce of anything else to offer.

"Wassup, man?" Holly gestured around the apartment and motioned Regina to his side.

"What you mean, wassup? I'm handling business."

"Whose?"

Charlie turned his full gaze on Holly. "You the police?"

"No."

"Is this your bitch?"

"No."

"Then what the fuck you up in here for?"

"Man, you can't be handling no chick like this. You want to get violated?" Charlie lived on parole. Leave it to Holly to know the only thing that might defuse him.

"Fuck my PO. My boy's dead, man." His voice cracked on the last word, and in spite of his wild dumbness I felt sorry for him. There were few people in the east Bay who could call Charlie friend. Matter of fact, Billy may have been the only one.

"We heard. That shit was foul, but you want to be locked up when they put him down? How's that gonna look? Your only boy and you don't show at his funeral?" I could see Charlie wavering while Holly talked, so I motioned Regina toward her bedroom. She slipped off as quietly as possible. Holly looked toward her retreating back. "What broad is worth that?"

"You know that tramp set him up." "Tramp" was Charlie's kind reference to Felicia.

"You think so?"

"I know so. Billy wadn't even fucking wit' me th same way once she got here. Me and him been tight sinc way back."

"You ever see her do anything scandalous?"

"Naw, but that don't mean shit."

"Did she have any shady partners coming around?"

He shrugged. "You can't trust women, man."

"I hear you." Holly paused. "But Maceo knows he roommate pretty good. Why don't you let him talk t her, and we'll get wit' you if we hear anything."

Charlie seemed to deflate as Holly spoke. He slumpe onto the couch and put his head in his hands.

I caught Holly's eye and slipped inside after Regina.

I found her in Flea's room curled up on the bed with her head buried in the pillows. I hated walking in there because the air was still charged with Flea's favorite per fume.

"You okay?" I sat at the foot of the bed and held on t the four-poster like an anchor. I planted my feet to kee my equilibrium, remembering what it had been like t make love to her.

We'd both finished a late shift at the bar a week befor she quit. Billy was out of town, and it was the anniver sary of her mother's death: a recipe for error. The two o us had just come home when she nonchalantly walke me into her bedroom. She gave me the go-ahead signa by allowing me to stay while she changed her clothes. sat in a corner chair with the remote control dangling i my hand. I tried to concentrate on the TV but all I coul see was her soft brown skin stretched to nearly six feet. knew her renewed interest wasn't about me but it didn matter. Her loneliness rode the surface of her body like second skin, but being a gentleman and being thoughtfu had cost me her once. I wanted her back under any circumstances.

"What you looking at, Maceo?" She'd turned around to reveal a perfect breast.

"Nothing." I dropped my head as desperate heat flooded my cheeks.

"Nothing," she repeated, teasing me with a dead-on imitation of my voice. "You don't see this?" She took my hand and placed it on her stomach. I held it there stiffly, afraid to move an inch.

She moved it for me. "You don't see this either?" She guided my hand to her breast.

"What about this?" She dropped her skirt to the floor and stood naked before me. Then she bent to look me dead in the eye.

"Why you scared?" she teased playfully.

"Because." I wanted to say, Because you're gonna leave. Because there's no way I could ever keep you. I kissed her instead. She let me.

Billy came back in the morning.

"Holly's handling Charlie," I told Regina. "We'll get him out of here as soon as we can."

"I ain't worried about him. I'll slice his ass if he gets too close." Her bristle had returned, the first sign that she was feeling better.

"Why'd you let him in?"

"I didn't. I left the door unlocked while I went down to the laundry. When I came back upstairs he was in the apartment. I recognized him as Billy's friend, but he still scared the shit out of me. Before I could say anything he started acting crazy. His fat ass never liked Flea, and now he's saying she set Billy up."

"A lot of people think that. That's why Holly and I came over here."

"You know Flea wouldn't do that."

"I'm not the one you have to worry about."

"You think she's okay?"

"As long as she got a head start."

In the front room Charlie stood at the door with his hand on the doorknob. He laughed at something Holly said under his breath.

He looked toward Regina and nodded, the only apology she would get. She rolled her eyes and started to pick up the shattered glass. Charlie looked away.

"I'ma head out." He moved to the top of the staircase.

"All right then." Holly held out his hand. When Charlie reached out to shake it he lowered his voice. "I'ma need a little help moving some shit out to Marin, things gonna be a little shaky in Oakland for a while. You know anybody can help me wit' that?"

Charlie's darting eyes betrayed his mouth. "Naw, don't fuck with Marin. Fools'll give you a life sentence for a traffic ticket."

"Well, holler if you hear anything."

"Peace."

He took three steps at a time going down. We waited until we heard his car start downstairs.

"Why the man lie like that?" I asked.

"We'll know soon enough."

After Charlie's departure the two of us helped Regina clean up the front room. She was skittish, which indicated that she was more spooked than she let on. We ordered a pizza, and while Holly went to pick it up I quizzed Regina about Reggie and Crim.

"You know how to get hold of Flea's brothers?"

She looked surprised. "Brothers? Why?"

"They're about the only ones that can protect her and get her out of Oakland safely if she's still here."

"You think it's that bad?"

I nodded. "Charlie talks a lot of shit, but we can only hold him off so long. I don't want him to run into Flea first."

"Won't Reggie and Crim make things worse?"

"That's better than the alternative."

She looked doubtful but she rose to go to the side table. A minute later she produced a notepad. "Flea and I keep our emergency numbers on this. You want to call or should I?"

"You call."

"All right." She hesitated for a minute. "You think you and Holly could stay tonight? That fool might start drinking and come back here."

"No problem."

"Good." She reached for the cordless and walked into the kitchen.

Moments later Holly walked in, carrying the deep-dish and the Sunday edition of *The Oakland Tribune* under his arm.

"Man, you check out the paper." He threw it down in front of me. Billy's face stared back at me with lifelike intensity.

It was eerie looking into the eyes of a dead man, but I met the gaze. Silently, I made a promise to him that I would find and protect Felicia.

The headline read: KINGPIN GUNNED DOWN. MURDER RATE CLIMBS. I started to read the article aloud.

"Billy Crane, 24, former basketball player at Albany High School and Laney Community College, became murder victim number 147 as the Oakland drug wars—"

Regina's voice interrupted my recitation. "I called."

Holly sighed, knowing the answer before he asked. "Who?"

"Reggie and Crim."

He shook his head. "Man, I got a bad feeling about them."

"You ain't the only one, but what else can we do?"

"If they can't find their sister there's gonna be plenty of bloodshed."

Regina sat down between us and picked up the newspaper. "They'll be here in the morning."

At the edge of my dream I hear someone moving about and talking to me softly, but for now I'm stuck on the baseball field in the middle of the cemetery. The headstones are gray and crumbling, giving way to knotty grass and clumps of dirt with bone fragments mixed in the soil. It's foggy, with a mist so thick and wet that I have to pull my jersey away from my skin in order to move. The outfield is empty and so are the stands and the dugout. There are only two people on the field, me and my catcher, just like it used to be. He's in position behind the plate, giving me signals that contradict what the coach shouts from center field.

"Take it easy, son. This guy ain't got nothing you ain't seen before." The coach's words circle around me, filtered by the fog.

At my feet there are at least three inches of bright yellow tennis balls. I'm bent over, rifling through them, trying to find the perfect one for my next pitch. I pick up one after another, weighing each one in my hand, trying to find the life force.

The catcher gives me the signal for a slider and then pulls off his glove in frustration. "Time!" he shouts.

I can see him moving toward me, but I ignore him and continue to look through the tennis balls.

Behind me the coach sighs in exasperation. "Jesus, what's this guy doing? Don't listen to him, Maceo. Don't lose your concentration. You know what's at stake here, fella."

On my back my jersey feels like a pound of concrete. I try again to pull it away from my flesh but I can hear the skin rip with the fabric. I shake everything back into place and kick a few of the balls away.

From the top of my eyelids I can see the catcher's dress shoes. They are black, with air holes around the toe and tassels on one foot. His cleats sink into the cemetery dust as he stands and waits for my attention.

I refuse to look up and meet his eye. I know he wants to pull me from the game.

"Wassup, Watch Dog?" he asks me in Billy's voice. "Want me to call the game?"

I nod with my eyes still cast to the ground.

"Well, I can't, man. We're in play." He shuffles his feet back and forth quickly. His cleats leave jagged grooves in the earth. "So, how you gonna fix this?"

He continues to stand in front of me while I toss around a tennis ball. It has the life and weight I need. This is the one, the perfect ball.

The coach continues to make noise from the outfield. "Take it easy, son. Take it easy. He's just trying to spook you."

I feel two cold fingers beneath my chin and Billy's voice again. "It might not be good enough to watch this time. You might have to get in the game, hear what I'm saying?"

He raises my face up to meet his. He's still wearing his mask, though I can see his teeth through the grating. "You might have to get a little dirty."

He pulls his mask away. His temples ooze blood from a fresh bullet wound. His eyes are closed, stitched shut with bloody thread.

He yanks his mask back down and trots away. I wind up into pitching stance, secure my pivot foot, not bothering to give him enough time to reach home plate. The ball feels good in my hands. I feel it breathe before I let it go. He turns around at the sound of it coming toward him. It has a life of its own. A fastball. A bullet traveling right to his temple.

CHAPTER

18

The article about Billy summed up what the rest of us knew by heart. I woke up sweaty from my nightmare to find myself on Regina's couch staring at Billy's newspaper photograph.

The end was approaching fast, but few people knew that. A drought season was coming, sweeping like a hurricane from the coca fields of South America, and only a few were prepared for it. Billy was the only one who seemed to stay ahead of the game. His savvy business tactics never left him without product or without competitive prices.

Regina came into the room holding two cups of coffee and looked over my shoulder at the paper. Holly was scrunched in a chair on the other side of the room. Neither one of us had wanted to sleep in Felicia's bed. "I gave them that picture of Billy. It was on Flea's dresser. Some reporter came by Saturday asking me questions."

"A reporter and Charlie." I exchanged a look with Holly. "Why don't you get dressed and ride with us to my grandparents' house?"

"What for?"

"It might be safer."

Regina nodded. She knew the drill, having grown up in New York. Death was death, and she might be next in line.

"You can stay in my cottage if you're not comfortable in the big house. You know my Aunt Cissy, don't you?" She nodded. "She lives there."

"Let me get my things."

After she disappeared into her room, Holly looked at me and then at his watch. "Countdown."

"Daddy Al, this is Regina Fowler, Felicia's roommate. Regina, this is my grandfather, Mr. Redfield."

"Nice to meet you." Regina extended her hand, and Daddy Al took her small one in both of his.

"How you, baby?"

She shrugged. "I'll feel much better once we find Felicia."

He guided her toward the house. "You'll feel much better once you taste some of Lady Belle's cooking. All the family here for lunch. Maceo, go 'head and take her into the house. She can stay upstairs in the twins' room."

I grabbed Regina's suitcase and led her inside.

"*C'est toi qui y connais, ma fille! Cre tonnerre!*" Gra'mère stood over a plate of *grillades* talking to my Aunt Phine. The two women were using their fingers to taste the sautéed veal while my grandmother praised it in

Creole. She always reverted to her childhood language whenever she was angry or excited about something.

The baby in a large family of beautiful women, my grandmother stands five feet eleven inches, with brassy hair and a smoky voice. She's been prematurely gray since the age of twenty-seven, and she wears her silvery locks down to her elbows.

Gra'mère's people on the maternal side, the Seigneleys, were members of Louisiana's *gens de couleur libre* because of a liaison between a female ancestor and a representative of the French crown. On her father's side the Tessier-Bouchaunds enjoyed freedom because of a Spanish nobleman's indiscretion.

The proud knowledge that royalty runs in the Bouchaund veins on both sides has less to do with Europe and everything to do with the Creole traditions of Natchitoches and West Feliciana parishes. I've been taught since childhood to be proud of my heritage, bloodstained hands and all.

"*Ça va, mon cocodrie?*" I moved forward to kiss Gra'mère, laughing at the nickname she wouldn't relinquish. I had been *cocodrie,* or "crocodile," since before I could remember. As soon as I learned to stand, I would hold on to the railings of my crib, lean my chin on the top, and peer at them. Gra'mère said it reminded her of the bayou gators floating in the water.

"What's up, Aunt Phine?" I called to Josephine.

"Same old." She offered a cheek for me to kiss and went back to her cooking. "I'm catering a bridal shower this weekend for some little pretend-Creole bride."

Like the rest of my aunts, Phine was not known for her patience or generous tongue. None of them suffered fools. In addition to the restaurant, Phine and her twin, Cornelia—or Nelia, as we called her—ran a successful troupe of male strippers.

"Everybody, this is Regina. Regina Fowler, Felicia's roommate."

Cissy wandered in while I made the introductions. Cissy is Gra'mère's late-in-life child, born six months before me. After my own mother died Gra'mère nursed me with the milk meant for Cissy. She never let her hatred of my father—the man who killed her daughter—affect how she felt about me. She took me to her breast as if she'd birthed me herself. I've heard again and again how she returned from her daughter's funeral to find me crying uncontrollably for my mother. "Hush, *bébé*," she said, and pressed me to her heart. She'd been saving me from grief ever since.

"Sit down, baby." Gra'mère motioned for Regina to take a seat.

"Regina's gonna stay here for a little while, if that's okay."

Gra'mère waved me away. "She can stay in the spare room."

Cissy turned to Regina. "Or you can stay with me. I have a computer in my room. I know you're in midterms this week."

"Anything is fine. Thank you."

"Y'all heard anything about Flea?" Cissy directed the question to Regina and me.

"Nope, but Noone and Charlie already been there," I answered.

She rolled her eyes at the mention of Noone's name.

"Hey, heifer, you ain't gonna speak to nobody else?" Phine stuck her cheek out to Cissy to receive a kiss.

"I got your heifer. What's for lunch?"

"What you bring?" Phine countered. "You grown and everything trying to have boys spend the night in Momma and Daddy's house. I think you can fend for yourself in the kitchen."

"Hush, Josephine." Gra'mère stirred a pot of stew at

the back of the stove. My nose told me it was shrimp Creole.

"You didn't hear the whole story," Cissy said.

Phine turned with her hand on her hip. "True or false. Was there some ratty-ass boy 'sleep on the couch at two o'clock in the morning?"

"True, but—"

"Uh-uh, no buts. You know better."

"We were studying, and he fell asleep when I went upstairs to get a sweater."

"And that's when Daddy Al came in from the garage," I added, remembering the shouts of anger he had directed at the sleeping boy.

"Shut up, Maceo. You just lucky you got that cottage before me." My occupancy of the cottage was the only point of contention between Cissy and myself.

"You don't need that cottage, Cissy. You think your daddy would let you have boys back there?"

"Why are we talking about my sex life?"

"Sex life!" Gra'mère dropped her spoon, as did Phine. "If I taught you right you don't have one!"

Cissy colored to her hairline, the one thing that saved her. Gra'mère's tone softened.

"I'm glad you got the sense to be embarrassed."

Cissy looked to me for help, but I raised my hands in surrender. She made a face and tried a new tactic. "I finished my biggest midterm this week."

Her announcement was met with silence. Neither Gra'mère nor Phine were ready to excuse her earlier mistake. Cissy was a senior English major at Mills College with dreams of becoming a playwright. She had bypassed Cal and Stanford for California's only single-sex college.

"How'd you do?" I asked.

Phine shot me a look. "There they go, thick as thieves."

"Been that way since I was nursing them."

"Momma's little titty babies." Phine laughed wickedly. "That's what me and Nelia use to call y'all."

"None of that in mixed company," I said.

"What? You shamed? We know you a different kind of titty baby now." Phine laughed again, and I remembered why I was glad she and the tart-tongued Nelia had moved out of the Dover house.

Cissy shot me a look that said, That's what you get.

Regina laughed. "This reminds me of my father's side of the family."

"That's enough, Josephine." Gra'mère spooned *grillades* over a plate of grits and poured shrimp Creole into bowls. "Maceo, Cissy, go 'head and set the table."

Cissy, grateful for the reprieve, rushed to the china cabinet. "How many?"

"Set the whole table. I think we might have a full house. And go tell Redfield to come in and eat something."

Phine took a seat across from me just as Nelia and Rachel came into the room. Rachel was dressed in the no-nonsense clothes of a high school principal while Nelia wore a sassy red sundress. While there were signs of Daddy Al in all four of the daughters present, Rachel definitely had a look of her own. She was darker than the rest, with soft brown eyes and an Afro she kept short and close to the scalp. In her ears, as usual, large Afrocentric earrings dangled.

She dropped her jacket over a chair and moved to the sink. I watched her and noted that she always went right to work without being asked. Sometimes I had the feeling that Aunt Rachel saw herself as more a boarder than a daughter.

Nelia, Phine's twin, was the flashiest of all the sisters. As she moved forward to kiss Gra'mère I smelled her perfume as it took over the kitchen. She winked at me with the big green eyes I'd loved since I was a little boy. Rachel walked by and pulled lightly on my ear, a greeting we had between the two of us. The gesture made my throat tighten. Wherever Felicia was hiding she didn't have the comfort of family, and Billy was far beyond it.

CHAPTER

19

Lake Merritt, a natural saltwater lake in the middle of the city, was working double time as a pickup spot. At its inception, the wildlife sanctuary had been lined with mansions, but they'd long since been replaced by restaurants, laundromats, apartments, a freeway overpass, and a movie theater.

I circled the north side of the water twice and gunned the Cougar at stoplights to get attention. The Cougar was a showpiece, and I knew once I parked I'd be surrounded by guys asking about the engine. Then the girls would come one by one. The Cougar had the same drawing power as puppies and babies.

I finally found a parking space on Grand Avenue, the center of activity and just below Grand Lake Theater. Holly fed the meter as I grabbed a pretzel from a street vendor.

Through the window of Faye's Alterations I could see Emmet Landry standing in front of a three-paneled mirror. Every new piece of information, every rumor, would put us closer to finding Felicia so we went inside. Besides that, Emmet was already an outright member of the fuck-Smokey team.

"Fellas." Emmet stepped down from the pedestal where he was getting his pants hemmed. "Wassup, Holly?"

"You, baby."

Emmet, more redbone than my aunties, was fair-skinned with a ruddy orange complexion. Freckles rimmed the outside of his gray eyes like circles, and he wore a low red fade. He made up for the oddity of his appearance with a stylish wardrobe.

The tailor continued to nip and tuck while Emmet stood in front of the mirror. "I'm getting hooked up for the funeral. You know everybody gonna be there frontin'."

Somehow in the busywork of searching for Flea I had forgotten about the funeral. Despite the evidence, the picture in the paper, and the steady build of danger I still couldn't imagine Billy as irreversibly dead.

"Emmet—"

At the sound of her voice, Holly and I glanced toward the dressing room as Emmet's legendary wife, Yolanda, stepped out. Only twenty-three years old, Emmet had been married for five years to Yolanda Perry. Holly had attended their Vegas wedding, two days after high school graduation. Emmet was proud that he never strayed, and she gave him every reason to keep it up.

Emmet was at least six feet tall and so was Yolanda, but she topped that with a Marie Antoinette hairdo strung with beads and pearls. Everything about her was exaggerated, from top to bottom: hips, thighs, lips, ass, calves, chest—it was like someone had created her purely for male enjoyment.

Holly, more than once, had said she was the only thing that would make him kill Emmet and not think twice. I doubt if he was joking.

"Hey, Mrs. Landry." Holly did not look directly at Yolanda when he spoke to her. I think he feared his eyes would betray the desire in his heart. Emmet, I guessed, was used to men speaking to the air above his wife's head. All in all he was a pretty level-headed brother, considering the ammo at his side.

"Holly, how you doing? And Maceo, I remember you. How are you?"

"Fine, and yourself?"

The two of us sounded like choirboys.

"Emmet, you think this is okay?" She held out the hem of her dress and twirled from side to side. I might have drooled.

"That looks nice, baby. You should get it." He winked at her, and she blew him a kiss, which he moved in to take directly from her mouth. When they came up for air they turned to admire themselves in the mirror. Besides being married they also had a wicked habit of wearing matching outfits. Same fabric, different dimensions. His as a suit, hers as curves.

"Man, we gonna get out of here," Holly said to Emmet, but he wanted us to wait.

We greedily took in Yolanda's assets while Emmet had his back turned.

"Hold up a second, y'all."

Yolanda returned to the dressing room with another dress handed to her by Emmet. She waved to us absent-mindedly over her shoulder. Already forgotten. Everybody wanted Yolanda, but few could put in the serious work that Emmet did.

He waited until his wife closed the door to her dressing room before asking the tailor to step away. He lowered his voice anyway. "I heard some shit went wrong out in Marin with them white boys and Charlie."

"How?"

"Don't know the details, but looks like Charlie was skimming from Billy to set that deal up."

"Serious?" Holly asked.

"You seen him?"

"Yesterday. At Felicia's house harassing her roommate."

"The boy's unraveling. Could be guilty about something. The fool definitely knows more than he's saying."

"You know anything else about the white boys? They related to anybody?"

"Not that I know of, but this is how I see it." He did a three-quarter turn in front of the mirror. "Folks just sitting at home. Deciding. Making choices about who falls where, who did what"—he looked meaningfully at Holly—"which means a lot of loose cannons on the road."

"Deciding?" Holly wanted him to explain his position.

Emmet accepted a shoehorn and a pair of loafers from the tailor, who quickly faded into the background. "This is what we got." He counted it off on his fingers. "Smokey could have shot Billy purely for drama, status, territory, take your pick. Then we got Charlie, who's been skimming drugs and money. Maybe he moved on Billy before Billy could move on him." Yolanda joined us for the second time. "Then we got his woman, and there's a million and one reasons she coulda had him smoked."

I spoke up. "It wasn't Flea."

"Hold up. Hold up. There's somebody to defend everybody on the list, but I'm just running down what the average nigga on the street think." Yolanda slipped away again after a quick kiss and a no to the shoes Emmet held up for himself. "Then, just to complete the circle, we got the two of y'all. I don't buy into it myself, but plenty of folks might."

"I hear ya." I hated that anyone thought either Holly or I could have killed Billy.

We heard a tap on the window and turned to find Crowley surrounded by a group of raggedy kids. I never got over the sight of him as the ghetto Pied Piper. His clients, as he called them, ran the brown gamut from Asian to Hispanic and back to Black.

Outside we stood on the sidewalk, engulfed by kids, eating pretzels and watching Yolanda through the plate-glass window. Emmet had disappeared into the dressing room so we feasted on her while she twirled in front of the mirror.

"That girl should be illegal." Crowley ran his tongue slowly around the edges of his lips.

"She is. 'Cause you'll definitely be on lockdown, permanent, if you fuck with Emmet's woman."

"He should put a fence up around her or something."

Yolanda turned and waved to us before disappearing behind the wall of glass.

With the spell broken, Crowley turned his full attention to us. "Crockett and Tubbs on the case, huh?"

Holly laughed. I laughed too. How many times had we arrived late to parties in order to view the last seconds of *Miami Vice*.

"Off-Beat know how to get in touch with the white boys if you need the information."

"Might could use it." Holly shot a glance my way. "You think they connected to this?"

"Who knows? Smokey thinks so. He came around manhandling Off-Beat."

"He get anything?"

"Not as far as I know. Off-Beat ain't too keen on the Grape Ape. But you, Holly, he wants to impress."

Holly frowned. He knew that asking a favor of Off-Beat would link them together. The look he gave me said,

You owe me. He turned back to Crowley. "Hook it up and call me at the bar."

"All right. Maceo, heard somebody took a shot at you, boy!"

"Something like that."

"Be careful, man. You know Holly made of steel but you a square." He used his pinky fingers to make the shape in the air.

I punched a hole through it. "Plan to stay that way."

"Not if you keep rolling with players, jocking beautiful women. Ain't you been schooled?"

I laughed.

"Here, let me give ya a little something for the road." He broke a weak beat box then whispered the lyrics with his back turned to the kids. "These bitches gonna do anything they feel / 'Cause if a game don't exist then a nigga ain't real."

Holly slapped the bill of Crowley's cap. "Calvin T. Appropriate to the situation."

"Rap always is, baby."

We watched Crowley and company disappear toward Fairyland, a park for kids on the shores of Lake Merritt.

"Mind if we go back over to Flea's? Regina gave me the keys yesterday."

"What for?"

"Ain't no telling what we might find."

Holly squinted his eyes to shield them from the sun. "You starting to suspect your girl?"

"Naw." But my answer was weak, my confidence shaken by the loud silence that came with Felicia's absence. "I just feel like I need to keep busy before I go crazy."

"Cool. You drive."

We pulled up at Felicia's apartment just as Reggie's Impala came charging down the street.

"Got damn, them niggas here already," Holly said.

We exited the Cougar and stood on the grass of the Victorian. Reggie drove over the sidewalk and parked his car at an angle on the grass. The Impala's bumper rested casually against our knees.

"Here we go," Holly said, as Reggie bounced from the driver's side with a chain wrapped around his left hand.

He was wearing his Crip uniform, as was Crim, and we could tell from the look on their faces that they hadn't slept all night. Reggie led the way, walking right up in Holly's face. "Where my sister at?"

"That's what we trying to find out," Holly answered coolly. There was weariness in his voice, a weariness that came from playing cleanup in other people's lives: his mother's, his crewmen, his uncles, and mine.

Reggie turned to me, and I could smell the mustiness on his body. On closer inspection I saw yellow rings under the arms of his T-shirt and stray hairs escaping from his cornrows. His breath was stale but his eyes were alert and focused on me in concentrated anger. "Square padna, how my sister get caught up?"

"She was with Billy the other night, not too far from here, and someone jacked them at the light. The police think Flea was there. The passenger door was open and one of her shoes was in the car." I paused. "Ain't nobody seen her since."

"Regina said something about some niggas looking for her."

Holly and I looked at each other, astonished that Regina had revealed that information.

I sighed. "Some of Billy's boys think Flea set him up for a hit." Crim stepped forward at my choice of words, and I took an automatic step backward. Holly moved in closer.

Crim spoke for the first time, in a raspy-dead voice that probably haunted many of his victims. "Wh-wh-where my sister at?" Since Crim had never spoken in my presence I was surprised to hear his stutter.

"We were hoping she called y'all."

"We ain't heard from her. I ain't seen Flea in a couple of months."

"Wh-wh-wh-who was looking for her?" Crim stepped even closer.

"Some of Billy's boys."

"You trying to protect somebody—"

Before I could answer, Holly said, "This motherfucker got a death wish." I turned to see Charlie's black Bronco at the corner light.

Time stopped.

Instinctively, Holly and I backed toward the open doors of the Cougar. I watched the Bronco hoping it would turn left, but I knew that would never happen.

After growing impatient, Charlie maneuvered around a car and ran through the red light and right up behind the Impala.

"Where that bitch Felicia at?" were the last words we heard before Holly and I dove into the Cougar and left Charlie to his fate. The dumbstruck look on his face almost made me feel sorry for him.

122 / NICHELLE D. TRAMBLE

Almost.

Through my rearview mirror I saw Reggie drop to the ground without even acknowledging Charlie and sweep him off his feet with his legs. As Charlie fell backward, Crim aided his fall with a series of blows right in Charlie's neck. Charlie's hands went up to protect his face while Reggie lashed him with the short end of the chain.

Just as we hit the corner we saw Charlie gasping for air as the two of them threw him in the back of the Impala. Reggie jumped into the driver's seat while Crim tumbled into the Bronco. If any neighbors had happened to look out of the window, the sheer fury of the beating would have made them retreat.

Holly and I rode in silence, too stunned to speak. Neither of us were strangers to violence, and despite the murder rate there was still something cartoonish about Bay Area crime. The participants still hoped to escape with a little something for the sunset, while the L.A. equivalent never expected to survive any of it.

As I turned into the Nickel and Dime I noticed for the first time that my hands were shaking. "Flea's brothers scare the shit out of me," I said.

I never drink and Holly could probably count every drink he's ever had on one hand, but we both walked into the bar with the same thing on our minds: liquor.

Daddy Al was there, working a crossword puzzle, while the Three Wise Men played dominoes.

Paulie was behind the bar, serving a lone customer at the far end. It was a slow day so only one waitress, Vicki, was on duty. The stage was empty, the band's equipment shoved against a wall covered with rows of aluminum foil.

On our way to the bar we stopped to greet the four old men.

"Hey, Daddy Al."

He didn't look up from the puzzle. "You working tonight?"

"I'm off."

The bones slapped heavily as Soup Can dished it out to Tully and Potter.

"How's everybody?"

They mumbled responses as I moved away. We took a seat on the street side of the bar. "Paulie, give me two beers."

He placed the mugs in front of us and reached under the cash register for three slips of paper. "Messages."

Two had the name Clarence Mann and the same phone number. The third was from Crowley, and it simply said *San Francisco. Nine o'clock. Tower Records. Marin boys.*

I grabbed the phone from beneath the bar and handed it to Holly. He paged the number and we waited as the Isley Brothers wailed from the jukebox.

The phone rang before they got to the end of the song. "The Nickel and Dime. . . . Yep. Hold on."

Paulie handed the phone to Holly and walked away. He busied himself with dirty glasses, eager not to hear a word of the conversation.

"This Holly. . . . Nuthin' yet, man. . . . We'll be in The City tonight. . . . Cool. . . . Tower Records. . . . Yep, nine o'clock."

He hung up, and we drank in silence. Behind us, the front door opened. I saw Black Jeff framed in the doorway.

"Wassuper?" His slang swung back and forth between hip-hop and skateboarder at unchecked intervals.

I gave him a pound. "What you doing so far from Rasputin's?"

"Oakland's my town, baby. I'm just letting y'all use it." He turned to Holly. "You hear? Funeral tomorrow."

"When you hear that?"

"This morning. His mama want it over as soon as possible. She ain't gonna wait for Felicia to show. Anyway, C.M.E. Cathedral, on Telegraph near Fortieth."

"You'll be there?"

He tapped his heart with his fist. "Without a doubt. Your girl got twelve hours to show or she'll miss them putting him down." I knew he was giving me info to pass to Felicia in case we were in touch.

"Peace," he said, and headed toward the bathroom.

"Peace," Holly and I offered back.

We could only hope.

CHAPTER

21

A trip across the Bay Bridge at ninety miles an hour, and we arrived in North Beach about five after nine. I wore a coat. As always, the twenty-mile difference between the East Bay and San Francisco meant a temperature difference of at least fifteen degrees. Add the fog and the icy winds sweeping through the Golden Gate, and we were cold. In a phenomenon unique to the Bay Area, it was possible to experience three different weather fronts within a forty-mile radius.

Inside Tower Records the aisles were crowded with late-night shoppers, couples, and teenagers out on dates. Clarence and the Samoans browsed the R&B section. From a distance I could see him having a heated conversation with his two silent pillars.

"That's some odd shit, him and them Samoans," Holly said, under his breath.

"Man, I thought I was the only one who thought so."

Holly and I laughed as we made our way down the aisle. Rap was in the back of the store under a wall of surveillance mirrors and security cameras.

Two White boys in khakis and bomber jackets conversed over Public Enemy. Chuck D was angry enough to get the bulk of his sales from the people he railed against.

"Wassup?" Holly stepped to the taller one, who continued his conversation as if Holly wasn't there. Holly's reputation was well known in Oakland but his physical appearance did little to alert those without knowledge of his background. The White boys made the mistake of labeling him a mark a little too early in the evening.

"Wassup?" Holly repeated.

The taller one turned around. "Wassup with you?"

Holly grinned, the same grin he'd locked on Smokey two days previous. The boys were already over the line and neither one of them had any idea.

"I'm Marc." Holly used the name to let me know he knew what they thought of him.

"No names, Marc. We don't fuckin' know you. Didn't they tell you . . . ?" He turned to his friend. "Jesus, this shit out of Oakland gets more amateurish every day. Who was that last idiot?" The man continued to speak as if Holly wasn't there. At the same time Holly's grin grew wider.

"Sorry about that." Holly managed to mimic the nasal tones of the guy's speech. "I'll just call you Guy then. Is that cool, Guy?"

"Whatever. Let's get out of here. You know your way around The City?"

"Sure."

"All right. Two blocks. Dead-end street. There's a tunnel boarded up on one end. Park your car away from the street and walk there."

He turned his back and walked away. Holly called after him, "That's perfect, Guy."

Guy didn't know how perfect it was. We followed them out, Clarence and his crew not too far behind.

I parked illegally and slanted my wheels to keep the car from rolling down the steep hill. Guy and his friend were just where they said when we arrived. They looked up as we approached and went back to their conversation. Something important. Something about a movie. Holly let them get to the description of the last half before he slapped Guy across the side of his face with the barrel of his gun. It took the partner a moment to register what had happened, but by that time Guy was on the ground clutching the side of his head and trying to keep Holly's fist away from his mouth.

"You think you can talk stupid to me, motherfucker?" Holly yanked the man up on his feet as the Samoans dropped from up above. They had taken another route, the top of the tunnel.

"Hey, I'm sorry. It was precaution—"

"How long you been fucking with Charlie?"

"Who?"

Holly whacked him again. "Charlie Carl, you know who I'm talking about."

"He just started coming around. We had to send him away. He was bullshit. He sold us bogus shit. I think you broke my nose."

"I don't give a fuck about that. What kind of bogus shit?"

"Drugs. It was shit, but we knew where to find him."

Bingo.

"Who else you know?"

"Nobody."

Holly raised his hand.

"Dude, I swear it. We only dealt with him a couple of times, but he told us the name of his partner. Billy something."

"Billy, huh? Who did you tell that to?"

"No one. Just us. It was just us."

Holly thought he was lying but Guy maintained his innocence until he was unconscious.

The ride through the city was surreal, a blur of lights, cars, people on sidewalks or looking out of the frosted windows of MUNI, as we raced through the hilly streets of San Francisco. The gaudy neon of North Beach disappeared behind us as we traveled south through the Tenderloin and the residential disarray of the Fillmore District. Like West Oakland's Seventh Street, the once-thriving musical area had gone the way of crack and mayhem.

We continued until the faces on the sidewalk got darker, as did the buildings—dark with grime and poverty because this was the San Francisco the tourists never saw. No need to scrub clean the Victorians and paint them the color of whores; it was just too far off the tourist track. Too far from the attractions that kept San Francisco one of the top five travel destinations. It was also a neighborhood that the two boys would never visit on their own.

To see Holly purely in his element provoked in me feelings of both envy and dread. In contrast to Holly I was too cautious, too aware of consequences to live solely by appetite, but Holly had no such boundaries. I didn't doubt for a minute that his actions weren't well thought out, but I knew his motivations were different from mine. If death, jail, or a serious beating were to be a consequence of his actions, that was the price to be paid. He would never dodge an outcome by showing weakness or fear. He lived by his reputation, something he was willing to die for, and he was comfortable with that. I knew it from the look of glee, the burning pleasure that surfaced in instances of danger. The one he wore as we rolled toward the murky waters of the San Francisco Bay. Holly's immunity to consequences was both his strength and his Achilles' heel.

The White boys, wedged tightly between Clarence and Holly, knew this too, not in the same detail, but in the certainty that their lives depended on how Holly felt from one moment to the next. They were terrified. I could see it in the way their eyes darted back and forth, searching the car for the one person who would hear their pleas. I could smell the terror on them. My own body was funky with the same odor.

Finally the silence was broken by Guy. "Where we going?" More silence and then a more desperate "Where we going?"

"I don't know," Holly answered. "Where you feel like going?"

"H-h-home."

We all had to laugh at that.

"You live this way?" Holly asked Guy.

"Uh, no. I—we live in Marin."

"Too bad then, 'cause this ain't the way to Marin." Holly ended the sentence with a quick jab to Guy's throat. He issued it without warning, but Guy, his partner, and I were the only ones unprepared for it. His partner squealed next to him and closed his eyes, while Guy twisted and gasped for breath. Holly rubbed his knuckles. The Samoan kept driving. In silence, with a clear destination, though no orders had been given.

Guy's face was tomato red as he regained his breathing. "I . . ."

"Say it, man," Holly directed. "You got something to say?"

Guy didn't answer. The car rolled to a stop in the

China Basin, an area filled with dark cranes, broken-down warehouses, and rusted-out ships that would never see another day at sea. Holly grabbed Guy by the neck and Clarence grabbed his friend. The second Samoan wheeled up in Guy's Mercedes.

As we stepped from the car I could smell the sea: briny, like the recesses of an unwashed body. The air was biting cold as waves washed loudly against the docks.

Guy started to stutter. "Please, don't hurt us."

Holly smiled and looked at Clarence. "Said please."

"I heard that. Don't mean shit, though. Everybody got manners when a gun pointed at 'em."

On cue Clarence pulled a gun from his waistband and handed it to Holly.

Holly aimed at Guy. "See this?"

Guy nodded vigorously.

"Know what it means? It means that if you talk we come after you. After you, ya' mama, your girlfriends, whoever we can find. And if it ain't us then it's somebody else. Understand?"

"Yes."

"Good, but I need your ID just in case you forget." He removed the IDs from both wallets and tossed the leather, including cash and credit cards, into the bay. "All right, strip down."

The boys hesitated only a moment before pulling off their clothing and shivering in the sharp San Francisco wind. The Samoans gathered both bundles and tossed them off the dock. They watched helplessly as Clarence popped the brake on the Mercedes and let it roll, slowly, until it hit a ramp, picked up speed, and hit the water with voluminous impact.

"Damn!" Holly uttered as he watched the car sink into the center of the whirlpool.

Clarence brandished a gun he'd pulled from the backseat of Guy's car. "Glock nine-millimeter, acid-wash serial number." He whistled low under his breath. "Nice piece. It got bodies on it?" He looked at Guy and waited for an answer. "The gun, White boy, it got bodies on it?"

"Uh, no, not that I know of."

Clarence aimed the gun at them both. "Y'all haven't killed anybody with it?"

"I just got it. It was for show."

"Cool."

Holly laid down on the horn and waved the confiscated IDs in the air. I noticed for the first time that the license plates were covered with black cloth. It was a mob car, anyway, a car used for crime. If the police did a trace, more than likely the vehicle would come up registered to a celebrity. Take your pick: film, music, television. A local joke.

They couldn't find us even if they wanted to.

CHAPTER

22

The twelve hours Black Jeff warned me about came and went without a word from Felicia. Tuesday morning arrived and I found myself dressing for Billy's funeral with a heavy heart. I dreaded the service. I didn't want to see him dead. I didn't want the day to come and go without Flea.

I hadn't encountered Billy in my dreams again, but he lived with me in my waking hours. I expected to see him around every corner, waiting on answers about Felicia. Hoping for us to learn why he died.

"Maceo?" Gra'mère knocked and entered the cottage. She came forward and took the tie from my hands. *"Brave homme, cocodrie,"* she said as she stroked my hair.

I took deep breaths while she worked to adjust my collar. After she was done she patted my chest and slipped a carnation inside my pocket. "I got one for you and Holly. Why don't the two of you ride over with the rest of the family?"

An hour later, with Daddy Al and Gra'mère in the front seat and Cissy and Regina sandwiching Mrs. Johnson in the middle row, Holly and I sat in the back of the van. Daddy Al took Telegraph Avenue to the church. I wasn't surprised to find traffic slowed all the way to Alcatraz, a good three miles north. A steady flow of people covered both sidewalks, heading in the direction of C.M.E. Cathedral.

The mini-mall at the corner was filled to overflowing with cars, the business owners too cowed by the mourners to chastise people about the parking. I looked at the crowds and realized I'd seen almost all of them at previous funerals that year. Not yet thirty, and my generation was skilled in the etiquette of mourning.

"It's going to be tough finding parking around here. Lady Belle, why don't I let you and Mrs. Johnson out here and I'll take the fellas with me. Celestine, why don't you and Regina go with your mother."

Daddy Al maneuvered to the side of the road and helped the older women out of the car. He was clean as usual, in a black suit with a black paisley vest and his Stetson.

Once the women were out of the car, the three of us circled block after block looking for parking. Everywhere we turned, men and women were dressed to the nines, carrying flowers, funeral programs, and somber faces.

"Looks like a lot of people loved Billy." Daddy Al surveyed the crowd as he made another corner.

Holly and I looked at each other. It wasn't just love. It was also envy, admiration, and curiosity. Daddy Al knew these things. He had made the comment to start a conversation, but this was one time neither of us felt like talking.

We finally parked five blocks away at the foot of Pill Hill, a cluster of hospitals cushioned between the boulevards of Telegraph and Broadway.

In front of the church every Bay Area dealer with a larger-than-life reputation stood on the steps profiling. Emmet Landry was flanked by Yolanda and Malcolm Rose. Malcolm's four henchmen brothers had all been killed the year before in a shootout with OPD.

On the step below, almost in the order of dominance, was Mosley Amos, a ladies' man strictly in the drug game for the free-flowing women. Mosley stood talking to Smokey, who'd done the ludicrous by bringing two snarling Rottweilers with him to pay respects. The breed was fast becoming the drug-dealing dog of choice.

Bilau Arafi, whose father was a prominent Muslim leader, was dressed all in white and flashing a wad of money between fingers loaded with diamonds. Extravagant displays of gold jewelry were everywhere, especially on the men. Even the most lowly of street soldiers were drenched in the spoils of the trade.

As I approached with Holly and Daddy Al, each man on the stairs acknowledged Holly's presence with a solemn nod. That he had a no-record, no-jail-time reputation while still being active and prosperous earned him solid respect in the Bay.

Standing in the doorway of the church with his usual entourage of twenty was Too Short, the diminutive rapper with the nasty lyrics and local-boy pride. His affinity for Oakland riddled all his songs and had made him a local hero.

As I looked out behind me I saw hordes of people waiting to pay their respects to Billy. Half of them wouldn't be able to enter the church, but they'd stake their claim at the graveside just to say they had been there.

Cissy and Regina were waiting in the vestibule of the church after seating Gra'mère and Mrs. Johnson. Reverend Mimms came forward to acknowledge Daddy Al.

"Mr. Redfield."

"Reverend. You preaching today?"

"Unfortunately, yes." A weary look took over his face. "I tell you, I'm getting tired of burying these young men. And from how it looks out front I have quite a few more to go."

Cissy pulled me aside and whispered in my ear. "Regina is going to sing for Felicia. Momma called Reverend Mimms this morning, and he spoke to Billy's mother. We felt like somebody had to represent her."

Just then the sound of horns alerted us that the casket had arrived. While Daddy Al went to find Gra'mère, Cissy, Regina, Holly, and I went out front to take our places. The receiving of the casket had become a tradition on the Oakland streets.

We walked outside to find everyone near a car leaning in to honk their horns in unison. The sound was deafening as the gray-and-black hearse made its way down the street. The funeral director moved at a snail's pace through the cars while the horns grew louder and louder. Behind the hearse was Charlie's black Bronco going equally slow. I dreaded seeing what shape Charlie was in.

For the first time I noticed the police stationed around the area, as well as television cameras and reporters kept at bay by hired security. Billy was big news. His death meant the possibility of a gang war, which translated into headlines. Mythmaking in progress.

Once the hearse drew to a halt and the driver cut the engine, the honking stopped. Silence took over the crowd as Emmet, Malcolm, Mosley, Bilau, Clarence Mann, Monty Quailes, and one of the Samoans stepped to the casket. They stood in silence, obviously waiting for the eighth man, Charlie.

"Damn," Holly muttered, realizing the same thing as me. "What happened to that fool?"

A nervous second stretched to a full minute as people craned their necks to look at Charlie's Bronco. The door swung open and Reggie bounced out of the driver's seat with a look of defiance on his face. Crim followed from the other side. Both men were dressed in blue, darker than usual, but blue.

Smokey stepped toward the hearse and spoke loud enough for everybody to hear. "Y'all need another man?"

Emmet, the unspoken leader, pointedly ignored him. He nodded toward Holly. "Handle this, man."

The lines were drawn then and there. It took all the willpower Smokey had to maintain even an ounce of cool. The carrying of the casket alerted the crowd to the new power structure, and he had been skipped over entirely.

Holly hustled down the stairs and took his place with the others. He couldn't resist a mouthed "Fuck you" to the seething Smokey.

Strike two!

The casket came into view for the first time, and the call went up from the back of the crowd—"Hustla!"—stretched to a twenty-five-letter word. "Hustla!" It came again, giving me a chill to the bottom of my soul. "Hustla down!" came the third call, the words that finally released tears for most of the crowd. I saw Emmet wipe his eyes before grabbing hold of the casket. Though the pallbearers might all be enemies again in the morning, it was a rule that anyone of Billy's status had to be carried out by his equals in the game.

Heads dropped and the casket made its way up the stairs. The crowd flowed behind it as Cissy, Regina, and I entered the church. As I took my seat I looked around to see who had made it inside. My eyes fell on a woman covered in black, a veil obscuring her face: Billy's mother, Delores. She sat stoic, facing forward, while two heavy-set women wept openly at her side. Reggie and Crim sat where Felicia should have been. I knew, wherever she was, it was killing her to miss Billy's funeral.

My eyes made another sweep and landed on Alixe, sitting next to Chantal and Patrice. She looked out of place, bewildered by the pageantry for a person who didn't rate in her world. I wondered why she was there.

Holly slid into the seat beside me as Reverend Mimms took the pulpit. "How many of y'all tired of coming here"—he paused—"for this? How many of y'all tired of laying these young men to rest?"

"Uh-huh, go 'head now," Mrs. Johnson said at my side. "Tell 'em, Preacher."

I glanced over at Alixe again to find her eyes sweeping the room and then focusing on the pallbearers. When she got to Holly she found me staring intently at her. She returned her focus to the pulpit.

Once Reverend Mimms finished his opening, Regina rose and took her place. She said defiantly before she began to sing a cappella, "This is from my girl. I had to represent her today no matter what any of y'all think." She looked at Billy lying in the casket and said simply. "Felicia loves you." Then she inhaled deeply and began to sing.

"You're my morning star / Shining brightly beside me / And if we keep this love / We will last through all eternity . . ." She held the last word and her voice reached the rafters of the church. I saw a tear slide down her face as the choir charged in with the chorus, still unaccompanied by music. As they faded out to a steady hum, Regina turned to Billy. It was obvious to everyone watching that she wanted him to hear Felicia's message, wherever he was.

She belted another verse and then the choir thundered through again and pulled several people from their seats. I saw Gra'mère drop her head and tap her feet as if she were in physical pain. Cissy put her hands to her face, but tears managed to make their way through. Holly placed his hand on her knee to offer comfort, and I was glad he sat close enough to provide it. Regina rocked back and forth while the choir boomed behind her.

Regina and the choir breathed new life into Natalie Cole's "Our Love" as she sang to represent her friend, Billy's heart, who could not show her face. There was barely a dry eye in the church. Once she finished, Reverend Mimms had to guide her back to her seat. Daddy Al rose to meet them halfway and let the sobbing Regina collapse in his arms. Through it all I continued to watch the casket. Regina's song was so powerful I half expected Billy to wake up and stand.

The funeral progressed, but not once did I see Billy's mother shed a tear. Even when it came time to view the body she managed to hold herself together. She walked alone, shrugging off the arm offered by the funeral director and her companions. The church was silent as she stood quietly before the casket, staring at the body of her son. She didn't lift her veil, but she pressed her fingers to her lips and touched Billy's forehead. She glanced at him one more time and then walked through the side door of the church.

The women followed, then Reggie and Crim, who stood shoulder to shoulder at the head of the casket.

Reggie leaned forward and whispered into Billy's ear. I hoped the message was from Felicia but something told me it wasn't. Crim finally pulled him away, but not before turning to glance into the faces of the congregation. He paused on Emmet, Malcolm, Clarence, Bilau, Mosley, Holly, and then me. He held my gaze and Holly's until Daddy Al leaned over and glanced down the aisle at the both of us. Once they departed through the side door the funeral director moved up row by row to allow everyone to go up and view the body.

When our turn came my grandparents remained seated, as did Mrs. Johnson. I moved forward, feeling like I was walking in sand. I knew people were talking and moving beside me, but I could not hear them. The colors surrounding me were faded, the voices muted until it was just a tunnel with me at one end and Billy at the other. I was him, save for a grandfather who continued to pull me back from the edge.

Holly stood before me, gazing into Billy's face like he was searching for answers. I knew Holly still loved Billy, just like I did, and admired the way Billy had stayed focused and true to his profession. I also knew that the murder touched him deeply. Billy was supposed to be exempt, his reputation and his way of doing business a safeguard in a ruthless environment. If they didn't work for Billy, someone at the top of his game, how could Holly hope to stay alive? Before Holly moved off he touched his heart lightly and made way for me.

I looked down to see a picture of Felicia stuck in Billy's lapel, the only piece of her present. I moved away quickly, leaving Cissy and Regina to fend for themselves, and rushed out the side door and stood in the parking lot. It was filled to capacity but I managed to find a spot in a far corner. Daddy Al found me moments later.

"You all right, son?"

"No." The tears I'd been holding finally slid down my

face. I felt like a five-year-old crying at my grandfather's side.

"Let it go. Let it go." He put a hand on my shoulder and turned his body to give me as much privacy as I needed. While I cried I didn't know if the tears were for Felicia, Billy, or myself.

"It wasn't suppose to be like this."

"Like what?" There was a touch of anger in his voice. "Like what? Did y'all think the game you was playing could cheat death? I look at all these young people here, and the way every last one of you is mesmerized by this. And as long as y'all don't see"—he shook his head and dropped his voice—"we don't stand a motherfucking chance."

Over his shoulder I saw Alixe staring in my direction. For once the bravado was gone from her face. I thought I saw compassion, but I wiped my eyes before I let my grief tell me another lie.

CHAPTER

23

It took over half an hour to wind the mile to Mountain View Cemetery. We finally made it up the hill to the burial site. The road around the grassy area overflowed with at least three hundred people. At the top of the hill a line of white chairs was set up for the elderly. Billy's mother sat in the middle, still veiled and quiet.

The buzz of the crowd dropped to a low hum as the cemetery pallbearers navigated their way to the open grave. The casket was placed atop metal lifts as Reverend Mimms took his place in front of the mourners.

He presented the folded blanket to Billy's mother and opened his Bible. As he talked a gentle breeze, a whisper, kicked up and sent a tumble of leaves across the hill. Reverend Mimms closed his Bible and turned to the pallbearers. The leader slipped on a pair of work gloves and placed his hand on the crank. As the first creak of the casket was heard, a shriek penetrated the crowd. And before anyone could say anything, Billy's mother was at the graveside on her knees.

"My baby, oh, Lord, my baby! Billy, Billy, oh no, baby, oh no!" While she wailed, Mimms and the funeral director tried to pull her away, but she was planted as sure as the grass.

"They killed my baby. Oh, Lord, help me, help him." She convulsed in tears, her head dropped onto her chest. Her arms flopped at her side, loose enough to allow the two men to lift her with the help of Emmet, who'd rushed forward. Her grief and the closed casket sent another wave of tears through the crowd. I felt my face burn hot with them.

Once the casket disappeared the crowd started to wander away, back to life, back to crime, back to the day-to-day that had brought Billy to his end.

As I walked I glanced here and there, hoping to spot Felicia hiding out, but she was nowhere to be seen. Reggie and Crim had also skipped the graveside, much to my relief. Their presence and Charlie's disappearance was too much dynamite in one place.

"*Cette pauvre femme.*" Gra'mère walked at my side. "If you have children you pray every night that you never have to bury them. Oh, my heart is with her."

"Lady Belle, you all right?"

"I'm fine, Redfield. It's just not right." Daddy Al

reached out and took Gra'mère's hand in his, and she leaned in a little closer to him. Cissy took his other hand.

"Holly, you got a minute?" Emmet had slipped up to us while I watched my grandparents. Malcolm and Clarence stood behind him.

"Yeah, wassup?"

"You know anything about Charlie?"

"You saw the same thing I did. Her brothers rode up in his car."

"Man." Emmet wiped his brow. "Who brought those niggas to town?"

"They came to get their sister. Charlie was talking to any- and everybody about waxing her."

"She still in the cut?" Emmet asked.

"Far as I know."

"What's the word on your side?"

"Ain't nobody saying. What about you?"

"Nothing. He didn't even have funk with anybody about territory. Billy was cool with everybody, looking to get out of the game after he hooked up with that girl."

"You think she set him up?" Holly asked.

"Either that or Charlie's trying to throw heat on her because he was living foul. Unless he's dead ain't no reason why he couldn't be here today."

I disagreed. I knew two blue-wearing reasons why he couldn't be there.

"You know, Charlie was fucking with White boys from Marin, and he conned 'em out of some dope. I don't know if Billy knew about it or if they knew about Billy," Holly offered. "You ridin' if we get word?"

Emmet never hesitated. "The second we know who did it, I'm riding on anybody."

Clarence moved up, flanked by the two Samoans. "Fellas." He nodded to all of us. "Billy was solid. This shit here ain't right. Y'all need me, you know where to find me."

Emmet gave him a pound.

"I'll be in touch wit' you. Feds trying to take me out of the game. They got leeches on my phone line—"

"I hear ya, man. They been filming all day." Emmet slipped on his shades.

Everyone stopped talking as Smokey approached.

Smokey stood directly in front of Holly. "Two of my boys, White boys, said they met up wit' some folks from Oakland the other night. San Francisco. Tower Records. You know anything about that?"

"Should I?" Holly countered.

"That's three times, motherfucker."

"Come wit' it then, fool. You ain't done shit yet."

Smokey looked toward the Feds lining the hills behind the grave. "You been lucky every time."

"It ain't luck. You a trick." Emmet, Clarence, and Malcolm laughed behind Holly. "Born a trick, gonna die a trick."

"We'll see."

Holly turned to his audience. "Ask him why his only son call me daddy. Matter of fact, ask that nigga why his son look like me!"

The group gathered around Holly broke into loud raucous laughter, laughter inappropriate and too sharp for a funeral gathering.

"Oh, you just saying anything now, huh?" Smokey tried to keep his composure while people snickered all around him.

Smokey had one child, a four-year-old boy named Kevin who cringed whenever Smokey was around. His mother, Cynthia, had an on-again, off-again relationship with Holly. Her interest in Smokey's rival peaked whenever Smokey neglected her or their son or greeted her with fists and open hands. I'd seen her with Holly more than once with sunglasses that barely covered the bruises on her face. She was a nice girl, pretty even, but pathetic.

"What? You don't believe me?" Holly laughed again. "Ask your woman. Or ask your son who his daddy is."

Sweat beaded on Smokey's forehead. His anger was apparent to all of us. "Just name the place, Holly."

Holly extended his hands out at his sides. "I'm wide-open."

"Gentlemen." Reverend Mimms stepped up to defuse the rising tensions. "Y'all wouldn't be thinking of upsetting Mrs. Crane any more than necessary, would you?"

A look toward Billy's mother squashed the drama instantly. Smokey moved away, as did the crowd that had gathered. Reverend Mimms followed.

"Everybody looking for bloodshed behind this," Holly said.

"And there will be plenty," Emmet answered.

"I give it to midnight," Clarence threw in.

"Yeah." Emmet slipped on his sunglasses. "And I hope for that broad's sake she ain't the cause of it." He looked at me over the top of his sunglasses. " 'Cause she won't be spared."

Felicia was officially marked.

I hear a voice at the edge of my dream, far off and muffled by the sound of rain, a heavy, thick rain that turns the intersection of College and Alcatraz into a pool of red, oozing blood. The street is deserted, as if it's the dead of night, but it's broad daylight. The sun blazes so hard that when the rain hits the pavement it sizzles like lava.

Billy is sitting on the curb, shoeless, his ankles caked with dried mud. He looks on as the red water washes into the storm drain. His car is parked in the middle of the street with the passenger door open and hanging from the hinges.

Felicia's tennis shoe lies near the front tire, sparkling white as usual, despite the mud. A stream of water envelops the shoe and moves it toward Billy. He snatches it up before it reaches the gutter.

"Heads up," he says, and tosses the shoe to me. It falls into my outstretched hand and burns a hole right through my Little League glove. I drop it and watch the skin of my palm bubble into the worn leather.

"Put some mud on it," Billy advises. I scoop up a handful of mud and use the sticky dirt as a salve. The tennis shoe, caught in a new stream of water, makes its way back to him.

Billy lifts his chin toward the car and his own corpse. "That's a damn shame." He shakes his head. "What you gonna do about it, man?"

I'm speechless.

"Ain't got nothing to say? I feel ya. I tried to dodge this shit myself, but it caught up with me."

A bullet whizzes past my ear.

"I knew it was coming," he continues. "I just didn't know when and why."

I try to work my mouth in order to ask him how it happened, but my lips are locked together.

He shakes his head as if he's read my mind. "I can't do it, man. This shit has to play out on its own." He throws his hands up. "I can't give you the reason and I can't help you. This train's been coming for a long time."

He drops his head and brings the dripping-wet shoe to his lips. He kisses it deeply and affectionately. Water runs down the side of his mouth—thick red water, like blood.

CHAPTER

24

I woke up to the bright, glaring sunlight and the stifling heat of the Cougar. I was slumped like a drunk over the steering wheel, the windows sealed tight as a drum with the car oddly angled under a sliver of shade in the parking lot of the Nickel and Dime. Against the protests of my grandparents I'd left them at the Dover Street house and driven my car to the bar. What started as a quick rest before entering the bar had turned into another haunting visit from Billy.

I wiped sweat from my forehead and noticed a shadow at the passenger door. Alixe stood there, bewildered, tapping lightly on the glass. She motioned for me to roll down the window, but I opened the door instead. She slid into the passenger seat and reached across me to roll down my window.

"It's a hundred degrees in here, Maceo! You'll pass out."

"I'm all right." My tongue felt thick and mossy in my mouth.

"No, you're not." She loosened my tie and unbuttoned the rigid collar of my dress shirt.

"I'll live."

She put a hand to my forehead. "And you're hot. You want to get out and take a walk?"

I shrugged her hand away. "I'm cool. Don't worry about it." I straightened up and popped the ignition. "I need to get out of these clothes, though, if you want to ride to the house."

"Sure."

We pulled out of the lot as a caravan of cars arrived from the funeral. I knew the bar would become the designated gathering place, but I wasn't in the mood for a crowd. As I hit the corner and headed toward the house I saw Holly stare after my car with a look of displeasure. I ignored it.

Clio was curled into a corner of the porch when I arrived. She jumped up eagerly when she saw I had company and followed us inside. I pointed Alixe toward the living room while I walked upstairs to change. She followed me instead. The heat had succeeded in wearing me down. My mouth was filled top to bottom with acidic cotton balls and my limbs felt heavy, like bricks.

My bedroom, little more than a closet with room for a bed and dresser, faced my grandmother's vegetable garden. Alixe took the director's chair beneath the window and looked down at the rows of plants. "What a pretty garden."

I didn't answer. Instead I dropped onto the bed and stared across the room at my St. Mary's championship jersey. It was stored in a glass case alongside the winning cleats and my mitt. Both items were still caked with the mud of a long-ago game. I focused on the cleats and used the memory of a simpler time to pull me back from the edge.

Billy and Holly were in the stands when I pitched my all-time best against Pius X High School. The southern California team hadn't stood a chance against an arm in perfect condition and an owner in his prime. The first two innings were no-hitters. I didn't even give my teammates an opportunity to break in their uniforms. When the game peaked at 5–0 in the ninth I stood triumphant on the mound, soaked through from the exertion of unfiltered concentration.

"You want water or something?" Alixe watched me cautiously.

"No, just give me a minute."

She moved closer to the bed. "Are you sure you're okay?"

I shrugged off her concern. "I'm fine. Maybe a little spooked from the funeral, but I can handle it." I moved my legs so she could sit at the edge of the bed. "Why you so concerned anyway?"

She shook her head, for once at a loss for words. "I don't know, something about today. Seeing you there with your grandfather. All the people in the streets. I've never seen anything like that."

"Welcome to Oaktown."

"How did all that make you feel? The honking horns, the cameras, the police? He was your friend, wasn't he? That's what my sister said."

"You've been asking about me again?"

"Here and there." She paused and looked at me. "I can't figure you out. It made me curious so I asked."

"Anything interesting?" I opened a drawer to locate a T-shirt and jeans. It wasn't post-funeral attire but I wanted to shake the remnants of the day as soon as possible. I watched as she climbed off the bed and studied the items in my room. She stopped in front of the glass case, flanked by the Bash Brothers poster of Mark McGwire and Jose Canseco.

"Baseball nut?" She reached for a baseball signed by the 1972 A's.

"Something like that. I'm gonna change. Then we can head back to the bar."

When I came out I could see her at the bottom of the stairs looking at the pictures that lined the wall. Gra'mère had done most of the decorating, making the cottage a small replica of the main house. There was little of me in the space besides the ashes of my baseball career.

"This place is nice," she said, as she took a quick look toward the kitchen. "How long have you lived here?"

"Since I was about fifteen."

"Did your parents live here too?"

"Gra'mère and Daddy Al are my parents. My mother died when I was born. My father died when I was four. I didn't know them."

"Well, both my parents are alive, and I don't know them either."

"How'd that happen?"

"How does anything happen? Are you sure you're okay to go back to the bar? We could stay here if you wanted, talk, have a drink . . ."

I moved to the porch and sat on the front steps. Alixe propped the screen door open with her shoulder and continued to look at the pictures just inside the door. She reached up to pull one down from the wall. It was the same picture displayed at Crowning Glory.

"Is that you and Holly?"

I nodded. "And Billy."

She let the screen door slam shut to come and sit beside me. She held the picture on her lap and traced the lopsided nine-year-old Afro I wore in the picture. I didn't bother to look. I had no desire to see Billy's droop-eyed, grinning face.

"You've been friends so long. I can't think of a single person I knew when I was that young."

"Part of being a nomad, ain't it?"

"Something like that. Were you and Billy close?"

I shook my head. "Not in a long time. But you couldn't separate us when we were little."

"When did that stop?"

"When we were about fourteen. Billy and Holly liked the same girl and it just escalated from there. No, actually it started before that." I thought of the death of John Claire, but I kept it to myself.

She reached for a cigarette stored inside her boot. "And you chose Holly?"

CHAPTER

25

We waited for the sun to go down before heading back to the Nickel and Dime. The place was surrounded by police cars and mourners from the funeral. In the center of the crowd I spotted two police officers, Phil Blakenhorn and Ron Sullevich. The duo were well known and hated within Oakland's Black community, especially in their North Oakland playground. The two of them embodied the worst stereotypes of White cops in Black neighborhoods.

Blakenhorn, the larger and more senior of the two, had a baton he referred to as his "nigger stick for nigger knocking." It hung vulgarly at his side as he rudely shuffled people around. He was proud of the notches created by splintered heads and cracked knuckles, and he loved to tell the stories of each indentation. At least two of them came from dark-alley encounters with Holly.

I drove backward down the street, until I was closer to Dover than Shattuck, and helped Alixe from the car. "We can walk from here." Our entwined hands were the first thing Holly noticed as we pressed through the crowd. He took a full minute to stare at our hands before speaking.

"Where you disappear to?" he asked.

"I went by the house to get out of the suit. What's going on here?"

"Same old bullshit."

"Jonathan."

Holly didn't bother to turn around at the sound of his name. Sullevich stood behind him, grinning at me and Alixe, his notoriously bad breath singeing my eyebrows. Dirty-blond strands of his hair peeked out from his hat, contradicting all rules of personal hygiene. He placed a firm hand on Holly's shoulder.

"Jonathan." He grinned sarcastically. "It's always nice to see you. I was sorry to hear about your friend, but it looks like someone's doing us a favor, picking off the lice one by one by one."

Holly shrugged free and slipped away. Sullevich turned to me but Noone stepped in before it went any further.

"Sullevich, can you assist Blakenhorn in breaking up this crowd? We need to get these people moved out of here as soon as possible."

"Yeah, okay." His reluctance was evident.

The three of us watched as he ambled roughly away, his right hand caressing the nightstick.

"What do you make of this, Maceo?" Noone looked me up and down. "You keep popping up at the center of things."

I remained silent.

"Have you heard from Felicia? She's the key to this, you know. We know she was a witness, and we know the two of you were close at one time."

I felt Alixe's hand slip from mine. When I turned to

look at her she glanced off toward the hills and refused to meet my eye.

"Maceo, look, I'll be honest with you." He tried the good-cop tone and lowered his voice. "We don't have anything on this. It's clean. There's a real chance this could go unsolved."

I let the lie hang between us. It might be classified as unsolved on the police books, but we'd all know, sooner or later, who killed Billy.

"You could help us—me—by letting me know if you hear anything."

"Sure."

He studied me, then looked at Alixe. "I know you were very close to Felicia, and I'm sure you're concerned about her safety. We all are, so we should work together on this."

"Yeah, yeah. Whatever. I'll call you."

"I'll look forward to hearing from you."

He walked away and left me and Alixe to our awkwardness. She spoke up. "Listen, I need to get to the hospital. Maybe I'll see you later."

"All right." I leaned in to kiss her but she backed away, gave me a weak smile, and walked off.

Holly came up to take her place. "Maceo," he said, "if you gonna be a player you can't fuck with chicks that don't know the rules. Trouble. Capital letters. Guarantee it." He hit me on the back. "Run me up to the Avenue."

"There he go." Holly pointed to Black Jeff, standing in front of Blondie's Pizza shoving a slice of pepperoni down his throat. Behind him his multicolored skateboard was propped against a wall. Jeff spotted the Cougar and pointed toward the campus. He took off on his board and turned on Bancroft. The new location allowed me to pull over without stalling traffic.

"Wassuper, Black men?" Jeff leaned into the car and

gave us both a pound. He continued to devour the pizza. "Man, I'm hungry as a motherfucker. I been practicing for a new tournament."

"Yeah? When you taking off?" I asked.

"I'll be outta here this weekend. Heading down to Orange County to show the White boys how to rock a board."

"You cool for money?" Holly offered.

"I'm straight. That funeral was something else, wadn't it? Everybody was out." He shook his head. "Man, what the fuck was up with them dudes from L.A.?"

"Who, Felicia's brothers?"

"Hell yeah! They looked like straight penitentiary-ass killas. I hope they getting the fuck out of here soon. You know, Charlie resurfaced looking beat down!"

Holly and I looked at each other. "When was that?" I asked.

"About an hour ago while everybody was at your spot. The man was butt naked, ribs cracked, face all swoll' up and shit."

"Got damn." Holly shook his head. "He say who did it?"

"Everybody know who did it, but Charlie wouldn't talk. You almost felt sorry for his crazy ass. The man got clowned."

"Who saw him?"

"Not too many folks. Emmet's boys found him and now they ready to rumble. It ain't like they got love for him, but the Bay got a rep to uphold. Can't have tricks coming from L.A. and trying to run shit."

"I heard that." Holly's eyes were vacant. He'd already chosen sides.

"You hear anything else?"

"Nope. Felicia still ghost, huh?" He directed the question at me.

I nodded. He grinned at me slyly. "What's up with

Chantal's sister? Girl is fine, with that big ass and them Chinese eyes."

"Japanese," I corrected, before catching myself. Holly looked at me like I was crazy. Jeff smiled like a fool.

"Man, did you hit it already? Maceo got game!" He yelled the last of it out to the passing crowd.

"It ain't like that" was my feeble attempt at damage control. If Black Jeff heard it, it was already in the street.

"Maceo ain't got no game." I turned to see Crowley approaching. He slid up to the car with a lyric ready: "I hold the microphone like a grudge / B'll hold the record so the needle don't budge."

Holly finished with "I hold a conversation 'cause when I invent / I nominated my DJ for president." Crowley smiled as Holly chastised him. "Rakim fool, you sleepin'. Give me something hard. Everybody know the master."

"Just lettin' you off easy, Black man." Crowley gave Holly a pound, then turned to me. "Maceo ain't got game unless you talking 'bout baseball."

Black Jeff hit him in the chest. "He got more game than you, nigga. He hooked up with Chantal's sister."

"Like that?" Crowley's eyebrows were raised in astonishment. "Damn! Maceo! How you pull all these fine chicks with your short ass? Must be the Sammy Davis factor."

"George Jefferson!" Jeff shouted. The two of them dissolved in laughter while Holly and I watched.

Crowley finally calmed himself down enough to lean into the car. "Jeff told y'all about Charlie?"

We nodded.

"They fucked him up." He threw a few air punches. "Beat the man like he was a slave."

"Hey, dawg." Jeff tapped Crowley. "I heard they tried to iron him."

"Word?"

"Word."

Crowley shivered. "That's messed up. Los Angeles should be burned down, if you ask me. Anybody try to fuck with that place come to ruin. I heard Billy was trying to move in down there. He hooked up wit' some Mexicans that was giving him a good price."

"Mexicans?" Holly's interest was piqued. "When you hear that?"

"At the funeral. Y'all know that Mexican from Vallejo. The one wit' the pit bulls." He snapped his fingers, trying to remember. "Damn, what's his name? He got the dogs and the scar above his lip. One of his dogs bit him in the face."

"Oh, you talking about Jorge!" Black Jeff said. "Got that Rico Suave accent."

"Yeah, that's him. Apparently, Jorge hooked Billy up wit' some of his cousins."

"No shit? Billy kept that on the under. I always wondered why he had such cool prices on dope." Holly hid his anger and amazement well.

"That's why, my man. He was hooking up wit' the source. Fuck the Colombians in the nineties. A brother need to get wit' the Mexicans."

Black Jeff tapped Crowley on the head. "But you know, dawg, Jorge isn't a Mexican."

"Ain't his name Jorge the Mexican?"

"Yeah, but that's 'cause niggas ignorant about nationalities."

"What's the difference?"

"History. Countries."

"No, I mean what difference does that make to me? To how much money I make or how I sleep at night?"

"None."

"All right then." He turned back to Holly. "Jorge *the Mexican* got all kinda hookup. You should check wit' him. Might know more than what's been said." He offered a pound by way of an exit. "I'm out."

"See ya."

Crowley slid away from the car as Black Jeff balanced on his board. "All right, y'all. Time for me to get in the cut." Slipping on a Rastafarian knit cap, he skated away, jumped a bus bench for our benefit, and headed off into the campus.

I pulled Felicia's house keys from my pocket. "One more time?"

Holly nodded, and we headed west.

"Nice to see you again, Jonathan."

Holly and I were stopped on the cramped staircase leading to Flea's apartment by Blakenhorn and Sullevich. Regina stood behind them at the top of the stairs looking shaken.

"What happened?" I spoke to her as if the two officers were not there.

Blakenhorn answered for her. "Looks like there was some sort of break-in while she was out today." He tilted his head to the side. "Would you know anything about that?"

Holly pushed his way past, his lips locked like a safe. Sullevich grabbed his arm and yanked him back down the steps. Holly lost his balance, which gave Sullevich the advantage. Holly was bent over, his arm at an unnatural angle, but he didn't let the anger show in his face.

"Lost your balance there, son?" Sullevich yanked up on the bent arm and Holly grimaced. "Don't mean to cause you any pain—"

"Sullevich!" The sharp command came from the bottom of the staircase. Déjà vu. For the second time that day Noone arrived to put his officers in check. I didn't believe for a moment it was a coincidence.

Sullevich didn't miss a beat. "I was just helping him

up. The kid stumbled. Uncoordinated." He turned to Blakenhorn. "The other one's the athlete, right?"

Blakenhorn nodded. "Baseball or something."

Noone made his way up the stairs as Holly shook himself loose and walked up to Regina and into the apartment. Noone hurried after him.

"That's a crime scene. Don't touch anything."

In the apartment I was shocked at the chaos. The couch was slashed open, the marrow scattered over the front room. The television lay on its side; cabinets and drawers were pulled out and emptied. The kitchen had also been overturned, with dishes broken and the refrigerator on its face, the contents piled against a counter like discarded garbage.

In the hallway paintings had been pulled from the wall and the frames splintered open. Regina's room was the first one at the top of the hall. I looked in to find nothing out of place. The bed was still made, pillows propped nicely, nothing discarded on her desk or dresser.

"They didn't touch my room at all."

"When did you get here?" I asked.

"Just a little while ago. I came by to pick up some more clothes. I asked my neighbors if they heard anything, but no one was home."

I doubted that and so did she. Most of them probably remembered the savage beating Charlie had received just days before.

Sullevich and Blakenhorn stomped into the apartment behind us. "The neighbors, of course, didn't hear a thing."

Noone looked at the three of us. "Maceo, you still keeping quiet? You can't tell me this isn't all related. Billy's murder, Felicia's disappearance"—he pushed open the door to her bedroom—"the specific way this apartment was ransacked."

Felicia's room was a direct contrast to Regina's. Nothing was left untouched. Her mattress and box spring had been pushed against a window—which had cracked from the pressure—and slashed open. The comforter, sheets, and pillows were spattered with blood, as were the papers and books from her overturned desk.

Noone pushed Holly and me back. "I'll need you both to leave the apartment."

Regina spoke up. "I'd feel more comfortable if they stayed."

"I understand that, ma'am." Noone's voice was patient, though his nose twitched with irritation. "They don't have to leave; they can stay in the hall. But I do need them to leave the premises."

Regina joined us in the hall out of earshot of the police.

"Where do you think the blood came from?" I asked.

"There's broken glass under the bed. I think the blood was an accident but they were looking for something that had to do with Flea. They didn't even touch my room."

"Do you remember Flea and Billy going to L.A. recently?" Holly shot a look my way.

"They went all the time, at least twice a month," Regina answered.

"What for?"

She shrugged. "Vacation. Flea wanted to see her Aunt Venus. She's been sick."

"Do you have her number?" I asked.

"I spoke to her yesterday. I called earlier to see if she'd heard from Flea, but she hadn't. At least she said she hadn't. Flea could have been there, for all I know."

"Her brothers would have said something if she was."

"I doubt that," Regina answered. "Venus doesn't speak to Reggie and Crim."

"When was the last time they went to L.A.?"

"The weekend before Billy got killed."

"Damn," Holly muttered from across the hall. I

thought his words were a reaction to Regina's, but he was looking out the window. "Speak of the devils."

A few minutes later Reggie and Crim appeared at the bottom of the stairs. "Y'all heard anything?" Reggie started up the stairs toward Holly.

He held up his hand to stop them. "The police are here."

Reggie stopped in his tracks. "They find my sister?"

"Naw, somebody broke into the apartment."

"For what?"

"Don't know, but the place tore up. Y'all heard from Flea?"

"Nope."

Regina spoke up. "I talked to your Aunt Venus, and she hasn't heard anything either."

"When did you talk to her?" Reggie looked back toward Crim with a raised eyebrow.

"Yesterday."

"We heard that Billy and Flea were going down to L.A. a lot," I said.

Both Reggie and Crim looked at me as if I'd farted.

"L.A.?" Reggie asked, his eyes wide in disbelief.

"Yeah. Regina said Flea told her your Aunt Venus was sick."

"W-w-wa-what?" Crim was blinking furiously in bewilderment. "S-s-sick?"

"Yeah. Flea and Billy drove down at least twice a month."

Reggie and Crim looked at each other. The news seemed a complete surprise to both of them. Holly decided then to play the trump card. "We heard on the street Billy was trying to move into the L.A. market with some Mexicans."

Reggie stepped back toward the door. There was no mistaking his fury. "Where you hear that?"

"Everybody was talking about it at the funeral. Billy

kept it on the under, but he had cool prices so it makes sense."

"Who hooked him up wit' the Mexicans?"

Holly shrugged. "Wish I knew."

Behind Reggie, Crim looked frantic. It was the first time I'd seen either of them at such a loss. Reggie wasn't as big as he thought if Billy and his own sister bypassed him in order to enter the L.A. drug market.

"L-l-let's get the f-f-fuck up outta here!" Crim pulled Reggie back toward the door.

As they stepped through the threshold, Reggie turned to me and Regina. "If y'all hear from Flea, tell her to call home."

"You do the same," Regina said, but I could tell from Reggie's expression that he didn't expect to talk to his sister.

I sat down on the top stair, which gave me a perfect view of Charlie's Bronco. When Reggie reached for the door handle I saw a white bandage wrapped roughly around his hand. It was hard work beating the shit out of someone. Reggie's injuries were probably minor compared to Charlie's.

Holly dropped his voice. "Sounds like your girl was living foul."

Though I didn't want to believe it, the evidence was starting to say otherwise. In my heart and mind, Felicia was nothing but innocent, but her mysterious actions and sudden disappearance threw suspicion on her recent activities.

Regina spoke my fears. "Y'all think Flea was involved in this?"

I refused to answer.

Holly told it like it was. "Without a doubt."

Jorge the Mexican looked more like an Indian than anything else. He wore his hair in a long ponytail with gold
pirate hoops in each ear. He cultivated a Raul Julia accent and suave *bolla* mannerisms but sported a big nasty
belly that shot it all to hell.

Jorge's house, which he liked to call the Compound,
was made up of two lots on a dead-end industrial street
in Vallejo. The front structure was made out of stone
blocks with a slanted stucco roof to cap the second story.
It looked primitive, as if it had been built by crackheads
working for extra credit. I always expected to see chickens and pigs in the backyard.

Behind the main house was a large converted garage
where Jorge held court and entertained wannabes and
his crew. As we approached we could see a few of them
playing cards on a rickety table. The open space on the
far side of the yard housed three pens of snarling dogs.
Underneath a tarp, treadmills were lined up in a row. I
watched as a man from Jorge's crew ran one of the muscle-
bound dogs at full speed.

"Hey, Holly. Maceo."

The voice caught us off guard. We looked up at the
second story, where a half-dressed girl leaned out of a
window. It broke my heart when I saw her.

"Wait there. I'll come down."

She did, and it was a sight to see. When Sera came

toward us, all I could recall was her untouchable status at Berkeley High School. She still walked with the remnants of that past in her step, but drugs had taken their toll.

Her look was that of a late-seventies *chola*. She wore her long black hair in plastered feathers that covered her ears. Two wings of black makeup shot out from the sides of her eyes. She was thin and papery-looking, her skin like cheesecloth.

"Man, it's been a long time." She greeted us with a friendliness that had never been present when she was one of the most sought-after girls in the Bay Area, but neither of us had the heart to shoot her down. "Y'all look good." Her teeth were covered with a gray-yellow film that reminded me of moss.

She was friendly, overly so, but there was also something mincing mixed in, like she expected us to send her away at any moment or ask her to give us something she was tired of giving.

"Hey, pretty girl." Holly used the same tone he charmed Chantal with. I was too stuck, too appalled to add anything. I'd heard rumors that Sera was a strawberry in Jorge's camp, but the evidence threw me for a loop.

She searched Holly's face for mockery but there was none there. "You still rollin', Holly?"

"Just livin', baby."

"Yeah. What y'all doing out this way?"

"Looking for the Mexican. He around?"

She frowned and looked toward the garage, where the group of men had stopped playing cards. When she turned and the sun caught her eye, I noticed the faint remnants of a bruise.

"He's here somewhere. He don't leave this place. Thinks he's Escobar or something." She rolled her eyes.

"You taking care of yourself?"

"Of course. My little girl upstairs. You wanna see her?" She asked the last question with a promise of something extra if Holly followed her into the house.

"I bet she's pretty like her mama." Holly squeezed Sera's hand. "Maybe after I handle some business."

"Sera! Get the fuck out of here. You left the baby by herself?" Jorge's voice boomed from the other side of an abandoned car.

"She's asleep."

He balled a fist and Sera slunk back despite the distance between them. Back in the day, Jorge wouldn't have been able to touch a girl like Sera, but crack was the great equalizer and he wasn't going to let her forget.

Sera scurried into the house while Jorge approached with his hand extended. "Lot of visitors from Oaktown lately."

"That right?" Holly replied. "Was Billy out this way?"

"Let's go up on the roof."

We took a rickety staircase to the top of the garage, where Jorge kept a pigeon coop. Two notches below the chickens I expected.

"Yeah, Billy was out here with his chick," Jorge answered. "Sera took one look at her and was depressed for two days."

Holly couldn't hold his tongue. "Man, why you got your girl smokin' that shit?"

Jorge dropped his congenial manner. "You judging me?"

"That shit is foul."

"Didn't you come here wanting something from me? And now you're gonna make decisions about how I'm living?"

"I'm just saying."

"You can't say shit."

Holly cracked Jorge across the nose. I knew it was more for Sera than for the outburst, but Holly had a reputation to uphold and he never allowed disrespect from someone below him on the food chain.

"Man, Holly, what the fuck." I remembered the crew of card players just below us. I stepped forward but Holly waved me back.

"This weak-ass punk ain't gonna do shit. This place'll be lit up by sundown if he tries anything stupid."

Jorge held one hand up and used the other to hold back the blood pouring from his nose. Holly grabbed his ponytail and tried to yank his head from his shoulders. "Am I right?"

Jorge nodded.

"Say it."

"Yeah, it's cool. I slipped on the staircase. Had a little accident."

Holly let him go. "So, Billy was out this way?"

"About a week ago. Came with the girl, like I said. He was looking for a way to move into L.A., and I tried to hook him up with my cousins."

"Tried."

Jorge flung the blood pooled in his hand off the side of the building. "Yeah. Tried. It was suppose to go down this week, but . . ."

"But what?"

"He got killed, man."

Holly let him go. "You have anything to do with that?"

"Hell, naw."

"Who else knew about the deal?"

"His girl. Just his girl."

"Felicia? Is that who it was?"

"That's not what he called her. He called her Flea, something like that." My heart sank. "She was here with him the whole time."

"She the only one knew anything about it?"

"From this side, yeah. I don't know how Billy was slippin' outside of here." Jorge's words had merit. I was surprised Felicia was so involved in Billy's dealings.

Holly pulled Jorge to his feet. "All right, then. We gonna get out of here."

"Sure. Sure."

Jorge started to follow us down the stairs but Holly held him back. "Wait up here until we gone."

Jorge nodded and went back to his pigeons. I expected gunfire to rain down on us as soon as we cleared the building, but Holly entertained no such fear. Jorge was too weak, too low on the scale to sustain a battle with anyone from the Town.

Out front as we climbed into the Cougar, Sera rushed out to see us. She leaned against the passenger door. "You sure you don't want to see the baby?"

"Another time." Holly motioned for me to start the engine.

"How's Oakland? Berkeley? I haven't been out that way in so long. Jorge like to stay out here with all this shit around."

"You should stretch your legs, get out some." Holly remained solicitous, though he was aching to go. "People in Oaktown probably miss you too."

She ran her hands across her hair and pulled on her bangs. "I'ma get my shit together, you know, fix things up a little."

"You do that."

She lowered her voice. "I was here when Billy came to visit." She smiled with her decrepit teeth. "He was nice to me too. Remembered me from junior high."

"You hear what they were talking about?"

"Yeah, I did. People ignore me now. They act like I'm not here but I still hear things. I usually know everything that goes on."

"Was everything cool between Billy and the Mexican?"

"Billy wanted Jorge's help in L.A. He said his other connection fell through, but he needed to get out there."

"Did he say who the connection was?" Holly probably wondered if Billy had been referring to him and the deal that never happened.

"No, but a lot of people came up here after that."

"You recognize anybody?"

"Not from the first crew, but Smokey came out a few days ago."

"Smokey?"

"Yeah. He came to get two puppies. There's a new litter and he got a male and a female."

"Did you talk to him?"

She looked away, and we both knew Smokey had used the opportunity to humiliate her. I wondered if the bruise came from his hand and not Jorge's. "No, we didn't talk."

"You recognize anybody else?"

Jorge yelled her name before she could answer the question. She glanced back anxiously at the house. "I gotta go. Maceo, tell your sister Cissy I said hi."

"I will." I didn't bother to correct her about the relationship.

Holly grabbed her hand. "You gonna take care of yourself?"

"Yeah."

She rocked from foot to foot, wanting to explain herself and her condition, but there were no words. She had just slipped like so many others.

Holly reached into his pocket and pulled out five twenty-dollar bills. He handed them to her. "You not gonna use this to fuck around, are you?"

"I'll try not to." She wouldn't look us in the eye—the reflection was too severe—so she looked off at the oil derricks that lined the bay.

"Try harder. You got that little girl."

A tear slipped down her cheek but she remained quiet. "This is the worst thing that ever happened, this stuff. This is the worst thing to ever happen to anybody." As she looked at Holly I saw a quick flash of anger directed at him and his charity. She might be a victim but he was a predator. He profited from the misery she had fallen slave to and she hated him even as her hands reached out for the cash. She hesitated for a moment but, ultimately, she didn't have the heart to refuse it.

Averting her eyes, she snatched the money. Our pity left bruises that ached just beneath the surface. Old friends, East Bay history, represented life before the pipe. She saw judgment in our eyes; there was no way to hide it. Maybe in her own mirror she could still see the proms and the boys lined up on her parents' porch, but the reflection cast back from us revealed Strawberry Sera and nothing else.

She turned without a good-bye and went back into the house.

We headed back to Oakland.

CHAPTER

27

The Nickel and Dime was cast in artificial light as the mute television screen flickered indecipherable messages throughout the room. On the big screen two blond sportscasters pantomimed the day's events to a nearly empty room.

Onstage the house band ended a run at the O'Jays,

then awkwardly moved into "Delilah," a famous blues tune with difficult vocals and chords. I looked to Vicki for explanation and she nodded toward the end of the bar.

I smiled to see Midnight Blue as he quietly watched the lead guitarist solo his most famous song. I couldn't imagine a more intimidating experience.

Midnight Blue was a master, a genius according to blues historians and layman musicians, and there he was in the flesh as Glenn, a weekend warrior of a guitarist, sweated and ached his way through the chorus.

Over a ten-year period, "Delilah" had been professionally covered by everyone from the Rolling Stones to college marching bands, and now Glenn strained his vocals and killed the riffs with his deadly fingers.

Blue was a member of the Redfield clan because of his fifteen-year relationship with my Aunt Desiree, Detective Noone's blue flame. Desi and Blue had found each other after she fled Oakland, a drug habit, and a string of dismal boyfriends for the comforts and safety of Louisiana. Desiree's visits to Oakland were few and far between, but we'd grown accustomed to Blue's unannounced walkabouts from the south.

Twelve o'clock noon or six in the morning, you could never predict when Blue would appear, somber-faced and expensively clad, on the front steps of the Dover Street house. He'd stay for a while, entertain us with tales of his travels, play a few songs at the Nickel and Dime, and then disappear without notice.

Desiree attributed his habits to the years he'd spent locked away on The Farm, Angola State Penitentiary in Louisiana, a former plantation that prospered by using the inmates as slave labor.

Blue's skills on the slide guitar and his haunting voice won him a governor's pardon from the place he thought would be his coffin. Blue left behind everything he owned except his lyric sheet, scribbled in an alphabet he'd taught himself, and memories of the real Delilah, a bona fide woman who'd granted him the only pardon that mattered.

Blue walked from the gates of The Farm into a lucrative recording contract, three Grammys, and induction into the Blues Hall of Fame. He met Desiree on his first night of freedom when he attempted to kick his habit, solo, in a New Orleans alley. Later Blue would say he knew that any woman who didn't run from his funkiness, his screaming curses, and the torment weeping from every hole in his body was a woman he would walk through fire to keep. Since then Blue's life had moved in a circle, beginning and ending with Desiree.

"Midnight Blue!" I yelled his name across the room. My shout cut through the music and startled Glenn into missing a few beats.

Blue turned and grinned a blinding-white smile. He was vanity personified in a charcoal gray suit, butter-soft loafers, and silver pirate hoops in each ear.

"Maceo Redfield!" He punctuated my name by slamming his mahogany walking stick into the ground. Christophene, his signature cane, had appeared on all seventeen of his album covers. "The bantam rooster!"

"What brings you out this far?"

Blue didn't bother to stand but he clasped my hand tightly to show his affection. "Oh, Blue goes where he's needed." His famous voice sounded like scotch and jagged ice, hoarse around the edges, a faded whisper that burned out at the end. His speech pattern gave the listener an impression of permanent distraction, but Blue was as sharp as they came.

"How you doing?"

"Blue's always fine. Ain't no other way to be. And yourself?"

"Good. Good." Wariness crept into my voice because Blue's gaze was too steady. Behind his concern I heard the worries of Daddy Al, Gra'mère, and Desiree. "You seen Daddy Al since you got here?"

He smiled to let me know he knew the root of my question. "And your grandmama, three of them aunties of yours, and Gloria Johnson. You say you good, but that ain't the way they tellin' the story."

"Telling stories. That's exactly what everybody doing." I shook my hand in the air. "Don't even worry about it."

"Of course not. Blue got too many of his own problems. But from what I hear, you determined to get killed behind that little gal I met last time out."

Flea had taken an immediate liking to Blue and he'd nearly charmed her into leaving Billy and going on the road with him, though she couldn't hold a note.

"It's not that deep."

"That's the way you see it?"

"That's the way it is."

"Y'all have a funeral out here?"

"Yep. Yesterday."

"And somebody tried to jump you?"

"Tried but I was too quick."

"Uh-huh." He nodded to Glenn as he segued into an easier Kool and the Gang song. Glenn nodded back, slinging anxious sweat halfway across the room. Blue wiped his own brow. "That boy there was killing my song. You have to know a woman like Delilah to be able to sing about her."

"Delilah? No woman like that exists." The joke fell flat before I even said it.

He shook his head. "Is that right?" He turned away from my dishonesty. Blue couldn't stand fools and liars. I guess at that moment he thought I was both.

The entrance of the Wise Men and Daddy Al allowed me a gracious exit.

"See ya, Blue."

"Uh-huh." He lit a cigar and went back to watching the band.

As I passed Daddy Al he put a hand on my shoulder. "You holdin' up, son?"

"What choice do I have?" I let the doors swing shut behind me as I stalked into the dimming sunlight. Daddy Al followed me out.

"Blue talk to you about going down South with him?"

"No."

"You been thinking about it?"

"No."

"Maybe you should."

He and I both knew I had no intention of going out to Red Fields, but I told him what he wanted to hear. "I'll think about it."

As he walked back through the swinging doors I had a quick flash of my last encounter with Billy. He'd walked through those same doors the night of the murder. The last time I ever saw him alive.

I'd been working a fill-in shift for Paulie, who had to attend a premarital counseling class at St. Ambrose Cathedral. He was engaged to another day-shift bartender and we all tried to accommodate them as best we could.

I was sleepily flipping through the midafternoon talk shows and soap operas, stopping longer on *Guiding Light* than I would admit to anybody. Thankfully, the show had gone to a commercial when Billy walked in. It took me a minute to place him, he was so out of context in my life and in the bar since Felicia quit.

"Hey, man." He slid onto a stool, waved to Daddy Al, and offered his hand for a shake. "Wassup?"

"You, big-time. What's going on with you?"

"Living, dog. Living. Can I get a Hennessy?"

I poured heavy, happier to see Billy than I would admit.

Our run-ins were few and far between, where they'd once been every day.

"How's baseball?"

"Swinging."

"Heard you dropped." He took a long sip. "That true?"

"For now. What about you? How's it going?"

"Can't complain. 'Bout ready to make some moves." He grinned, a slow, wide grin that I had missed.

"What you grinning about, fool?"

"My girl, man, my girl." He searched my face, to make sure his reference to Felicia wouldn't stall the conversation. I showed nothing in my face though my heart beat a mile a minute.

"Wassup?"

He reached in his pocket and retrieved an unmistakable black velvet box. All I could do was stare. She was gone, yet again, and I didn't have the strength to feel the loss a second time.

"That what I think it is?" I picked up the box and filled my voice with what I knew he needed to hear.

"That's it, baby. No reason to sleep, *know-what-I'm-saying*?"

"I hear ya." I opened the box and looked at a ring I remembered seeing on his mother's hand. She wore that wedding ring from Billy's father well into her second marriage.

"It's my mama's. I went by there and got it today. I'ma see my girl tonight and hopefully, couple of months from now, you'll stand up for your old boy."

I gave him the ring back and shook his hand. "You know it, brother. Wouldn't do nothing less."

He held my hand tight, a bridge to the missing years. "I'd do the same for you, man. Ain't nothing ever came close to me, you, and Holly back in the day."

"You gonna talk to Holly? He'll wanna be there too."

He shrugged. "Don't wanna cause the man no distress."

"Can't be me and you without Holly."

"I got ya." He downed his drink, then looked into the empty glass.

"Maceo, man, if it wasn't like it is I woulda never stepped to her. Felicia." I recognized the look in his eye. "Felicia is mine." He said it in truth, not to provoke me but to convey that there was no one else for him. Too bad I felt the exact same way.

I reached under the counter and felt around for a cracked wineglass that housed the butterfly anklet I'd given her. She'd lost it here last week in the bar and had come back several times, hoping to find it. I'd found it the same night—I'd seen it slip from her ankle as she moved around the bar—but each time I'd told her I hadn't seen it. It was my last link to her, and I didn't want to give it up.

While Billy waited I closed it in my fist and placed it on top of the counter. "Give this to Felicia." I tried to joke. "It's not the same as that big ol' ring, but she might want it back."

It disappeared into his pocket. "Thanks, man." He stood to go. "All right then. I gotta hit it." He gave me a heartfelt pound then nodded to Daddy Al, who looked up absently from his card game with Tully. "Time for shit to unfold."

"Keep in touch, man."

"Without a doubt." He smiled and headed for the door.

CHAPTER

28

Twenty minutes later I was searching the West Oakland neighborhood for Holly's car. I wanted to tell him what I remembered about Billy's last visit. I wanted to tell him that they were going to get married and that Billy and I had reached a certain peace.

I was surprised to spot his car parked recklessly close to his house. It brought dread back into residence but I proceeded anyway. The sun was going down, and commuter traffic clogged the streets around the BART station. In the distance the big construction dinosaurs of West Oakland loomed against a burnt-red sky. Local lore had it that Marin filmmaker George Lucas used them as inspiration for the Walkers in the *Star Wars* movies.

The gate was cracked open alongside the warehouse, another testament to Holly's uncharacteristic carelessness. I backed up. Then I made a decision, a decision that put me farther over the fence, but I knew Holly wouldn't hesitate if I were in danger.

In the car I pulled on a batting glove and reached for the gun underneath the passenger seat. I'd forgotten since my encounter with Smokey to dispose of it, and now I was grateful.

The steel felt alien to my hand, hands used to the grip of a bat or the roundness of a baseball, but I stilled my fears and held the gun low at my side.

Alongside the warehouse I kept to the shadows, grateful that the opposite side was lined with a tall hedge.

Before rounding the corner, I stopped abruptly at an alien sound, a sound that didn't fit the circumstance.

A woman's laugh.

A familiar laugh.

For a moment I thought it was Felicia.

Holly and I had never kept secrets between us until her arrival, and I didn't want to know why he kept them now. But my feet kept moving me forward until I could see the silhouette of two people near the clay wheel.

The girl was stretched backward and fully dressed, with her legs open wide to give him access. He leaned over her with his shirt off and his face buried in the side of her neck. Kissing was not Holly's style. He'd said more than once that he didn't see the point of it. It was more intimate to him than fucking, as he put it, so I was surprised to see him rise up and cover the woman's mouth with his own. She responded, and I watched with my heart beating as they tried to devour each other. That's what it seemed like to me, desperation fueled by something other than desire.

Secrets.

When they came up for air I looked straight into the face of my Aunt Cissy. She didn't see me and neither did Holly, so I moved back into the shade. I went toward the front gate, careful not to make a sound. I stopped again when I heard them laugh together. I bent to leave the gun in the center of the walkway, clearly visible. A message.

Let him wonder.

Secrets between brothers?

At the car I realized my body was clammy with sweat, from exhaustion, like I'd just run a race I had no chance of winning.

I drove aimlessly through the streets, not sure of my destination until I stopped at a phone booth and dialed local information.

"What city, please?"

"Oakland. Can I get a number for Alixe Hunter?"

A recording came on and recited the seven digits. Moments later Alixe came on the line.

"Hello?"

"Wassup, girl?"

She paused to clear the sleep from her head, maybe to decide who I was. "Maceo?"

"Yeah. You 'sleep?"

"Not too. Just tired, mostly. Sounds like you're out on the street. Where are you?"

"I don't know." I looked around and realized I wasn't too far from Chantal's house. "Not far from your sister's."

"You all right?"

I thought of Holly and Cissy entwined in the yard of his house. "Been better."

"Want me to meet you?"

"Not if you already asleep."

"It's okay. I'm dressed. Just need my shoes. Why don't you meet me at Chantal's. I'll call and tell her you're on your way. Okay?"

I didn't answer. I wasn't sure if Chantal was the antidote to my black mood. "I can't take your sister right now."

"I'll warn her. See you in a minute, okay? Give me twenty minutes." The line went dead before I could talk her or myself out of the meeting.

I redialed but her answering machine picked up on the third ring. "You know who you called. Leave a message."

Five minutes later Chantal opened the door of her apartment dressed in a black-and-white Adidas sweat suit and pink high-heeled slippers. Her hair was pinned into sections and loaded down with white globs of straightening perm. Behind her Donna Summer blared from the speakers while Scottie played PacMan with a friend. I put on a game face before walking inside.

"Donna Summer, Chantal? You trying to bring disco back?"

"Donna Summer found the Lord, fool. What you about? You trying to be a heathen till you die?" She kicked the door closed with the heel of her shoe and walked away. "Come on if you're coming," she shot back over her shoulder.

The small living room was funky with the pungent smell of hair relaxer. I recognized the odor from growing up in a houseful of women.

"What's up, waterhead?" I flicked the bill of Scottie's cap and took a seat.

He looked perplexed. "You here to see my mama?"

"Your auntie."

"For real?" He smiled, pleased at the possibility of a new union.

"Why you up so late?"

"It ain't late. I go to bed at eleven."

"Oh, you grown?"

"Don't mess up my game." I watched him concentrate on the screen figures as I tried to get the image of Holly and Cissy out of my mind.

Chantal returned with an ancient hood hair dryer in her hands.

"Damn, you dig that out of a time capsule?" I hadn't seen a contraption like hers since blow dryers hit the market.

"You got money to buy something else? How you gonna come up in my house trying to talk shit?"

"I was just kidding."

She rolled her eyes. "Don't get me started on you"— she pointed her brush and raised an eyebrow—" 'cause you living kinda foul your damn self."

I knew immediately that she meant Alixe. "What are you talking about?"

"You know, punk, but if you want me to break your business down, come on in the kitchen."

I followed her into the cramped cooking space, where one rickety table was shoved against a far corner. She set the dryer on top of the counter, opened it, and put her hands on her hips. She gestured for me to take a seat.

I could tell she enjoyed keeping me waiting. It wasn't very often that she had my full and undivided attention.

She gave me a wicked gleam. "I told my sister I had a little bit of you myself." She ran a vulgar tongue back and forth across her lips. "Me and you did the nasty." She winked. "Keep it all in the family."

"What?" The thought of Alixe knowing about my indiscretion with Chantal made my stomach hurt. "Why would you do something like that?"

"Just to fuck with you." She sectioned her hair off and used her fingers to work in the small clumps of pungent lye. "I didn't tell her nothing till she came in here talking all about you. But let me warn you, brother man, my sister ain't at all what she seems. She ain't homegrown so you gonna have problems. Trust me."

"You throwing salt in the game?"

"It don't change what I said."

"I'm not trying to hear all that ying-yang."

"Whatever. All I'm saying is that sister-girl is notorious for getting in the cut when thangs gets rough. If you looking for a female to watch your back through the rough-and-tough, she ain't the one."

"It ain't that deep."

"And it ain't gonna *get* deep, you keep rollin' with ballers. There ain't an ounce of ghetto in that girl."

"That's a positive."

She shook her head. "Ghetto ain't all bad, baby. It give you coping skills."

"She's coped with a lot."

"White people shit. What you dealing with, despite your bougie-siddity-high-yellow family, ain't the same. We both know it."

"You finished with your lecture?"

"Did you hear what I said?"

"I heard ya."

"Good. Don't get blinded by that big old booty of hers."

Scottie wandered into the kitchen then, so Chantal cut her lecture short and stuck her head under the running water in the kitchen sink. Her words hadn't found a place in my head anyway. I figured that anything Chantal had to say about Alixe was laced with jealousy.

"When we going to the park to pitch? 'Member I talked to you about that?"

"I remember."

"When?"

"I got some things going on. I'll get wit' you after that."

Scottie looked at me with reservation but decided to give me the benefit of the doubt. "All right. Don't keep me waiting, though."

Alixe walked in dressed in her nurse's uniform as Scottie exited. I hadn't bothered to ask her if she was working. I was sorry I'd interrupted her sleep before a shift.

Alixe held her nose. "It stinks in here. What's that smell?"

"All of us ain't got that half-Japanese hair." Chantal shouted from the sink.

Alixe turned to me and smiled. "Did you just get here?"

"A couple of minutes ago."

"Everything all right?" Her words brought Holly and Cissy back to my mind, and I grimaced. She took the bait. "Let's get out of here then."

She waved to Chantal, who pretended not to listen but waved back, dismissively.

"Remember what I said." She looked me in the eye before returning her head to the running water.

On the way down the stairs, Alixe turned and slipped both arms around my shoulders. She gave me a hug with her full body and held on to me so long I almost forgot my troubles. Almost.

Chantal's voice blasted me back into reality.

"Maceo! Y'all out there?"

Alixe sighed. "I knew it wouldn't be easy."

"Yeah, I'm right here. What's up?"

"Cissy. Your Aunt Cissy is on the phone."

"Tell her I'll call her later."

I grabbed Alixe's hand and tried to hustle her down the stairs.

"She said it's an emergency."

I hesitated.

"She's crying."

I gave in and walked back toward the apartment. I grabbed the phone from Chantal, who looked genuinely worried. Before I had the receiver to my ear I could hear Cissy's sobs.

"Cis, wassup? What's wrong?"

"Maceo. It's Holly."

I steeled myself. It couldn't be possible to lose two friends in one week, but logic had stopped being part of my reality long ago.

"What happened?"

"They picked him up." She took a deep breath in an attempt to calm herself. I saw visions of Smokey, even the White boys, until she said, "Noone. He picked him up."

"Why?" At least he was still alive.

"Jorge. Jorge the Mexican is dead and somebody fingered Holly."

"Damn!"

Chantal and Alixe searched my face for clues. I noticed that Alixe had remained near the front door, as far away from me as possible. Maybe Chantal was right.

"Where are you?"

"At the Tombs." The Tombs was the nickname for the city lockup at the base of downtown Oakland.

"All right. I'll be there in a minute." I hung up the phone and headed for the front door. Alixe stayed put. "I'll call you later" was all I could manage as I raced down the stairs.

The Tombs had the dour gray walls of most government buildings, moldy green windows, and the lethargic movements of employees on a city payroll. Cissy looked out of place in that environment and for a quick moment, when I caught my own reflection in the glass walls of a trophy case, I realized that I did too.

Cissy was sitting between two disgruntled women, women familiar with the air of despair and the patronizing attitude of the people in charge.

One of them was a young mother, nineteen maybe, with gold braids that swirled into a beehive and twin boys who used her as a scratching post. She stared angrily ahead and ignored their kittenish whines for a bottle or, at the very least, affection.

On the other side of Cissy, a bedraggled older woman, also Black, fingered a string of grimy rosary beads and mumbled to herself.

And above them all Huey P. Newton, the once formidable leader of the Black Panther Party, glared down at them in youthful defiance. He was perched famously in the rattan chair, beret at a rakish tilt atop a beautiful Afro, a rifle in each hand.

Newton was a Louisiana boy, named for a former corrupt governor, but he rose to power in northern California with a battalion of committed brothers at his back.

Who knew back then that he would take himself out

of the game? Huey P. Newton's pathetic demise on a West Oakland street corner in August was representative of where we were and all that was yet to come for us. The night of his death he was out searching the streets of Ghost Town for drugs at a dangerous hour, in a dangerous city with a dangerously short memory.

Cissy jumped up when she noticed I was there. Her pretty gray eyes were rimmed with red and her nose ran unchecked while she tried to tell the story. Her wild head of curls, which had been pulled back in a ponytail, had come undone on one side. It was the most unkempt I had ever seen her.

She wrapped her arms around my neck and cried for a full three minutes before letting go. Over her shoulder I saw the young mother roll her eyes in irritation. Why the hysterics? her eyes said. Shit happens.

I edged Cissy across the aisle and sat her down.

"What happened?"

"We were together." She looked sheepishly at me but I ignored her discomfort. "And we were leaving Holly's house when four police cars surrounded us. They dragged Holly from the car. They made me lay on the ground after they pulled me out. Noone was with them, but he acted like he didn't know me. I tried to talk to him but he wouldn't say anything."

"Did you call a lawyer?"

She nodded. "I called twice. He should be here soon." She looked toward the empty front door.

"Did they book Holly?"

"I don't know. They asked him about Jorge, though. I heard them. Him and Sera were killed yesterday." She wiped her eyes and took a deep breath to still the hiccups that peppered her speech. "Were y'all up there?"

I nodded. "For a minute."

"Did Holly and Jorge get in a fight?"

I flashed back to the quick flurry of fists on the roof. Jorge's broken nose would have been obvious to all his boys when we came down from the chicken coop. "Shit," I muttered. Any one of them could have set the police on Holly. Or on me.

I jumped out of my chair like it was on fire.

"Watch it, son."

Winston Lamb. I shook his hand, glad Holly's lawyer was in the building. Lamb was famous throughout the Bay Area, as much for his clientele—career criminals in high-end tax brackets—as he was for his style. No shame in his game. He had left a prestigious teaching post at Boalt law school to practice criminal law and enjoy the financial good life that went with it.

He looked like a Black Garfunkel, hair-wise, which made his appearance somewhat cartoonish, two nappy puffs three inches straight out from his ears, and bald as a globe in the center. He wore expensive suits, though always a little too tight, and was openly gay—not a big deal for San Francisco, but Oakland was geographically on the moon in that category.

"Mr. Lamb, I'm Maceo Redfield, Holly's friend, and this is his girlfriend, Cissy Redfield."

I saw Cissy look at me sideways but she didn't correct the introduction.

"Pleased to meet you both."

"Do you know anything?" Cissy interjected.

"My client is here for questioning." He said the word as if it were a discarded tampon, useless. "That means they don't have anything solid, but they want to play with him." His manner indicated that the idea was absurd.

"Can we do anything?"

"Not here. Let me handle this, and if I need you I'll call."

"Can I wait?" Cissy objected to leaving Holly behind.

"Come with me, Cis. Holly will call when he gets out."

"I think that's best." Lamb put a comforting hand on Cissy's shoulder. "Trust me. It won't take long. You'll see him in no time."

Lamb moved past us, ready to do battle. The desk sergeant, encased behind bulletproof glass, looked up and shook his head as the lawyer approached. Lamb was a familiar sight at the Tombs.

"Let's go." I grabbed Cissy's hand, then dropped it. The poster of Newton still played on my mind. I walked across the aisle to the young mother with two kids. I was curious, after Newton's death, to find out what he meant to people. Young people.

"Hey, girl, you know who that is?" I pointed to the poster.

She didn't bother to look up. "Yo' mama."

I left it at that.

CHAPTER

31

"They brought you over here in a police car?"

Cissy and I stood in front of the police station and tried to ignore the circumstances and that I knew about her and Holly.

"Yeah. Noone wanted to question me too. I guess it was all part of his act."

"This is what you want, huh?"

"Don't start with me, Maceo. Not tonight. I can't deal with defending me and Holly right now. Not now."

I gave a dismissive snort. "You and Holly."

"Yeah, me and Holly. Holly and me. You got a problem with that?"

"Do you? You the one keeping secrets."

"It's not about secrets. It's about the two of us being sure about how we feel."

"That's what y'all tell each other."

"Maceo."

"Secrets."

"Maceo, not now, okay? We can get into it tomorrow, whenever, once Holly gets home."

"How long this been going on?"

She didn't answer. She walked away from the station, looking for my car. "Where are you parked?"

I stood my ground. "Answer my question."

"I'll catch a cab." She walked toward Fourteenth and Broadway, the city center where cabs congregated.

"You'd rather catch a cab at eleven o'clock at night than answer the question?"

"Maceo, I'm tired. I just want to go home."

"Damn, Cissy, it's been that long?"

"Six months. Since April. The last time you went out to Louisiana. We hung out together a little bit and then we just kept hanging out."

"You didn't feel like you could tell me? Holly neither?"

"We knew you wouldn't want to lie to Daddy, and neither one of us wanted to put you in the middle. You understand that? As long as it remained between the two of us we could contain it, control it. Daddy loves Holly, but he's not going to love him with me. You know that! You remember how he put Holly out of the house."

"Daddy Al loves Holly."

"Not with me, Maceo. It's like your mother, Ellie, with your father, like Celestine with Earl Ray. It's too much for him. He doesn't act like it, but he's an old man. I didn't want to put you in that position. I didn't want to put myself in the position of defending Holly. Not yet. Okay?" She reached for my hand. "Okay?"

"Holly's not safe, Cissy. He has too much to pay for." She and I both knew I spoke of John Claire. I had never, even at my most reflective, let my mind wander to Holly's role in John Claire's death. But now it was out there for the first time since it happened. Another debt.

"Don't say it, Maceo. You were the only one who believed him without question. Don't say it just because you don't want him with me."

I wished it were that simple. "The car is this way." I unhooked my fingers and let her hand drop away.

We were silent. The radio took the place of conversation as I drove down Broadway to the intersection where it split in two. I was halfway to Alcatraz before I realized where I was going. Cissy had fallen asleep in the passenger seat. Her head was turned to the breeze that filtered in from the open window. The heat had tapered off but not enough to match the calendar month. Our Indian summer looked as if it might stretch into November.

When I stopped at a red light, Cissy opened her eyes and gasped. "Maceo!"

I'd driven there without direction but it made sense. College and Alcatraz: the scene of Billy's murder. The place where it was all set in motion.

"I'ma get out for a minute." I pulled over and parked illegally in a handicapped zone in front of a corner store.

She reached for me but I was already out of the car. "You can stay. I won't be long."

I saw the door open but she thought better of it and closed it quietly. I walked away with the sound of the radio ringing in my ears.

On the corner I stopped for a moment. I could imagine, in my mind's eye, Billy slumped over the steering wheel, the horn blaring into the quiet hills above. Straight ahead, and visible because of the Campanile, was UC Berkeley. I closed my eyes and tried to imagine what he saw, what the last thing he focused on was before it went black.

I turned away and walked south on Alcatraz, toward the hills, in the direction I imagined that Felicia ran. The killers would have been on the north side, on Billy's side of the car, so she must have sprinted south for the hills.

As I walked I heard the tinny sound of music, not the bass-heavy beat from the Cougar but the small, faraway aluminum sound of a transistor radio.

I kept my hands in my pockets and never looked toward the source of the music, but I knew what it was: a faceless member of the Berkeley homeless. I was right. Beneath a bundle of dirty blankets and old clothes was a person and a dog, a dog with a simian face to match his owner's. Both of them were covered with soot, so much that I couldn't tell the gender of either one. They appeared to be hunkered and comfortable there, like it was familiar, not the perfect place but a spot that was theirs.

I turned back toward the car, cut into an alley behind the Buttercup Cafe, and came out into the bright lights of the Safeway supermarket parking lot. The store was due to close at midnight and I slipped in just before the doors were locked.

I pulled a ten-pound bag of dog food and a gallon of water from the shelf and paid for them. I retraced my steps down the alley and came out just on the other side of the storefront. The transistor played on and the dog eyed me with new interest as I approached.

"Hey there. I got the wrong brand for my girlfriend's dog. Can you use this?" I asked the question in a distracted manner as if it was an afterthought, an act of charity that occurred to me just at that moment.

The bundle of material bubbled beneath the surface and a hand reached toward me. I tore open the bag and poured a little, just a little, onto the sidewalk. The dog looked once at its owner, hoping for an okay but prepared to pursue its own course if it didn't get what it wanted.

"It's all right." I kept my voice low as I kneeled. The dog inched forward, hungry but leery. I wasn't that excited about it either. It looked to be infested with everything the Berkeley streets had to offer.

"You can give her more than that." The bundle moved enough for a head and torso to appear. "She'll eat it. She got a good appetite. I can go all right without food, but she can't. What I get I give more than half to her."

"I got a dog eat like that too. A girl. Doberman named Clio."

"Doberman, uh-uh. Turn on their owners. Not her, though. Sweet. Had her since she was a puppy. She had a litter too but animal control got 'em."

The dog nudged my hand with her nose: more food. I poured again, the same amount as last time. "What's her name?"

"This one? That's Lana Turner. You say your dog is Clio?"

"Yep."

"No last name?"

"Nope."

"Oh, that's not good, man." The bundles were moved away and a man emerged. Hippie burnout. Shaggy hair. All his clothes layered on his body, creating an illusion of bulk. "All my dogs had last names. They want to own themselves too."

"Never thought about it like that."

He tapped his temple. "You got to. You got to. They depend on us. Lana Turner appreciates that I took the time. Think about it."

"I will."

"Good."

"Hot enough for you out here?" I handed over the water container. It disappeared quickly under the rags in case I might change my mind.

"Been hotter."

"Last Friday. Last Friday was hot."

"I don't know nothing about that." He shook his head and made to go back undercover.

I rolled the top of the dog food bag closed. He and the dog watched me. "Didn't mean to get in your way." I lifted the bag under my arm.

"You gonna leave that? Thought you said it was the wrong brand."

"I can mix it in with the regular stuff."

He came back out of the clothes pile. "Dogs don't like that, man. Just leave it here."

I stood my ground, with the dog food the deal point between the three of us. They wanted the food and I wanted information. Lana Turner looked hopefully at her owner.

He finally conceded. "It was hot."

I sighed and opened the top of the bag. Maybe he knew something that could bring the nightmare to an end and let Felicia come home.

"It was so hot I wasn't in my usual post." He pointed down the street toward a gas station. There was an alley that ran parallel to the pumps. "Too much movement. We came up here to this spot and hunkered down for the night."

"Lot of people on the streets?"

"At first. Then, right after midnight, it slowed down. By one o'clock there were hardly any cars. Nobody walking. Like everybody disappeared."

"What happened? You know what I'm talking about."

His eyes shifted from side to side in avoidance, but we were engaged.

"You talking about the guy in the car?"

"Yeah. And a girl. There was a girl, right?"

He nodded. "She's the only one I saw. I slept through everything else, but she ran right past me and spooked Lana Turner."

"She ran by here?" I looked down at the ground as if there might be clues in her faded footsteps.

"I looked up just as she passed. She scared me. My dog too. Looked like a ghost. Wide-open eyes, no tears, and gasping for air."

"Was she hurt?"

"I couldn't tell."

"Did anyone come after her?"

"No, but I could hear them calling from the corner."

"Them?"

"Yeah. There were two of them. I couldn't see too well. They stayed out of the light but they kept calling her even after she was gone. Then they drove away."

"Did you see what they were driving?"

"A black Chevy. Muscle car. Loud."

"But you didn't see 'em?"

"Not like you want. Dark skin, I think, but there wasn't a moon so I couldn't be sure. They stayed away from the light, then drove away."

"And the girl ran thataway?" I pointed toward the hills.

"Far as I could tell."

I set the bag of dog food on his pile of clothes and scooped a generous handful out for Lana Turner.

"Thanks, man." He smiled as his dog greedily devoured the morsels scattered on the cement.

"No problem. Did you tell the police any of this?"

"They never asked. We went up in the hills soon as we heard sirens."

"All right." I reached in my pocket and pulled out a twenty-dollar bill. He snatched it away before I could change my mind. "Be safe."

"You too."

I was halfway down the hill before he called out to me. "You know the girl? Felicia. That's what they called her."

"Yeah, I know her."

"Felicia. Nice name. Maybe if Lana has some puppies."

The car was exactly where I left it, but something was different. Something was wrong. The air had changed. The entire street was charged with danger, the pungent smell of a predator locked onto his prey. I knew someone watched me.

I took another step toward the car before I realized Cissy was gone.

CHAPTER

32

The blow came out of nowhere.

I was so focused on the empty car I'd forgotten to check my surroundings. The fist slammed into the weak spot behind my ear while a foot connected to my ribs. I went down, fast and hard, on my shoulder. Another foot met my spine, and a scalding-hot pain shot straight to my brain.

"Cissy?" I muttered weakly, aware that my attackers probably held her life in their hands.

I was rolled onto my back, where I struggled helplessly with my arms pinned beneath me. A foot came down hard on my throat and collapsed the walls of my windpipe. I could barely get air through my nose or mouth.

I kicked outward and tried to connect with some part of the man's body, but he danced away swiftly and laughed, a deep menacing chuckle laced with pleasure. As he bounced under the streetlight I saw the mask and knew it was the guy from the Nickel and Dime there to finish his job. Another kick to the ribs sent bile up from my stomach and into my mouth. It made it to my lips before retreating down to puddle in my throat. I gagged and sucked for air like a fish.

"Can't breathe, motherfucker? Let me help you." He bent down and closed my nose together with his fingers while keeping his foot pressed to my throat. Someone came up behind him and a new pair of hands held me down. I heard a knife flick open and its steel tip was pressed into my inner ear.

"Maybe we can cut you a new breathing hole."

They laughed and hauled me to my feet. My shoulder was out of its socket and one arm dangled at an odd angle. It didn't matter. They snatched both arms behind my back and tied the wrists.

"We got something for you to see," the first man said. The second one stayed and pulled a Molotov from his coat. I knew the Cougar would be his next victim.

I stumbled along, dazed. My feet were kicked from under me at every other step but I managed to stay upright. I spit into the face of the man on my left. He let it hang there and then punched me once, quickly, in the ear and I saw a flash of light. I learned instantly that sharp pain is always met with bursts of color or flashes of whiteness like shooting stars.

"Fuck you," I said through clenched teeth. "Fuck you."

"Think so? I got a better idea." They laughed again and dragged me into an alley that ran behind the liquor store. I saw Cissy as soon as we turned the corner. She was bound and naked from the waist up. Tears ran down her face though her skin was unmarked—not a single blemish, as if they had been extra careful with her. She dropped her eyes to the ground, and I noticed tufts of hair, like the guts of a pillow, scattered around her knees. I wondered where they came from.

Then my stomach rose up to my throat for a second time. Cissy was completely bald. The jagged lines of a razor ran an ugly path across her scalp.

I was stunned. I knew instantly that it was Smokey's work. Cissy's humiliation was directed point-blank at Holly as if she weren't even an entity. A cold-blooded drug dealer's weapon of torture. A rival's woman. His weakness. Holly and Cissy hadn't been as secret as they thought.

I couldn't look at her. I was just as responsible for her condition as Holly, if not more so. Hot tears streamed down my face but I wasn't ashamed. "Cissy."

She flinched at the sound of crunching gravel. An unmistakable bulk stepped from the darkness: Smokey. He pulled the mask from his head just so I could be sure.

"Maceo, you the cryingest bitch I ever met." He laughed. "I gotta say this 'bout your boy Billy, though. He was a true all the way to the end." He gave me a minute to let the words sink in. Billy. He was talking about Billy. "Yeah, rolled up on that nigga right at this same corner." He laughed at the memory. "Bam, before he even knew what hit him. He was gone just like that and his girl got in the cut. So much for true love, don't believe in it myself.

"And if I was you, Maceo, I wouldn't trust that bitch Felicia to spit on me if I was on fire."

I blocked his words. I needed to concentrate on Cissy, somehow get us both out of that alley alive. Cissy tried to move away from Smokey but with her hands tied behind her back she couldn't get far. He reached out and grabbed her by the neck.

"Smoke, man, what the fuck are you doing? Let her go." I said the words without hope. I knew there was no chance of compliance, but my helplessness was castrating.

"Let her go?" He laughed. "Aw, naw, baby, we got plans." He unceremoniously shoved her face in his crotch. I railed up against the grip of my captors but they held me tightly in place and forced me down to my knees. In the middle of that she tried to keep her exposed body turned away from the two men at my side. Smokey grabbed her again and ground her face into his crotch. He made a lewd face at me.

"Wanna go first, Maceo? Heard y'all Louisiana boys like it that way."

His goons laughed behind him. He shoved Cissy backward and her head hit the wall with frightening force. A sickening sound escaped her lips before she slumped to the ground like a rag doll, unconscious. All I could wish was that she stayed that way.

Smokey pulled a knife from his pocket and cut away the last of her clothes. She didn't move, not once, while he yanked her body from side to side. Once she was completely naked I lost any composure that I had left.

"Come on, Smokey, man, please. Don't do this. Don't do this. Leave her alone."

"No chance of that, brother man." He kicked Cissy's leg and then grabbed hold of her ankles. "Get up." He dragged her toward him on the gravel. A streak of blood from the gash in her head left a gruesome trail. I thought immediately of John Claire. His ghost was in that alley. I felt the presence, just as I knew that Holly and I both had set these events in motion.

"Smokey!" I yelled once, loud, before a hand was clamped over my mouth and I was kicked in the shoulder that had been popped grotesquely out of its socket.

"Got damn, Smokey! You motherfucker! Let her go!" I cried without shame, begging and pleading for my aunt.

"Hold her up." Smokey motioned to one of his boys. He stepped forward and pulled Cissy up by her armpits. I saw him strain under her weight. She was unconscious and offered little resistance to his manipulation. Smokey slapped her hard across the face. She didn't respond.

"She ain't breathing. She ain't breathing!" I hoped my words would get to him, but they had little effect. *"She ain't breathing!"* I shouted one more time and finally got a response.

A bark, sharp. Pointed. Followed by a single low growl. At the end of the alley the homeless man stood at the street entrance, Lana Turner at his side. They stayed long enough for their presence to be noted before jetting off toward the hills. I couldn't expect anything more. It was all we needed.

Smokey's boys dropped Cissy to the ground. She lay just as she fell, arms crooked with one leg bent awkwardly outward.

Smokey stood and backed away from Cissy's discarded body. "Fuck. Let's get out of here." He kicked Cissy once, hard, to show his disappointment, then moved toward me like a bulldozer, and used one kick to the chin to send me backward to the ground. I landed on my bound hands. That time the pain was yellow, the yellow of vomit and piss as I rolled onto my side.

Smokey pulled out his gun but stopped when he saw people running along the end of the alley. "Fire! Somebody call 911! Fire!" The yells came from the running neighbors who bypassed the bowels of the alley and ran toward the fire on College Avenue. I could smell the smoke. The Cougar had gone up in flames.

I crawled to Cissy. Shards of glass ground into my knee but I kept moving. I wobbled upright and used my feet to move her clothes closer to her body. I could see the wound in the back of her head, open and weeping blood. "Cissy."

She didn't move. I used my feet to drag her shirt over as much of her body as possible. All I could think was that it had all started because of love—my blind, relentless love for Felicia and a misplaced desire to protect her. My single-mindedness had made everyone else in my life vulnerable. I'd left everyone, including myself, wide-open, and now Cissy had paid.

A boom sounded behind me. A car explosion, I was sure. Smokey's boys ran off into the night as the activity increased on the street. Smokey followed behind them. I knew he would leave me alive. He wanted Holly, not me. He didn't even want Cissy, though he would have taken supreme pleasure in her abuse. He wanted Holly, and he wanted me to be able to tell him what had happened.

On his way past me he lashed out and caught the bridge of my nose with his pistol. "Another time," he said. Then raised the gun again. The second meeting of metal and flesh finished it off. I spiraled down into blackness.

"Maceo." It was a hollow sound, with a hint of mocking laughter at the base. "Maceo, you fucked up."

I looked down to find myself standing knee deep in water. The cool, clear water of a water fountain. The fountain in the center of Cal's campus.

"Maceo."

I hated the sound of my father's voice. It reminded me of failure. "Maceo, Maceo, Maceo. Where's my love, boy?"

I stepped from the fountain and walked away. I kept my back to him, refusing to give him power by looking into his eyes.

"Turn around, Maceo." Then, quieter: "Don't make me say it! Don't make me say it!" Another round of spiteful laughter and then the word that locked me in place.

"Greg! Greg, you hear me talking to you?"

My father's use of my real name was his favorite sport, a way to keep control and clarify the mark he'd left behind. "That's right, I said it: Greg. Gregory Samuels, Junior. You think because that old man changed it, it changes you. You think it's not the truth. Gregory Samuels, Junior. That's you."

He stepped in front of me and I ducked my head. I felt his palms on my chest pushing, pushing me backward until I fell underwater. I reached a hand out for his help, *hoping he would pull me up. He laughed instead and spit a stream of putrid water into my eyes. He grabbed ahold of me with his arms and legs, using all his limbs to grip me like a vise. We dropped toward the bottom at break-neck speed.*

I strained for air. He watched my struggle with pleasure.

Then we hit bottom. Solid earth.

"'Beneath the cypress lies the heart of my life.' What kind of shit is that?" My father read the words carved into the tombstone of my mother's grave. The words were written on the first page of Gra'mère's prayer book.

I looked around to find that we were in the cemetery at Red Fields. My head rested at the base of my mother's tomb. Blood clouded my vision as it poured from a gash in my forehead.

"Did you hurt yourself? You weak motherfucker. Get up! I was going much faster than you when I crashed. Ninety miles an hour—after begging that old man to let me see you." He spit at the ground, then wiped quickly and frantically when he realized the spit had landed on the Sophia of my mother's name.

"Look what you made me do. That old man raised a sissy. I told him you needed to see me. And not like this. He wouldn't let me near you.

"When I crashed they pulled me from the car with a crushed skull, but I held on for two days. You know why? I wanted to hang around long enough to see that old man's heart stop.

"I should have taken Eleanor when I had the chance, but you came sooner than we thought so I blame you too. Just as much as I blame him. Now you owe me, so get up and help."

He dragged me to my feet. I watched as he pierced the earth with a jagged shovel. "I can take her with me now.

Help me. Pick up something, use your hands. You owe me, Greg."

He knocked me to my knees and shoved my face in the open dirt.

"You owe me."

I could tell by the way my father's arms shook that he meant to kill me.

CHAPTER

33

I was moving.

"He's coming to. He's coming to." I didn't recognize the voice, but it was male and authoritative.

Not the voice of my father.

"Maceo? Oh, my God!" That voice I knew. Alixe. I knew it was her but I didn't know how she'd gotten there. I tried to move my mouth to tell her about Cissy but I couldn't. My head throbbed with nauseating intensity, and for the first time ever I could feel my nose on my face.

"What happened?" I heard her ask.

I listened to the rush and movement around me and couldn't contribute a thing. I heard a gurgling sound from my own body and then a sticky liquid traveled out of my mouth and onto my neck.

"Move, people, move!" The voices became faint again, softer and far away. I dropped into another blackness.

* * *

"Maceo."

The voice was frightened. I could hear it. I could even smell it. I knew that if I reached out it was possible that I could even touch it. It was that strong, that heavy and palpable.

"Maceo."

I groaned in response and opened one eye. Alixe was there out of focus, in a hospital room.

"Can you hear me?"

"Where's Cissy?" I tried to sit up but felt dizziness.

"Cissy's here. Don't get up. You have a concussion and a dislocated shoulder."

It all came back, rushing back: Smokey and the alley. The homeless man and Cissy. Everything that had been done to her. "I need to get up. Help me up."

"You need to stay put." She eased me back on the pillow. "You need rest."

I sat up anyway. It took all the strength and effort I had, but I couldn't stay in the hospital bed. "How'd I get here?"

"Ambulance. Some people found you in an alley."

"How long have I been here?"

"About half an hour. You also have bruised ribs."

I swung my legs off the side of the bed and ripped away the hospital gown with my good arm. I stood naked in the middle of the room, but it was the least sexual experience of my life. "Where are my clothes?"

I stood up and took a moment to get my balance. I caught sight of myself in the mirror while I searched for my clothes. My nose was packed with bloody gauze and my face was bruised with broken blood vessels from ear to ear. My torso was wrapped tightly and my arm was in a sling.

"I'm going to call a doctor."

"I don't care what you do. I'm getting my clothes." I grabbed my jeans and the bloodied shirt from the closet.

Alixe watched but refused to help as I struggled into my pants. I dropped into the chair, wracked with frustration. "Help me."

"I can't do that, Maceo. The doctors want you to stay."

"Alixe. The guys who did this. If I stay here they'll come back. Do you understand?"

She blinked twice, hard, and backed toward the door. "What?"

"I cannot stay here." I pronounced each word with precision to try and make her understand. "Help me, please."

She inched forward, tentatively.

"Alixe, please."

She sighed and helped me get my jeans up to my waist and my shoes on my feet.

Alixe guided me to the third floor, where Cissy was in Intensive Care. She hadn't regained consciousness in the ambulance or in the hospital, and she was being watched closely. The family had been notified and the staff expected my grandparents to arrive at any moment.

Just as I reached the glass window of Cissy's room I saw Holly burst through the doors on the other side. He stormed down the hall, frantic, already expecting the worst. He nearly lost his footing when he saw me. He ran the last yards, then looked through the window at an unconscious Cissy, a freeway of wires and tubes, her head wrapped entirely in bandages. He slammed his fist into the wall repeatedly until two orderlies approached from either end of the hallway.

"What the fuck?" His voice broke and he let his forehead fall to the glass. "What the fuck."

Alixe watched us both, silently, at my side. I felt her fingers graze my elbow in comfort. She was still in uniform. I knew she was expected somewhere else in the hospital but she hadn't said a word about it.

"Lamb had just gotten me out and my pager was blowing up. I called the numbers back and they kept saying, "Where ya girl?" He looked at me with more pain in his face than I'd ever seen. "Who did this, Maceo? Smokey?"

As I nodded, Daddy Al, followed by Gra'mère, Rachel, Phine, and Nelia, stormed in through the double doors. A security guard ran behind them, waving a sign-in sheet that was ignored by everyone. Daddy Al's faced was riddled with anger. He'd set his sights on Holly and myself. I took a step backward but he was on us both before we could say a word.

His open hand met the side of my face, sore from the encounter with Smokey. His palm stung worse than the gun butt had. I went sprawling onto the ground, landing once again on my shoulder. Gra'mère screamed and Rachel rushed forward to calm Daddy Al, but he shook her off. He yanked me up from the floor and used the other hand to pin Holly to the wall by his neck.

"That's my baby in there! My baby! She's hurt behind shit everybody told y'all to leave alone."

As my throat closed beneath his strong fingers, the words "my baby" rang in my ears, separating his blood child from me. It spoke directly to the fear I'd always harbored in my soul.

Me and them, separately.

"Al, please," Gra'mère pleaded softly, as if she was in prayer. "Al, please."

Daddy Al stuttered with rage and didn't hear a word she said. Rachel stepped forward and tried to unlace his fingers from Holly's neck. His grip intensified the more she tried. "Come on, Daddy. Let go."

"Let go? I ought to choke the life out of both of them."

His eyes flashed like fire. The veins in his fingers and hands pulsated as he slammed Holly against the wall. It shook from the blow. He still held me tightly with his other hand.

"Redfield!" It was a command. Another man's voice. I hadn't seen Midnight Blue enter the hospital. I had thought he was gone, back to Louisiana. "Redfield!" he repeated again.

Daddy Al responded, not by letting go but loosening his grip enough for Holly to breathe. He swung me around and pinned me alongside the sputtering Holly. "You two think it's okay to play games with my girl's life?" He knocked our heads together like rocks. "Ya think it's okay for my baby to be laid up in there?"

Neither one of us spoke. Gra'mère continued to plead behind him.

"We raised you both with everything we had, and you think it's okay to pay us back like this." He swung me around so that I faced Gra'mère.

"That's the only mama you ever had, boy. The only one! And a child she carried might die because of you!"

"Daddy, you need to let those boys go." Rachel stepped in between me and Gra'mère. Phine and Nelia kept their distance. Rachel had always been the only one fearless enough to approach Daddy Al in moments of extreme anger. "We need to deal with Cissy right now."

He let us go, but not before a final powerful push of disgust. Holly stood silent, as did I. Neither one of us had the nerve to walk away. Daddy Al turned his attention from us and looked for the first time into Cissy's room. He seemed to deflate and grow old right before our eyes.

"Oh, my God. Sweet Jesus," he said, at the sight of her.

"Come on, Al." Gra'mère grabbed his arm and pushed open the door of the room.

Rachel reached a hand out toward me and whispered, "Y'all get out of here."

Daddy Al stopped and turned to us before he disappeared inside. In just that instant he had withered, multiplied in age, and come out a very old man. His voice was laced with venom as he railed at Holly. "You came to us like an alley cat and we made you family." He spit at his feet.

Holly took off, running full speed down the hall. The aunties stepped quickly away. They must have thought that he was running away from Daddy Al's words, the family's anger and disappointment, but I knew different. He ran with a purpose. He was going to get Smokey.

I was left in the hall with Alixe and Midnight Blue. Blue wouldn't look at me. He just stared through the window at the family gathered around Cissy. "Maceo," he said, "you don't need to be here."

Alixe left the top off the Jeep as we sped through the streets of East Oakland toward Jack London Square. I didn't know where we were going and I didn't ask. I wondered briefly where Holly was, but it didn't seem important. My mission had lost its purpose. Not even images of Felicia's frightened face could jump-start my heart.

Alixe wheeled into the parking lot alongside Ole Spaghetti Factory in Jack London and jumped out of the car. I followed, listless, not even tired or in pain. We walked away from the restaurant down a path near the water. Boats bobbed darkly in the marina. She moved with purpose. She was still in uniform, and I hadn't seen her check out or tell anyone she was leaving.

At the last boat in the slip she stepped aboard and motioned for me to do the same. "This is where I live."

I looked around. Any other time I might have been impressed or curious but not now.

She kept talking to fill in the silence. "I look after the place for one of the doctors. He lets me live here rent free, and I take care of things. Have a seat."

She cleared a place for me on the bed. I sat.

"Lie down if you want. I'm going to jump in the shower."

I did as I was told. I fell asleep to the sound of running water coming from the bathroom.

I awoke hours later to find Alixe at my side. She mumbled and slid into me perfectly. I absorbed the warmth of her skin. "Maceo." She blinked to clear the sleep from her eyes. "You okay? You need anything?"

"I'm fine."

"Are you in any pain?"

"Sore all over." It was more than soreness but I deserved it. Even if I had access to painkillers I wouldn't take them. I deserved to feel every inch of the pain.

"Do you think they'll catch the guys who did this?"

Holly flashed through my mind. "I don't know."

"How safe is it for you to be here?"

"Not too. My granddaddy wants me to go to Louisiana, out to the farm, until everything calms down."

"Are you going to go?"

"I can't leave Holly here."

She looked me right in the eye. "Yes, you can, and you should. If you have a place to go, you should go as soon as possible."

"It's not that easy."

"Yes, it is, it *is* that easy. It seems to me your only other option is death. I don't know how you could look at Cissy and not see how important it is that you leave for a while."

"Alixe."

"You never want to hear what's right. I don't understand that."

"You never want to let things go."

She glanced at the blood splattered across my T-shirt. Her voice softened. "Let me help you out of that." She sat up and I noticed she was wearing only a T-shirt.

Her legs brushed against mine as she moved to pull the shirt from my head. "You want to get out of those pants?"

I stood and undid the buttons of my jeans.

"I called the hospital while you were sleeping. No change."

"How long I been asleep?"

"Three hours." She brushed my cheek with her hand. I moved it to my lips and kissed the open palm. She glided up, careful of my ribs, and kissed me. It didn't take long for us to get to where we were going. My body was a solid wall of aching pain but I'd once pitched an entire series with swollen elbows and sprained wrists. I thought at the least, for my own sanity, I could make love through the soreness.

I covered her body with mine and guided her hands down to help pull away my shorts. She slipped her T-shirt off and let it fall on the pillow above my head. Her skin was soft, her lips wide and generous.

I dropped my head to her breasts and took one in my mouth. She attempted to move my face back up to hers but I resisted. I moved from one to the other, feeling like I'd been rescued from a famine.

Her hands moved down my body until she reached the very center. She took me in her hand and guided me to her core. When I slipped inside I heard a sigh from deep within her throat. It made me harder. She sighed again and I went farther inside. She was tight and shallow enough to make me feel safe.

Her lips spurred me on and I moved with a fury. I knew it was all fueled by Billy's death, Felicia's disappearance, and Cissy but I needed a way to disappear. As the bed rocked beneath us I knew deep down that I played a fool's game. I was gambling with raw emotions as chips, and the house held my sanity as collateral.

But I went on, moving like a blind man, desperate, choosing to let everything ride on the woman beneath me.

"Maceo." Her eyes were closed, her upper lip damp with sweat. She delivered my name to me as the sweetest sound in the world.

"Damn, Alixe" was all I could say in response. She matched me stroke for stroke until I was close to the edge. The sound of her voice, her body, her smell—it all worked with me to keep reality at bay. I raced to the finish line.

CHAPTER

34

First thing in the morning I made a call to the hospital. Cissy had regained consciousness once, briefly, but no one in my family was willing to speak to me. I left four messages for Holly and reached out for my clothes.

I pulled the keys Regina had given me days ago from my jeans and held them in the air. Alixe walked in with a cup of coffee and found me holding them. She handed me the coffee and pulled a videotape from behind her back.

"I made this for you the other day. I don't know why but I did. Maybe it's really to help me understand you and the world that holds so much appeal for you." She shrugged. "Maybe it's for your friend if she ever comes back."

"What is it?" I took the tape.

"The funeral. They were running it yesterday on Soul Beat." I should have been surprised, but I wasn't. Soul Beat was a ghettoized Oakland channel where news correspondents showed up notoriously unprepared for various events with microphones visible above their heads.

"Thanks."

"Maybe something there might give you a clue to what this was all about. Maybe not."

"Thanks."

"What do you want to do now?" She flopped down beside me and kissed the side of my neck. I wanted to stay, to climb back under the covers and hide from everything, but I knew the reprieve was over.

"I need to go home." I held Regina's extra keys in the air again. "But I need to make a stop on the way."

Yellow police tape was still strung across the door of Felicia's apartment, but I whacked it down and used the key from Regina to enter. Alixe was behind me. The living room had been returned to normalcy, just a little more disheveled than before.

"What are you looking for?"

"I want to get a phone number."

I went to the stand near the couch and opened the drawer. There were fragments of a cracked figurine inside. I moved the pieces around until I found the paper with the emergency numbers. I tore it from the pad and shoved it in my pocket.

I heard Alixe move down the hall and then I saw her disappear into Felicia's room. I gave her a minute and then went inside. She stood near the shattered bed and looked at the cracked photographs atop the mattress.

She picked one up. "Is this her? Is this Felicia?"

It was, one of her best pictures. It made her vivid again, seeing the photo. A smiling face with still no indication of whether she was dead or alive.

"Yeah, that's her," I answered.

"She's beautiful." She searched my face. "You loved her, didn't you?"

I turned away and walked to the door. "We should go."

"Don't do that, please."

I sighed. "Yeah, Alixe, I loved her."

She returned the picture to the pile.

Out in the car we were silent. I knew her next question before she asked it. "Do you still love her?"

I answered simply, truthfully. "Yes."

She wheeled onto Alcatraz and headed toward my house. "Even after all that's happened? Even after seeing Cissy like that?"

I didn't answer.

She pulled up in front of my house and kept the motor running. "I hope you find her, Maceo."

I believed she meant it. "Why?"

She cut the engine but didn't get out. I took the lead and got out onto the sidewalk. "Because I like you." She continued, "I think we like each other."

"Alixe, I appreciate everything you did last night. At the hospital. Everything."

"I wasn't fishing for a compliment. I like you, independent of how you feel about me. I just hope you find her, even if her coming back means I don't get to keep you."

"Why would you wish that?"

" 'Cause Felicia is too potent as a ghost. Who can compete with that." She dropped her voice at the end of the sentence. "What fool would want to?" She popped the engine. "You should go to Louisiana, Maceo. As

soon as possible." She handed me the tape of the funeral
I had placed on the dashboard. "Find what you need."

I watched her drive away.

CHAPTER

35

Rachel sat on the front steps of the cottage. She stood up
when I came through the gate and wrinkled her nose at
the sight of me. I still wore the bloodied shirt from the
night before.

"You just getting home?" she asked.

"Yeah."

"You been by the hospital?"

"No. Is everybody still there?"

She nodded. "They've been there all night. You heard
from Holly?"

"No."

"How long have Holly and Cissy been together?"

I was surprised that she knew. Was I the only one in the
dark? "How do you know about that?"

"Noone came by the hospital. He told us about Holly
being picked up. How he and Cissy were together and
how the two of you went down to the jail."

"Oh."

"Cissy came to for a minute this morning. She kept
asking for Holly. Daddy's crushed, and Miss Antonia
too. How long have they been together?"

"Six months."

"Did you know about it?"

"Not until yesterday."

She moved out of the way so I could make it up the stairs. I saw an envelope stuck in the screen door. My name was scrawled across it in angry script. Rachel pulled the envelope out of the door. "I was going to leave this here if you didn't come home soon."

Inside the house, the answering machine flashed with eight messages. The first was straight to the point. "This is Sterling Travel calling to confirm your flight arrangements from Oakland International Airport to Shreveport, Louisiana on flight—"

I turned the machine off and Rachel handed me the envelope. "You should pack."

I expected Rachel to be gone when I got out of the shower but she sat at the top of the stairs with my duffel packed with clothes. "I got your bag together for you."

"I didn't say I was going."

"Yes, you did. You agreed to go as soon as you and Cissy arrived at the hospital. It's not your choice anymore. You think Daddy can stand for that? Can you face Miss Antonia right now?"

I couldn't.

"I called Numiel and Donna, and he'll pick you up this evening."

"Just like that?"

"Just like that."

"And what am I supposed to do, all the way out there?"

"Be safe. Helping Cissy is all Daddy and Miss Antonia can deal with right now. It's all they should have to deal with. You're a grown man, Maceo, you can make your own decisions, but leaving is the *right* thing to do."

I knew she was right but I was still angry. It felt like running away from trouble, leaving Holly, yet again, to clean up my mess.

"You know, Maceo, when Ellie died you were very important to this family. You helped us all heal and we loved you, at first because you were a link to Eleanor. Then, of course, we started to love you because of *you*."

"I know that," I said, but my heart said otherwise. Daddy Al's "my baby" had rung in my ears all night.

"Do you? Sometimes it seems like you're trying to punish yourself." She grabbed my chin and forced me to look into her eyes. "Like you're trying to punish yourself for something you had nothing to do with.

"I know about your burden, believe me I do, but what Ellie and Greg did after you were born had nothing to do with you. They chose that life, not because they loved you any less but because they didn't love themselves enough. It had nothing to do with you."

I understood her words, I even heard what she said, but my heart didn't quite translate it the same way. It was abandonment, pure and simple. The two of them together had chosen a life that didn't include me.

"I don't blame *my* mother, I don't agree with what she did, but I understand it." Rachel rarely referred to her birth mother, Elizabeth, or her suicide.

"Well, I don't agree and I don't understand" was my angry reply.

She reached a hand out. "Miss Antonia and Daddy know that, and they've spent a lifetime trying to make up for it. They made you a priority, Maceo, and you've treated them like their efforts don't mean anything."

"This has nothing to do with them."

She rolled her eyes. "The ignorance of youth. You can still say that after everything that's happened?"

"Cissy wasn't meant to get caught in the crossfire."

"I'm sure she wasn't, but *somebody* was meant to. And that's what has everyone confused. You knew that someone would get hurt but you still made the decision to keep going. You and Holly both, like nothing and no-body else mattered. That's what Daddy can't forgive."

I had no answer. She was right. I picked up the plane ticket and shoved it into my bag.

Rachel drove me to the airport, eager to get me away from the house before my grandparents came home or more violence could erupt. I hadn't heard a word from Holly, and the streets were eerily quiet as we passed through town. Oakland was boiling around me, and not just from the heat. Guns would sound at nightfall, and I was going to be as far from it as possible. The idea of running made me cringe, but I also felt torn by loyalty to my family.

At the airport I kissed Rachel good-bye and jumped from the car. Halfway to the ticket counter I turned and made a beeline to the pay phones. Louisiana was the right choice, but it wasn't my choice. Not by a long shot. It was time to stop hiding.

I pulled the crumpled paper I'd taken from Regina's notepad from my pocket and dialed L.A. I knew Felicia's aunt as Venus, the pet name Flea had bestowed on her, but Regina had written Venestta Bennett on the paper. I dialed the number.

"Hello?" A smoky voice crawled through the telephone wires.

"Can I speak with Venestta Bennett?"

"Who's calling?"

"Maceo Redfield, Felicia's friend from Berkeley."

"Maceo. I remember. What can I do for you?"

"I'm on my way to Louisiana, but I wondered if I could come out and see you. I'm at the airport now. I can make it out and back and take a later flight to Louisiana."

There was a long pause. "This about Felicia?"

"Yeah. I haven't heard from her, and I—"

"What time you coming in?"

I looked at the departure bank near the phones. "There's a flight leaving in thirty minutes. I'll be there in an hour and a half."

"You need directions to the house?"

"Yeah. Let me grab a pen."

I wrote down the directions and shoved them into my pocket. Another split-second decision, but I had to play the hunch to the end. Louisiana could wait. It would have to wait. I had to right a wrong—three wrongs as I saw it: Billy, Felicia, and Cissy.

CHAPTER

36

The plane circled LAX for a total of thirty minutes, giving me a bird's-eye view of the freeway-choked city. It had been years since I'd set foot on southern California soil, and the previous trip had been one of pleasure, a round-robin tournament of the state's best collegiate athletes. The tourney had been played on the UCLA campus, set smugly in the middle of the manicured lawns of Westwood, but this trip promised no such glamour. The South Central home of Felicia, Reggie, and Crim was a breeding ground for gangstas.

I made my way through the airport, ignoring the curious or horrified stares as I passed among the travelers. At a magazine kiosk I caught sight of my bruised and swollen face in the polished chrome of the cash register and slipped on my sunglasses in defense.

A half hour later, after two DMV checks and an obvious reluctance on the part of the counter agent to rent me a car, I was on my way. I entered the web of cars, circling the terminal trying to find an exit and avoid an accident all at the same time.

I propped Venus's instructions on the dashboard and managed to find my way east to the 110 North, until the exit for Slausen Avenue loomed above me like a beacon.

Felicia's childhood home was on Fifty-ninth Place in the middle of a high-security street. The address for each house was visible atop the roof in five-foot numbers to make the location of criminals easier for LAPD's aerial patrol. Venus's house was a small Spanish-style structure with a red stucco fence and wrought-iron gate strung with heavy rusted cow bells.

Venus waved to me through a small window in the middle of a tightly locked metal door; then she waited until I was on the step before opening the gate.

I should have been afraid. The new territory, the unfamiliar graffiti, being alone—all of it added up to danger, but I was numb. I wanted answers.

"Oh, what happened to you, baby?" she purred when she saw my face and arm.

"Car accident."

"Uh-huh." She motioned me inside, and I crossed the threshold to step backward into Felicia's childhood. The room was painted a dull yellow, faded to a dingy white over time, with unframed family pictures taped or thumb-tacked to every surface. In pose after pose, Felicia smiled alongside her brothers, Venus, and, in one, her mother and father.

"Come on in. Have a seat. You want anything to eat or drink?"

"I'm fine, thanks."

Venus took a seat across from me in a recliner chair. To say that Venestta Bennett was heavy was an understatement even in a community where heavyset women were commonplace. She was at least three hundred pounds on a five-foot-five frame with a towering cascade of red-brown curls adding the last two inches.

"Have you heard from Felicia?" I asked.

"I heard from her right when all this nonsense happened, but I haven't heard a word since. She didn't tell me too much, but she was scared to death. I have my whole congregation praying for my baby girl."

"What did she say?"

"Nothing. She just cried. I tried to get her to tell me where she was, but she wouldn't say nothing. I must have sat on that phone with her for about an hour."

"Hadn't you seen her the weekend before?"

She looked puzzled. "No. Why?"

" 'Cause her roommate, Regina, said Flea had been down to see you at least twice a month for the last few months."

"I haven't seen Felicia since June, when she came out after school ended."

"Haven't you been sick?"

"Me, sick? Baby, I ain't been sick since 1972."

"Then why would Flea say she'd been down to see you?"

Venus took her time before answering. "I raised my niece and nephews but sometimes I don't think I know 'em at all. Reggie and Crim I don't even allow over my house no more. I love them boys, but they more trouble than a little bit."

"I met them."

"Then you know what I'm talking about. And Felicia, she always had a mind of her own. Plus, me and her had a few words about that boy of hers. I liked Billy and everything, but how could I turn my back on my nephews for doing what *they* did and then turn around and accept *him*?" She shook her head. "I wouldn't do it, and I told her so. And now that Billy's dead she might not want to come home."

A tear rolled down her cheek but she quickly wiped it away.

"I tried, you know. I tried so hard with them three babies, but it was only so much I could do. They wasn't mine. I loved them like they were but they wasn't mine, and them boys needed a strong hand from the beginning. Both of them was old enough to know what happened with they mama and daddy and that damaged them. Big Reggie thought he was saving them when he left, but he did more harm than good."

"Why did he leave?" I asked.

"Felicia didn't tell you?"

"Tell me what?"

She looked away to avoid a direct answer. "You and she was close, I know that. She talked about you even after she met Billy. You were the first real friend she made out there. She loved you. She told me one time that y'all was the same but she didn't tell me why."

I'd often felt the same thing but had never been able to explain the connection beyond the absence of our mothers.

"She talk about her mama to you?"

"Not really. She told me she died when she was a little girl."

"You know her daddy is my older brother: Reggie. That's who Li'l Reggie is named after. The two of them was thick as thieves. I think my brother's disappearance affected Reggie the most but I might be wrong. Crim was always to himself and Felicia was just a little girl. She changed after he left, but Reggie just combusted. It wadn't too long after that he started to get in trouble."

"What about her mother?"

Venus looked at me, surprised I was still in the room. The conversation had become one-sided while she talked.

She used the opportunity to voice her concern about her brother's children.

"Their mother." She snorted. "She wasn't but a little whiff of a thing. Women in my family is big, prone to meatiness, but she was"—she snapped her fingers—"that big on a good day. Big Reg met her when we was teenagers. She came to our school from out by San Clemente, and he just couldn't get enough of that little nappy-headed girl. I couldn't see it myself. She was too lightweight for me. There didn't seem to be anything holding her to the ground.

"And I was right. She gave Big Reg more trouble than you could imagine. She was plain to ugly on a good day, now. You look at Felicia and you think her mama must've been a movie star, but that's not the case. Felicia got all her looks from our side of the family. And underneath all that death and destruction Reggie and Crim are nice-looking boys too."

I kept a straight face. Crim could never be considered a handsome man.

Venus went on with her story. "Well, Big Reg married Felicia's mama about 1964, right out of school. They lived with the family. That's how you did it back then until you could get on your feet. They lived with us my senior year of high school, and I saw her go from being a little wallflower to a September tornado. She didn't get no cuter, mind you, but after that first sex she got a better sense of herself and her powers. Some women ain't equipped for that knowledge, and she was one of them. Boy, she started giving Big Reg hell after that. She didn't run the streets or nothing but she always had somebody sniffing around while he was at work. Mostly neighborhood mens and a few of Big Reggie's friends.

"I didn't like her much but I don't think she fooled with any of them. Big Reg wadn't the kind of man you did that to unless you was fool enough to face the consequences, but she liked the attention so she didn't run 'em off.

"They finally moved out of Mama and Daddy's house when Big Reg got on as a longshoreman out of Long Beach. He worked his tail off and bought them a little house. This house here. He gave it to me when he left.

"Every time he came home from a trip she'd be pregnant when he left again: one, two, three. She had all them babies one after another, and it cooled her out for a while. But when Flea was about four years old she up and left. Finally, one of them men of hers had turned her head with Big Reg gone all the time.

"Now, can you imagine that? A good man working his ass off for you and you decide it's too much trouble to wait on him." She sniffed. "I always said that girl wasn't about shit, but I stood by my brother 'cause that's what family does.

"He lost his job trying to track her down and almost lost this little house, but I started driving buses, and it paid good money. Plus, I did hair out the kitchen for extra cash here and there. We made it. Became a little family: me, Big Reg, and the kids. We kept the house, built up a little savings, but he wasn't satisfied. He had a fire burning inside about finding that girl and nothing could put it out. Not me, not the kids, not other women. Nothing. He started drinking and leaving on weekends chasing down leads about her. When he'd come back on Sunday nights ain't no tellin' where he'd been. Up and down California, even Mexico, but there was no sign of her nowhere and she never called to ask about the kids. Just disappeared, just like that. And while he was gone I maintained things. I couldn't afford a baby-sitter for Felicia so I took her on my bus routes with me. She'd ride up in the front so I could keep an eye on her."

Venus pushed away the stray curls that fell across her forehead.

"Everything, every problem one way or another, can be traced to how a man and a woman treat each other. Whether it's husband and wife, father and daughter, mother and son, brother and sister, whatever, most problems I've come across have been born out of one of them combinations.

"And now I see it happening all over again, and I don't know what to do to stop it. I wish I did, Lord, I wish I did."

"Did Big Reg ever find his wife?"

She turned to me again as if she'd just remembered I was there. "What you think I been talking about all this time? Of course he did. It took him two years but he found her up in Fresno in a motel. She wasn't even with a man, just livin' by herself, waitressing, like her life and family in Los Angeles didn't exist."

"Did he bring her home?"

"No."

"Why?"

" 'Cause he killed her."

I shouldn't have been surprised, but I was. If anything, my existence should have taught me there was no end to violence. It circled around like wagons, a noose of wagons. No matter which way I turned, waking or asleep, death was there to greet me.

"You didn't know?" Venus seemed truly surprised.

"Felicia didn't talk about it."

"Figures. She wouldn't talk about it with me either. Reggie asked a million questions. He wanted to know the how and why of everything, but there wasn't much I could tell him.

"How was I suppose to know what was in somebody else's heart? I barely got a handle on mine, and every time I think I do I find some little dark corner I didn't even know about."

"And you haven't heard anything from Felicia?"

"Not since that first call. Her daddy did the same thing. He murdered that woman and disappeared. Ain't nobody seen Big Reg since he left, and that was in 1974."

I thought back to 1974, the year when Felicia's world fell apart, and remembered it as one of the best ones of my life. The A's had won the Series yet again with a team made up of storybook characters with names to match—Vida Blue, Rollie Fingers, Catfish Hunter—and Daddy Al and I were front row center at the games and at the victory parades that wound through the streets of Oakland.

"Has he ever tried to contact you?"

"Once or twice." She looked off through the window.

"But not Felicia?"

"No."

"Do you think Flea was involved in Billy's business?"

"His business?" Her voice rose high enough to crack. "What the hell is that suppose to mean? You think Felicia was selling drugs?"

"The alternative is worse."

"Why's that?"

"If she wasn't involved in his business, what would make her stay away so long and not contact anyone? Can you think of anything?"

"No." But she wouldn't look me in the eye. We were both thinking the same thing as the new knowledge about her family history sat between us. "But then again, I'm tired of the truth lying to me."

I dropped my voice another notch. "Do you think Felicia could have killed Billy?"

The phone rang before she could answer. Venus rose heavily from her chair and hurried into the kitchen to answer it. I stood up to take a closer look at the pictures.

Venus was right. Felicia looked nothing like her mother. The woman in the photograph wore an elaborate beehive, horn-rimmed glasses, and a white blouse with a bow at the collar of the same material. She was plain, just as Venus said, with a grim, sour set to her mouth that poisoned the entire photo.

Felicia sat in her mother's lap, smiling into the camera, a ring of pigtails circling her head.

"Maceo?" I turned to find Venus standing in the doorway. "That was the bus company. I'm a relief driver this month. I got to take a route for somebody who called in sick. I'll only be gone two or three hours." She moved quickly to remove a brown-and-tan uniform from her closet. "You be okay?"

"I'll be fine."

"You need a place to stay tonight? You're more than welcome to stay here."

I understood then that Venus thought I planned to stay in town. I decided to play along.

"I hadn't looked into it yet."

She smiled. "Just like a man. Well, I got this big old house all to myself. You can stay here." She squeezed my hand to let me know the deal was sealed. I hadn't realized it until then, but it was what I'd wanted ever since I left Oakland.

"Thank you."

"Don't mention it. There's no reason for you to go spending money when I got all this room."

"You need me to do anything for you while you're gone?"

She looked pointedly at my bruised and battered body. "Why don't you just get some rest. Help yourself to anything you need in the kitchen. I got movies in that case over there, I tape them off cable, and a stereo in the corner. If you get tired, grab any of these blankets and lay yourself down. The boys' room is straight back at the end of the hall if you want to get some real sleep."

She went into the back room to change into her uniform. When she came out I saw her test to make sure her room and the room opposite hers were both locked. "Help yourself to anything you need. There's roast beef in the kitchen. Make a sandwich, eat some potato salad."

"Thank you."

She paused at the front door before unlocking the three deadbolts and removing the chain. She mumbled so softly I wasn't sure she had spoken, but I heard the words. "Maybe you was meant to come here, Maceo."

Before I could question her about the comment she was on the other side of the door snapping the locks into place. I stood in the center of the living room and watched her go.

I waited until her car cleared the corner. Then I set out to get answers.

I started in the living room.

I shuffled through papers and drawers. I overturned cushions, replaced them neatly, then moved to the next area. I repeated what I'd seen in movies, running my hand under desks looking for bumps in the surface. I emptied drawers and opened the backs of picture frames.

In the kitchen it was much the same, also in the hallway and the sewing room, and then I came to the end of the hall. The room—the boys' room, from what I gathered from the decorations—was open with the beds neatly made. But the two doors on either side were closed tight and locked.

I went back into the kitchen to get a knife and found an ice pick to help me with the lock. Since the murder, since the search began, I had taken a backseat, following behind Holly, waiting for the dust to settle, clues to come my way, or answers to appear to me in a dream, but my passiveness, the guise I employed to slide quietly through life, had failed me.

The truth was that I asked everyone around me to go

out on a limb on my behalf while I stayed safely in the shadows. I wasn't proud of cowering beneath a garbage bin while Soup Can was pistol-whipped or of my performance during Cissy's attack. Living as a little man with a big name, keeping life compact and close to the vest, didn't work anymore. I knew that.

I dropped to my knees in front of the locked door with the ice pick pointed at the hole in the center of the doorknob. The door would be easy, I knew that; they were similar to the ones at the Dover Street house, but it was hard to angle with my injured shoulder. It took about five minutes of jiggling the lock and gasping from pain before I felt the knob give. I opened the door and walked into what had obviously been Felicia's room as a young girl.

I had to still myself. I felt dizzy from exertion, and row upon row of Felicia's smiling face was an assault on the senses. Just like in the living room, Venus had pictures taped to every surface: school photos, Polaroids, snapshots, and a large graduation photo right above the bed.

I went over to the desk and sat down. I opened drawers, again repeating what I'd already done in the other parts of the house, but I found nothing. I didn't expect to. The room had an air of stillness, like a crypt, as if it had been preserved for someone who would never return. I closed the door behind me and used the same procedure to enter Venus's room.

The elaborate four-poster canopy bed revealed nothing. Neither did the lace-covered dresser or nightstand. The connecting bathroom with layers of talcum powder on every surface did nothing but make me sneeze. I crawled under the bed and encountered yet more dust, a bag of dirty laundry, and paperbacks with the covers torn off. I gave up, sure that clues to Felicia's whereabouts existed in the house but not certain where.

My shoulder ached with pain and my stomach growled with hunger so I retreated to the kitchen for an ice pack and sandwich. I found the roast beef front and center in the refrigerator, potato salad, and a thick slice of lemon cake. I went through the drawers for a second time to find a plastic bag to make an ice pack. I wrapped the plastic-covered ice in a dish towel and sat down to eat.

The roast beef melted in my mouth like butter. I was on my second double-decker before I realized it had been over twenty-four hours since I'd eaten. I mowed through the potato salad and the cake with the ice pack dripping onto my shoulder and chest. When I opened the dish towel I found a hole I hadn't seen before.

I pulled the wet shirt away from my body and reached into the drawer for another plastic bag. My search was met with a sharp intense pain. I pulled my hand back. A thumbtack protruded from beneath the nail on my index finger.

In the bathroom I shuffled through Venus's cosmetics drawers, hoping to find a Band-Aid. At the bottom of the last drawer I saw a stray Band-Aid wedged into the crack of the drawer. My only hope was that it wasn't used. From the looks of Venus's makeup and jewelry she never threw anything away. I pulled it out and tried to close the drawer but it wouldn't budge.

I tried again and met the same resistance. I stuck my hand all the way back and felt a piece of paper rolled into a ball. I pulled it free.

It was an envelope, addressed to Venus but otherwise empty. The left edge was torn away. The zip code started with a 9, California, but the last three numbers and the name of the city were missing. The paper was old and felt flimsy in my hand. It was also slick from powder and smudged around the edges with face makeup and lipstick but something made me hold on to it. There was plenty of evidence throughout the house that Venus saved everything whether it was significant or not, but I knew the envelope was key.

I ran my finger beneath a stream of cold water and then pulled the drawer all the way out. I turned it upside down and found a jagged piece of paper stuck in the corner. Bingo. My heart raced. I knew before I flipped it over that it would lead me somewhere.

1198 Allen Lane. Fresno, California. I picked up the envelope and noticed that it was addressed to Venus at a post office box. There wasn't a name above the return address, but I knew it was from Big Reggie.

"Maybe you were meant to come here, Maceo."

Venus had slipped in without me hearing her. In the doorway she sagged against the frame. She looked tired but also relieved. "I left out of here because a part of me is tired of the burden."

I didn't respond. I couldn't respond. I felt like I'd walked into a trap. I was tense. I half expected her to pull a gun from her pocket, but it wasn't meant to be dramatic. Venus was a woman who was ready for someone else to carry her load.

A tear rolled down her face as she dropped into a chair in the hallway. "Do you know how hard it is to keep a secret like this? For fifteen years?" An anguished sob escaped her chest. "I watched each one of them babies, one by one, get lost. Felicia held on the longest, but I always knew it was just a matter of time. I tried to tell Reg, again and again, but he's so stubborn he wouldn't hear me. This time I didn't let him talk me out of what I knew was right."

I found my voice. "You sent Felicia to him?"

"I made it easy for her to find her way."

I already felt myself in motion, in the car, shooting toward Fresno. "Do you think she's still there?"

She looked me in the eye. "I honestly don't know. I'm done, though, I'm done." She cried some more. "Let her daddy save her. I've done all I can."

CHAPTER

37

I entered the Grapevine, the winding mountain road that marked any journey between northern and southern California, just as night fell. I aimed my car north and watched ink spread through the midnight-blue sky.

I drove with a clear destination, a purpose, for the first time since my search began. I knew what lay at the end this time. I knew it was also possible, finally, to get some long-deserved answers.

I ignored the pain coursing through my body from my shoulder, face, and rib cage as I moved on. In reality, the pain I carried in my heart was the most potent of all, but I needed it there, tangible and on the surface, in order to remain focused. I needed the pain to remind me of my goal: to find Felicia and learn the details of Billy's murder.

Fresno was a logical conclusion, once I pieced it all together. I'd known that Felicia's mother was buried there, far away from her childhood home of San Clemente. But I hadn't known, until my conversation with Venus, that her death was the result of her husband's rage.

The knowledge made me sad, hollow, and more aware than ever of the ways in which so many of us were linked by tragedy. It was like a bloody, contagious game of connect-the-dots. I'd lost my mother through drugs, and so had Holly, though his mother was still alive, a skeletal strawberry on the East Oakland streets. All her maternal instincts had long been compromised by the pipe. She had little regard for her son beyond his accessibility to high-quality narcotics. He refused to sell to her but he never acknowledged to me, or maybe even to himself, the anger that probably fueled his choice of career.

Holly rarely saw his mother, or his equally smoked-out uncles, but I know she was a continual thorn in his side. He had chosen the sanctuary of the Redfields to re-place what was missing in his own life, but after Cissy's attack, and the exposure of their affair, the family would never again provide what he'd taken for granted.

There were ashes all over Oakland, the ashes of re-lationships, lives, and futures. A part of me, the weakest part, was glad to be away from The City. Holly's rage could be all-encompassing. I'd seen the look in his eye when he'd slammed through the doors of the hospital; it was like seeing a caged animal spot his prey on the other side of its bars, just out of reach.

On the other side, the murderous side of connect-the-dots spiraled out to bind me to Felicia. I considered my father's giving a highball to my mother to be murder, plain and simple. And Felicia had known all along that we shared this link.

The three of us, at twenty-three years of age, were con-nected by abandonment and pain. Our parents, in their own unique ways, had made the choice to disregard us and forever relegate us to orphan status. It was a feeling I couldn't shake, even in happiness, an emotion I could never trust, even in sleep. It was there, always there, the realization that I was not worthy of the good things in my life.

From memory my gut knew the good things would all disappear one way or another, and they had, bit by bit: my mother, my father, baseball, school, Felicia, Billy, and one day Alixe. The signs were already there. Some of the loss was my own doing, I couldn't argue that, but it all stemmed from the same place.

As I wheeled off the highway and into the nearest gas station, I realized I was too exhausted to continue the emotional game. I didn't want to explore the ways in which Billy was linked, or Chantal, or Scottie, or even Smokey, but the bottom line was drugs, the common denominator for us all. Drugs and a self-hatred so deeply embedded in the psyche of our community that we gave away the souls of our children for a golden calf.

The rental's tank was nearly empty as I turned off the engine and climbed from the car. I stood up and stretched to release tension and ease some of my discomfort. Around me the streets were deserted, the rush of highway traffic making the only sound in the still night.

The attendant watched me warily, and I remembered the bruises on my face and my disheveled appearance.

"Listen." I spoke for the first time in hours. "I need to know how to get to this address." I slid the ripped paper and twenty dollars for gas across the counter.

The man studied the paper for a moment and then pulled a map from one of the racks. He opened it and pointed to a road that ran alongside a river.

"It's an odd part of town," he said. "Mostly abandoned railroad shacks, houses for migrant workers, and such."

I nodded as he wrote directions on the map.

"No need to pay for this. Most people around here know their way around." He slid the map to me, eyeing my face. "Car accident?"

"Yeah," I responded. "Couple days ago."

"Well, good luck." He put the money in the cash register and returned to his magazine.

I got to the door before he spoke again. "There was a

girl in here not too long ago looking for that same part of town."

I knew it was Flea. "Thanks."

"Not a problem."

I stepped out into the night.

CHAPTER

38

The man's directions were precise. I found myself at my destination in a little under twenty minutes. He was right. It *was* an odd part of town, a mixed bag of single-family homes and trailers along a nearly depleted riverbed that looked baked through and weathered from the notorious Central Valley heat. By moonlight and the glare of the streetlamps I could see the hay-colored lawns that marked the stationary position of the lower middle class.

It all looked unkempt, forgotten, a neighborhood where the inhabitants didn't bother to invest themselves. Cars were parked across front lawns; curtains were tightly closed with only the blue light of television seeping through.

I drove to the end of the block, searching the numbers, until I came to a red stucco with an attached wooden porch. The house was neat, or at least neater than those of the neighbors on either side, but it still carried an air of neglect. The driveway was empty and all the lights were off, but I saw a dog sitting calmly on the front porch. I slowed down, rechecked the address, and parked a couple of houses away.

I waited for flickers of curtains or for porch lights to

come on and indicate that I was being watched. None came. It was definitely a place to disconnect, where TVs and stereos were turned up loud to drown out cries for help or the sounds of someone being beaten. This was a neighborhood where people came to forget and be forgotten.

I contemplated knocking on the front door or looking through the window, but I knew there was a good chance my arrival would be met with violence. I didn't know the state of Felicia's mind; I didn't know who she was with or if I would be a welcome presence. I decided to wait for the sun.

I was awakened by the sound of activity on the street and light beaming through the rear window. The dashboard clock read ten o'clock and I was amazed to have slept ten hours in the cramped hindquarters of a rental. When I stepped from the car I noticed that the dog was still in the same spot. He didn't budge even as I approached the house.

"Hey, boy," I said. "Easy, boy."

The pretense wasn't necessary. The dog looked as if he'd been waiting for me. Under his watchful gaze I knocked on the front door several times but got no response. I thought I heard something inside but I couldn't be sure. I peered through the window into a spartan house.

Around back, my knock was met with the same silence. I twisted the knob, and the door opened with ease into a small kitchen with a rickety table in the center of the room. Every inch of available counter space was filled with liquor bottles, neatly stacked and grouped by color. A transistor radio played softly, tuned to a sports station announcing the pitchers for game one of the World Series. I had to chuckle. The series seemed as far away and unreal as my chance of suiting up to replace Dave Stewart.

I moved through the house quickly. There wasn't much to see and less to indicate that anyone had been there.

Just as I reached the front door, I heard a sound behind me. The dog? I stopped to consider it, and whatever or whoever was making the noise stopped too. My body tensed. I'd been ambushed twice, and I knew the signs. A glance to either side revealed nothing that could be used as a weapon. My only chance was a quick exit out into the wide-open street and a prayer that at least one neighbor would be compassionate.

I pulled the front door open, ready to move quickly, when I felt myself yanked backward by a hand over my mouth.

"Be still, boy." The door closed in my face, but I instinctively reached out for the knob. "Be still, hear me." The man dragged me backward. I felt the strength in his arms, the solid mass of muscle in his chest and shoulders. At my best I couldn't beat him without a gun, and I was doomed by my injuries.

"What you doing in my house, huh? What you sneakin' in people's houses for?" He squeezed down on my shoulder until I felt the bone shift beneath his fingers. A pain shot through me but I wasn't giving up. I swung backward into his rib cage.

He swept my feet from beneath me and delivered one forceful blow to my spine to stop my attack. As I fell forward, scrambling for balance, I landed on a dinner tray. It collapsed like a board, and I threw it at him. He punched the tray away and kept coming. I moved like a crab, trying to make it to the lamp on a side table. I wanted something, anything, to throw at his head. I aimed the lamp and watched it graze off his forehead.

Blood sprang from a cut near his eyebrow but even with blood dripping into his eye he kept coming.

His hands were at my throat before I could move. He pinned me to the floor with his hands, hands that reminded me of my grandfather. I reached for the tray again and beaned him twice before I felt him let up.

I saw his fist spiraling down toward me. Then I heard a soft, steady voice from somewhere in the house. There was no urgency in the words, just direction. "Daddy. Don't."

Two words, two beautiful words, and Felicia stepped into my view.

"Let him go."

I focused on the red in Big Reggie's eyes, the red rage of fifteen years and no relief from his guilt. Now here he was, right before his daughter's eyes, sinking into the same murderous state that had cost her her mother. He let me go and fell back against the wall, his head in his hands. Felicia watched him from her position across the room, a coldness in her eyes I'd never seen before.

I scrambled up and away toward the front door, coughing the entire time.

"Did that feel better to you? How long have you had to wait for that?" I watched in amazement as she baited him with cruel words that recalled her mother's death. She dropped into the chair beside him so she could look him in the eye. "Does it feel the same?"

She held on to the cruelty for a minute like a hard-won toy. Then I saw her lip quiver, and she dissolved into a vulnerable heap. I didn't know if I should move forward or run. I looked at Big Reg, who remained on the floor, silent and spent. Before I could decide she ran out the back door toward the riverbank.

I hesitated for a moment, only a moment. My goal was and always had been Felicia, but I was stymied by the sight of her father, crumpled in the corner and weeping loudly into his hands. His sobs were filled with anguish, the anguish of facing a daughter he had managed to avoid for over fifteen years.

"I'm sorry. I'm sorry," I could hear him mutter through the tears. "I'm so sorry." It sounded inadequate even to me. I could only wonder what it sounded like in his own head.

I found Felicia down by the river, sitting on a slab of rock with the dog at her side. The fire that usually burned within her looked to be forever extinguished. She turned to look me over and there was absolutely no welcome in her face.

Something told me to stay where I was.

She looked as if she might bolt or kill me if I made any sudden moves. She reached into her pocket, removed a lone cigarette and a lighter, and lit the end. When she caught my eye the usual trust and happiness that lived in her face was gone.

I moved closer but she drew the cigarette up between us like a shield. I got the distinct impression that she would shove it in my eye if I provoked her in any way, so I took a seat on a rock a couple of yards back. Felicia lit a second cigarette with her first and flung the first one into the river.

"Did you see him in there? That mess of a man?" She picked up a pebble and tossed it off to follow the cigarette.

I rubbed my neck where his fingers had been less than ten minutes before. "I saw him."

"All these years I imagined someone bigger than that. Someone who could still fix all my problems despite what he did." She didn't bother to wipe away the new tears.

"How did you find him? Did you always know he was here?" I asked.

"No. Venus kept his secret." She flashed a smile filled with ice. "Family secrets." Again the ice. A grin without mirth, a joke I could not understand. "Did you go to Billy's funeral?" It was an abrupt change of subject, and she held her hand up before I could answer. "Just nod. Don't talk."

I nodded.

"Got damn!" She was up like a flash and at the water's edge. Her feet crunched pebbles and twigs as she paced back and forth. "The funeral was Tuesday?"

I nodded again.

"I wanted to go. I couldn't." She wrapped her arms around her middle and doubled over. She stayed that way, bent at the waist and moaning. "Oh, baby, baby." She sank to the ground and put her head on her knees. The dog moved in to nuzzle her with his nose. She didn't object to his presence, but he wasn't providing comfort either. Felicia gave the impression that comfort was something she could never know again.

"As long as I didn't see you I held out the hope it wasn't true." She looked up and I saw her eyes brim with tears. "I didn't think I could cry anymore. I haven't stopped crying since I started running."

I took a tentative step toward her. She didn't object so I took another. The dog issued a low growl of warning, and I stopped in my tracks. Felicia's body started to shake but no sound came from her. She sank to the ground and pulled her knees up tightly to her chest. She tucked her head so low that I thought she might fold in on herself.

"Felicia." I said it as softly as I could.

She moaned in response. "Billy."

"Flea." I moved closer, careful to tread lightly. I knelt at her side, the sharp pebbles like slivers of glass in my knee. I was close enough to feel the heat from her body. The dog had inched away to give me room, but I expected him to lunge for my throat if I caused her any more grief.

"Maceo." My name was a plea. "Maceo." She sobbed, and I leaned forward. She let herself go and melted into me. I rocked her for I don't know how long, out in the open with the dog at our side.

"Is he dead, Maceo? Is he dead?"

"Come on, girl." I tried to raise her up but she was anchored to the ground like dead weight.

"He was looking at me. He was looking right at me when he got killed." I remembered from my dreams that Billy's corpse had been slumped on the steering wheel with his head turned toward the passenger seat.

"He tried to protect me. He was still alive when I ran. I couldn't stay." She started to heave as if the tears had drained all the moisture from her body. I could feel her muscles tighten against my hand.

"Come back in the house," I said.

She shook her head. "I have to stay out here. I can't go inside. I don't like being walled in."

"Then let's move into the shade."

She made a motion to stand so I helped her to her feet. She leaned heavily on my good arm as we made our way to a tree closer to the property. I sat down with my back against the trunk and pulled her into my arms. She fit easily, though the smell of her hair and the feel of her body made my knees weak.

Once she relaxed against me I gave in to how much I had missed her, to how my life had been driven and over-taken by her disappearance. With Felicia in my arms, Al-ixe faded away. I couldn't remember her face, her smell, the reason she interested me in the first place. Felicia had captured a part of my soul that wasn't available to any-one else, not even family.

Blue told me once, when describing his love for De-siree, that if you're lucky you get one person who is all yours. It's too much to ask that you meet this person when you're young, and greedy to hope that the person feels the same way about you.

The simple fact was that I loved Felicia with every-thing I had, heart and soul, and she loved Billy the same way. The three of us were a triangle where the points were connected only on one side, but it didn't matter. My flame for Felicia would burn long after I was dead.

I closed her tighter in my arms. The feel of her skin brought back the nights long ago when she had been mine for just a moment. I didn't want to let her go.

Ever.

We stayed together under the tree for over an hour, silent, afraid to talk about the most obvious thing be-tween us: Billy. For her it would mean he was gone yet again and for me it would drive home the knowledge that he would always be there. I welcomed the delusion, but finally the silence became too big.

"Felicia," I said. "Felicia, tell me what happened."

She turned all the way around and threw her legs over my knees. We were like tangled crabs, limbs locked together. She leaned forward until her forehead rested on my chest.

"Felicia." I pushed her backward until we were eye to eye.

"I can't." She locked eyes with me.

She seemed to be searching for a promise in my face, but I didn't know what she wanted. My best guess was that she wanted me to take her burden like a baton. A quick exchange, like in a relay race, and one of us would sprint off into the wind, away from the trouble.

"What happened?" I asked again. "I know about Smokey, but who was with him? Why?"

She sighed loudly. A long exclamation of breath as she released her last bit of hope. Her eyes flickered off into the distance, and I read something else, something quick and fleeting that I didn't trust. It made my skin crawl with fear, a faint cold fear that there was a lie right behind her eyes.

"Tell me later," I said, before she could open her mouth.

She nodded, a little too grateful for the reprieve, and I knew my guess had been right.

CHAPTER

40

Big Reggie had restored the house to normal, but he was nowhere to be found.

"He disappears like that all the time." Felicia came down the hallway holding a wrinkled paper bag in her hand. For the first time I noticed that she was much slimmer than the last time I'd seen her.

"What do you mean?"

"I mean, he just gets up and walks out, disappears, comes back drunk and incoherent. Crying." She grimaced. "He's pathetic, isn't he?"

"I don't know anything about him."

"You know enough. You know plenty."

"No, I don't."

"I was arrogant, you know, always thinking that if I just saw him once, talked to him, I could forgive him and it would be okay."

"You were wrong?"

She nodded. "I couldn't have been more wrong. You know what happened when I got here? He opened the door, drunk; I could smell it all the way out on the porch. He opened the door, but then he fell over backward and scrambled toward the wall. He kept putting his hands up over his eyes and crying like a baby."

"Did he say anything?"

"Ophelia." She saw the confusion in my eyes. "Ophelia is my mother's name. He thought I was my mother. I guess he'd been waiting all these years until she came back."

I didn't say anything. Felicia and I knew she didn't look anything like her mother.

"Do you know what you would say, Maceo?"

"To what?"

"To your father. What would you say to him if you could speak to him?"

"I don't know."

"I know you think about it."

"Naw, Felicia, I don't. My father doesn't mean anything but bad news to me."

She didn't believe me, but I saw my father on a regular basis; that was the problem. He had always been present, and he usually laughed whenever I tried to ask a thing about my mother.

"You know what the worst thing is about seeing him?"

"What?"

"That I can't take it back. Now I don't have a safe place to go even in my head. All these years, he's been the only one I thought could make it all better."

"He's just a man."

"That's the problem." She licked at tears that had fallen to her lips. "He's just a man, and that's the worst thing he could've been. I needed him to be bigger, so I could forgive him. I didn't realize that until I saw him. Fifteen years of anger, resentment, all built up to face a simple broken-down old man."

"Maybe he was always just that."

"Not in my mind."

We locked the door behind us, and for all purposes Felicia closed the door, permanently, on the past that included her father. I envied her that. My mother and father and their mistakes would live with me until I died.

We got through lunch, a half-hearted drive through Fresno in search of Big Reggie before coming to rest beneath the California 99 North freeway entrance.

I turned off the engine and looked at Felicia. "You got to tell it, girl." She pressed her body into the door and avoided my gaze. "Felicia, what happened?"

"What happened to you?" she countered. "I been with you all day, and you never said a word about all those bruises. Look at your arm. Your pitching arm."

"It's a sprain."

"It's more than that, Maceo. I haven't been gone so long I forgot what baseball means to you. How did it happen?"

"A fight."

"Maceo, tell me the truth. The more ... wering my questions, the more I know this ... g to do with Billy and me."

... matter now."

... else got hurt?" I didn't answer. "Who else got hurt, Maceo?"

"Cissy. Cissy got hurt; she's still in the hospital. Unconscious."

"Who did it?"

"Smokey Baines."

She sucked in her breath loudly. "Oh, man. Because of Billy?"

"Partly. Mostly because of Holly."

"Holly?"

"Him and Cissy been together for a while, so Smokey went after her."

"And you?"

"I was there. We were together." I paused. "On College and Alcatraz."

I watched the effect of my words. I waited for the location to sink in. While we were talking she had regained some of her bravado. In between the cracks of despair and hardness, glimpses of the old Felicia peeked through, but she disappeared again as my words sank in.

"College and Alcatraz?" she asked.

"Yeah. I drove there the other night, without thinking. I guess Smokey followed us."

She whispered, more to herself than to me, "They followed us too." I kept quiet, knowing the story would come out piece by piece. "They followed us too. They didn't know I was in the car. I had the seat back. I was tired, so Billy told me to go to sleep.

"Billy had a gun in the car. I went to sit up when I saw him reach for it, but he told me to stay down. I did but I kept my eyes open. I don't even remember breathing. But then—then he put down the gun, and I relaxed." She looked at me, desperate. "I mean, he wouldn't put down the gun unless he felt safe, right? That's what I thought, otherwise I wouldn't have closed my eyes. If I had been paying attention."

The rest of the story was lost in tears. I waited for her to continue. Her grief was real, I could see that, but I couldn't understand why Billy would put away his gun at the sight of Smokey. They weren't real enemies, like Smokey and Holly, but they weren't friendly. It didn't make sense to me for Billy to drop his guard that way.

"Come on," I said. "Just let it go."

She shook her head. "Maceo, he was right there. Right there next to me. One minute he had his hand on my arm and the next minute I was covered in blood."

"Why did he put the gun down?"

She hesitated for just a moment. "I don't know. I go over that in my head all the time. I don't know. He didn't hate Smokey, but he didn't trust him either."

"Who was with Smoke?"

"I didn't see. He told me to stay down so I did. I heard a gunshot, and he fell on the steering wheel. I saw his hand reach out. I don't know if he was trying to push me out of the car or if he was trying to touch me. I don't know. I ran. He wasn't even dead yet, but I was scared. Why, Maceo? Why did this happen?"

I didn't have an answer. In quick flashes I imagined his last actions. I felt the fear that must have gripped him when he realized he was being followed. The feel of the gun, its cold steel providing tangible reassurance. Looking over at Felicia to make sure she was safe and then a quick calculation of the best streets to make a getaway. How far to the freeway? The open highway? And, then, finally, the act that cost him his life. Easing up on the gun, maybe even putting it away after recognizing a familiar face. A friend. It had to be a friend. A friend to put a bullet hole in a set of rules that never worked in the first place.

"Did anybody come after you?"

"No. They only wanted Billy."

"You keep saying 'they,' Felicia. Who was with Smokey?"

"I don't know. I didn't see but he wasn't by himself. I heard him talking as he approached the car. I saw his face a second before I ran. He looked surprised to see me. He raised his gun up, though, and the other person knocked it away."

"So you ran?"

"I ran."

"Is that why you disappeared?"

"It wasn't planned. I just ran. Billy made me memorize an escape route in case anything like this ever happened." She smiled weakly. "I used to hate when he talked about stuff like that. Who was gonna kill Billy? Nobody in the Bay hated him like that. I saw how people reacted to him all the time. The way they reacted to me once we got together."

"Where did you go from there?"

"I went to a car Billy kept parked near my house. I wore the key on a chain around my neck. I drove to a safe house where we had clothes and money stashed. I traded the first car for another one, and then I went to see Mrs. Johnson."

I listened, knowing that Holly had a similar plan. They all did, but few of them ever benefited from the elaborate safety nets.

"Then I started driving. I didn't even know where I was going. I was driving blind. I ended up here in Fresno. I called Venus from a truck stop off Highway 5 and she told me to come here." She hugged herself. I tried to move closer to her but she put her hand up to stop me. "It won't help. Nothing helps. Nothing works anymore. Billy. My daddy. Venus. Everything's gone. You know, Maceo. You know how it feels to live without wishing."

She went on, not waiting for my confirmation.

"I got that finally for a little while with Billy. He made me feel safe enough to do that. I felt good enough to imagine things. I haven't felt like that since I was a little girl. After my daddy left I stopped feeling like that altogether. It didn't make sense after that to believe life could be good."

She spoke what I had always believed. She was right. It didn't make sense to imagine anything good. Calling attention to what made you happy, trusting that feeling, was the surest way of losing it.

"I loved my father," she continued. "My mother's not that vivid to me, but I loved my daddy so hard. He had those hands, trustworthy, kind of like Daddy Al's. I noticed that immediately about your grandfather. My daddy even smelled safe to me. Billy was like that too." She tapped the steering wheel with impatience. "I should have known. I should have known by the smell he was gonna leave me."

I dropped my open hand into the place between us in the car. I held it there, open, until she reached for it. I closed my hands tight around hers and she finally moved close enough to put her head on my shoulder. But it didn't rest there. It was perched on the edge, her body tensed for flight. On guard.

"My family has secrets like yours, Maceo. I think that's why we liked each other."

I wanted to correct her simple words but it wasn't the place or the time. It was never "like" on my part. I loved Felicia Bennett from the moment I saw her. And now I listened as she told me that my arms, the love I offered, never represented safety.

"Let me drive, Maceo."

"What?"

"Switch places with me." She climbed across the front seat without waiting on an answer. Once she was settled she looked up at the freeway sign that loomed above us. Whatever it took, whatever she decided in that moment of silence, gave her the strength she needed. She took only a minute to decide her next step. Then she turned on the engine.

"Where we going?" I asked.

"Oakland," she said, as she wheeled the car onto the highway.

CHAPTER

41

With Felicia at the wheel we made it to Oakland in less than four hours. The sun had already gone down, and as we broke through the mountain pass I remembered, yet again, how beautiful the Bay was.

"You know," Felicia said, "when I got here from L.A. and saw this I couldn't believe it. Mountains. Water. San Francisco. Los Angeles could never be this beautiful, not where I grew up. I saw where the Black people lived out here, and even when it was bad I thought to myself that they could still see all this. And I thought it would mean everything was different."

"That's too much to ask."

"I know that now."

"Pull over and let me drive. You need to stay down."

"What about you?"

"If they wanted me they had me already."

* * *

Without asking I drove Felicia to Mountain View Cemetery, where Billy was buried. She was quiet in the car as we approached the iron gates at the entrance. I gunned the engine past a maintenance man who tried to wave us away.

I wound my way up the hill until I came to the flagpole I used as a signpost. Five yards away a lone tree sat at the top of the hill. Billy's grave was three plots down. I stopped the car.

"It's right there, midway down, with the fresh soil."

She had to watch her step because of the steepness of the hill, but there was another sort of caution in her walk. I stayed by the car to keep watch.

Behind me the maintenance man screeched to a halt and jumped angrily from his truck. "The park is closed! We close at five thirty!" he yelled.

"Five minutes, brother," I said calmly.

"Five minutes, my ass."

I turned and looked him in the eye. "Then you tell her that."

He looked to where I pointed. Felicia was bent forward with her face buried in her hands. The grave was new so a marker had not yet been set.

"All right then, man. Look, just don't get me fired." He returned to his truck.

Felicia sat up, dried her eyes, and pulled Billy's ring from her finger. I'd noticed it in Fresno but hadn't said anything about it. She kissed it and shoved it in the dirt at the foot of the grave.

"Felicia," I said, when she got to the car, "Billy wanted you to have that ring."

"I don't deserve that ring, Maceo." Her eyes told me not to question her, so I didn't.

"Felicia."

"Let's go, Maceo. I'm ready."

She climbed into the passenger seat and looked straight ahead. As we made our way to the front gate she never looked back. Not even once.

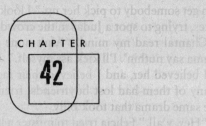

CHAPTER

42

We killed time until well after midnight. Not talking, we sat down by the marina looking out at the water and San Francisco sparkling in the distance.

"I'ma take you to a friend's house, then I'ma try and find Holly. As soon as I can get ahold of Clarence I'll have him pick you up. He can keep you safe."

"But will he?" she asked, knowing that there was probably a price on her head.

"More than the others. All he wanted to know was that you didn't kill Billy yourself."

She winced at the absurdity of that as I rolled to a stop in front of Chantal's. It was after two o'clock in the morning, but the lights of her apartment blazed out into the night.

As we walked up the front steps I heard loud, animated voices through the door. Female voices. I had to knock with my foot to make myself heard over the party. Chantal opened the door, drink in hand and attitude at the ready.

"What—!" She stopped short when she saw Felicia. "Oh, girl. Oh, girl. Turn the music off!" She yelled the command back over her shoulder. It ended abruptly.

We entered a room full of astonished eyes. The silence

was deafening. Everyone stared at Felicia, who must have looked to most of them like a ghost.

"Chantal, I need a favor," I said.

"What you need?"

"Felicia needs to stay here for about an hour until I can get somebody to pick her up." I looked at the gaping faces, trying to spot a Judas in the crowd.

Chantal read my mind. "Ain't none of these bitches gonna say nuthin'. I'll kick ass myself."

I believed her, and I believed their faces. I knew that many of them had lost boyfriends, friends, relatives, to the same drama that took Billy.

"Hey, y'all." Felicia tried to muster a little personality, but it failed her.

"Wassup, girl." Patrice, the nasty baseball fan, made her way forward. She had to bypass two racks of clothing and three card tables to greet us. "I'm sorry about Billy."

"Thank you." Felicia said it to close the subject, and Patrice took the hint.

"You want some Tanqueray? We got plenty. Chantal's ass was too cheap for anything else."

"Ya drank it up, didn't ya?" Chantal shot back.

"Can't get my buzz on wit' water. Of course I drank it."

They gave each other a pound. "That's what I'm saying." Chantal laughed.

"What's going on?" I raised my chin to indicate the party.

She lowered her voice. "I supplement my income every once in a while with a little poker and shopping."

I would have laughed if life wasn't the way it was. Leave it to Chantal to be up on the latest trend. I'd heard about a circle of ghetto-fabulous Oakland women who threw elaborate all-female parties filled with racks of boosted designer clothes. All top-notch labels. The women lost their money by shopping off the rack, gangsta style, or by playing high-stakes poker.

Shopping bags were lined up against the wall with each woman's name written in black marker. Patrice had a total of five bags.

"You ain't nothing nice, Chantal." I meant it as a compliment and she smiled.

"Felicia, why don't you pick out something, and if you tired we can clear out the room."

"Y'all go 'head, I'm fine," she answered.

"Chantal, can I use your phone?" I asked.

"It's in the bedroom"—she paused a minute—"with the stripper. We had entertainment too."

"Maceo!" Big Slippery, Phine and Nelia's star act, was getting dressed in the cramped bedroom. "I thought this was a women-only party." He looked me eagerly up and down and licked his lips. "Unless you done switched teams?"

I shook my head. "I'm just here to drop off a friend."

"Well, don't tell your aunties I'm moonlighting. I couldn't resist. These little Hot Clothes Hot Body parties pay a nice piece of change."

I laughed at the greedy giant. Big Slippery was famous among Oakland's male strippers, a tough circuit to crack. Most of them were cliquish, competitive as hell, and straight. Big Slippery was everything but the last, which made his success so ironic. The twins knew he was gay and so did his clients, but he brought in the most money.

"I won't tell 'em," I said.

"Good."

"I thought you moved to New York anyway." Phine and Nelia had been mad as hornets when Big Slippery announced his plans to dance on Broadway. Far as I knew, he had gone to New York around the same time as Billy's murder.

"New York. Puh-lease! Made a punk out of me, and I'll be the first one to tell it. It was too buck-wild for me. My first day there, the cabdriver took me to Ho Stroll. Motherfucker, the hookers was ass-naked in broad daylight! Ass and titties and shit, just *out* flesh-and-blood to the world.

"I got my behind back on the plane, okay? I'm staying right here in Oakland. Oakland's the only place for me in 1989. California, North Oakland, Fifty-first Avenue. Corner house on the left. Third bedroom on the right at the top of the stairs."

The door opened and one of the partyers slid in to retrieve her purse. Price tags hung from her collar. Big Slippery didn't miss a thing. "No, mommy, the Gucci you had on before was fierce. Black girls got to let go of Ann Taylor, she don't mean y'all nothing but harm."

The girl nodded and left the room.

"I saw your boy Holly today. He like to run me over in front of Flint's Barbeque on East Fourteenth."

"Holly? You sure?" It was too much to hope for. I hadn't known where to start in my search for him.

"Yeah, it was him. That nigga looked like he was on his way to kill somebody or had just come from doing it."

I walked out of the bedroom intent on searching the Kill Zone for Holly. Holly's silence when I paged him made me nervous. He always answered his pages; I'd even used the emergency code of 911 twice.

In the living room I stopped dead in my tracks. Alixe stood at the front door, not yet aware of my presence or that Felicia was in the same room. She slipped off her coat and went to the clothing rack nearest the door.

"How did you think of this, Chantal?" As she browsed the labels there was nothing but admiration on her face.

"Girl, you on Tokyo time. We been doing this in Oakland for ages." I noticed that Felicia had changed into black pants and a white sweater. Simple. Beautiful as always.

She eyed Alixe quietly, noting from my demeanor that the new arrival was more than just a late shopper.

Alixe pushed aside a row of skirts and spotted me in the empty space. "Maceo!"

"Hey, girl." I stayed put in the hallway entrance.

"Funny place to find you."

"Ain't it, though."

She look puzzled but I was too stuck to offer guidance. Patrice nudged her way past me, holding a pair of black shoes in her hand.

"Felicia, these'll work fine with what you have on."

Alixe held my eye for what seemed like an eternity before turning to Felicia.

Chantal graciously stepped between the two women. "Felicia, you see anything else you like? Why don't you grab a couple of things?"

Alixe turned her crosshairs on me. "Maceo, can I talk to you for a minute? Outside."

"Yeah, I was on my way out anyway." Then I made a mistake. I crossed the room and knelt in front of Felicia's chair. All around me I saw the Black-girl-tilt-of-the-head to indicate that I'd just dissed Alixe. Felicia smiled, a real smile, for the first time in ages.

"Glad you think it's funny," I whispered. "Listen, I'm going to try and find Holly. You gonna be cool?"

"I'll be fine." The smile played around her mouth as she looked at Alixe. "*You* be careful."

CHAPTER

43

"What's going on?" Alixe waited for me on the sidewalk. "How long have you been back? How come you didn't call?"

"I just got here."

"Why didn't you call?" she asked again.

"I had something to take care of."

"Something or someone?"

"Something. I haven't even seen my family yet."

"You haven't seen your family?" She looked confused.

"No."

"Maceo, what's going on?" She looked back toward the apartment. I saw that Felicia had stepped out and was watching us from the balcony. "Where'd you find her?"

"Fresno."

"Fresno? I thought you were going to Louisiana?"

"Change of plans. I'll explain it later."

She scanned my face. "I want to believe you."

"Believe me or don't, I got somewhere to be."

"Why are you mad at me?" She grabbed my arm when I tried to turn away from her. "You don't think I deserve an explanation?"

"Nobody's getting what they deserve tonight."

"I'm not just anybody. And I do deserve an explanation. I thought you were gone. Out of state. Then I see you here, with her, and you can't explain to me what's going on? That doesn't wash.

"Where you going? I'm talking to you." Her voice rose in anger.

"I got business to take care of."

"It can't wait?"

"Alixe. I don't have time for this." My own voice rose in response to hers.

"Nobody can save Felicia but you, is that it?" Her words were laced with contempt. "She takes precedent over every other thing in your life."

"I owe it to Billy" was all I could say.

"Don't use that excuse. Billy's not here, and I can't imagine if he was your *friend* that he would want this."

"That's the difference. You can't imagine it, but I know it. He would do the same for me and so would Holly."

Her eyes darted around in desperation. I wanted to make her understand but there weren't enough words in the dictionary. This knowledge came from an innate code of ethics that was alien to her universe. If I died the way Billy had, Holly would ride into his own death to right the wrong.

"I owe Billy," I said again.

"You only owe yourself." She answered me with an innocent's certainty.

"That's how you live," I told her.

"It's how I survive, Maceo."

Felicia came quietly down the steps while we argued. Alixe turned to stare pointedly at her and then she looked back at me. "Don't do this, Maceo. Whatever happens is not going to be worth it. It'll cost you too much."

"Meaning you? It'll cost me you?" I asked, but I already knew the answer.

"More than that."

I stood and looked at both women, knowing I was making a choice, knowing also that there had never really been any question.

"Maceo," Felicia interjected. "I changed my mind. I'm going with you."

Alixe's gaze was steady, locked on mine and awaiting answers. She ignored Felicia, who stood patiently at my side. My head started to spin. Both of them wanted something from me and I could only give to one. I saw tears pool in Alixe's eyes because we both knew the answer. Felicia stepped around her and slid into the passenger seat of the car. She rolled the window up tightly to give us privacy but there wasn't any. Everybody present knew what was being said in the silence.

"Alixe, this doesn't have anything to do with you."

"Yes, it does." She smiled weakly. "I love you, you know." She paused. "But you don't deserve me."

"Alixe."

"Let me finish. You don't get to play this game and get the good things too, and believe me I'm one of the good things."

She was right, there was no denying it. She was a good thing but the timing was bad. "You *are* a good thing," I said. I stepped toward her but she backed away.

"I love you, and I have no idea who you are."

"You knew who I was when you met me."

"*You* don't even know who you are, Maceo. How could I? If you did you wouldn't run so hard into this madness. You would realize that you have too much to lose." She looked at Felicia, seated in the car. "Even when all this is over you still won't get her."

I flinched visibly, and she realized she'd struck a chord. "That's it, isn't it?" She shook her head in disgust. "I never took you for one to believe in fairy tales, but you got your white horse out of the stable. Guys love that, I guess. The damsel in distress, even if she's a black widow. With me there's no rescuing. I'm just by your side."

"I'll call you."

"No, you won't"—she wiped a tear from her cheek—"and I wish I didn't care."

She walked into me until her face rested on my chest. I was forced to wrap my arm around her. It would have been so easy to stay there, to walk away with her, but the mess was mine just like it was Holly's.

"She's your past," Alixe whispered into my chest. "I wish you could see that. She's everything you should run away from."

I tried to break the embrace and push her away, gently, but she held on tight. I found myself doing the same thing. I wanted them both, and the reality was I didn't have either one. Alixe was what I wanted waiting for me on the other side, but I needed Felicia now.

"I wish I could wait, Maceo. But whatever happens tonight is going to poison you, and I can't be a part of that." She finally stepped away, and I saw her eyes glisten. "I remember that first night at your house when I saw all those pictures of you, your family, and Holly, and I was envious. I don't have ties like that. But maybe those are ties I don't need."

I smiled at her and touched her face. She brought my hand to her mouth and kissed my fingers. "Be safe," she said and leaned in to kiss me. It tasted like good-bye before our lips even met.

Alixe, as an outsider to Oakland and to me, had exposed my shallow, insular world in one conversation. I resented that. If she opened me up what would she find? A map of Oakland where my heart should be. That's all the definition I had: my neighborhood, my city, the like-minded friends with our sticky web of unwritten rules. Despite my talent, my family, or even myself, all any of us felt we had was the game. A sport with its own set of regulations. Invented manhood. Winner take death.

Alixe's words exposed it all like a surgical knife.

I watched her walk away. I was set to call out her name when the car horn blared behind me and broke the spell. Alixe flinched at the sound, but she didn't turn around. I waited until she got in the house before I drove off into the night with Felicia at my side.

CHAPTER

44

The Kill Zone bumped with activity as I made my way down East Fourteenth. At a green light I maneuvered around a drunken couple having an argument in the middle of the street. Business as usual in the ghetto.

I turned off the boulevard and headed into the numbered streets lumpy with speed bumps. The speed bumps were the city's lame attempt at fighting crime. The theory was that three speed bumps on each street would cut down on high-speed chases between criminals and the police and thus combat crime. It didn't matter that a large portion of dealing, stealing, and general mayhem was done on foot.

Slowing down as I came to the end of the block, I watched a group of three young men eye me to determine if I was friend or foe. There was no identifying color or gang sign, like in L.A., just my demeanor. I was either there to enhance their lives by purchasing rock or get in the way of profit by being an undercover. I ignored them to show that I was neither. Just a brother out with his girl.

I got out and leaned into the car window to speak to Felicia. "You gonna be all right? I'll only be a minute."

"I'll be fine."

I walked to the end of the block, made a left, and cut over two blocks to the apartment building where Holly's mother, Sylvia, lived with two of her brothers in a relationship assumed to be incestuous.

Holly hated his mother. It wasn't hard to see why but he played the family card during emergencies, and apparently she had come through for him. When I walked up the stairs I could see him inside the apartment. He sat on the couch with the front door wide-open. The light from the TV screen made him look bloodless.

It took him a moment to place me when I stepped into the doorway. He watched me, blankly, making no move to reach for a gun, run away, or acknowledge me. He had retreated into the recesses of his soul to recover from whatever activity was fresh on his brain. He was either contemplating Smokey's fate or recovering from it.

It spooked me to know another person so well, but my knowledge gave me the tools to deal with him. Holly thrived on violence, living on the edge gave him sustenance, but once in a while he had to work extra hard to erase the effects of his actions. He called it rebuilding.

"Holly."

He looked at me without speaking.

"Holly," I said again. "It's Maceo. I got Felicia in the car. We gotta roll."

I watched as he fought his way back to the surface in order to respond. He went into his reserve to pull himself past Cissy's attack and Smokey's fate.

"We gotta roll, man. I need you to contact Clarence." I stepped into the room and turned off the TV. I couldn't stand to look at him under the artificial blue light of the screen. I flicked on the overhead, and the room danced with light.

He blinked sleepily like a man under anesthesia before looking directly at me.

"When you get back?" he asked with deliberateness. His speech was slurred, like his tongue was swollen.

His surroundings made my skin crawl. The place was filthy, as if wild dogs had used the apartment as a storage unit. East Oakland was notorious for roving, overbred dogs abandoned by their owners who then merged into packs, traveling the streets day and night, dodging cars and navigating red lights like New Yorkers.

There were clothes scattered around the room, dirty, torn, some covered with spatterings of blood that could have been from sex, needle usage, or a fistfight. I didn't want to think about any of it. In one corner, the only neat spot in the house, shoe boxes were marked in black: one for Sylvia, one for her older brother, Dom, and one for the younger brother, Vernon. They were lined up in a row and contained all the paraphernalia needed for dedicated drug use.

Holly caught me staring at the storage units. "Ain't that a bitch, man." I could tell he was resurfacing slowly, fighting his way back. He used contempt to get there.

"Where are they? You the only one here?" I asked him.

He nodded. "Ghouls out roaming the streets. They tried to hit me up for some product when I got here."

He slowly came back to life as he told me about his mother. Some children born into heinous families tend to overcompensate with love for their parents, but not Holly. I think it gave him undue pleasure to have so much money and so many pure drugs. He loved being able to turn a deaf ear to his mother's pleas. To say no to her at will.

It was a sick game, but Holly loved it. He loved being

in control of something she wanted so badly and holding it back. It was his paycheck for the love and care she had withheld from him since birth.

"You see how these people living, man?" he said. "Don't even go in the back of the house. The three of them sleeping on the same mattress."

He stood up and shook his arms and legs awake. I watched as color seeped back into his face and life into his limbs.

"I got Felicia with me," I said again. "She's in the car."

"Felicia?" He sounded surprised. "You find her in Louisiana?"

"Fresno. Never made it to Louisiana. I went to L.A. instead, and her aunt told me where she was hiding."

"What's the word?" I saw him brace against the answer I was about to give him. "How'd it go down?"

"Smokey. Just like we thought. She didn't recognize the man wit' him. She said it was him, though, and one other person."

"She didn't recognize him?" He looked doubtful.

"That's what she said. She heard the gunshot and ran before Smokey could fire at her."

"Who does she think it was?"

"Probably just one a his boys."

"Hmm." Holly was a skeptic to the end.

"You find Smokey yet?" I asked.

"Nope, but I know how to get him."

"How we gonna do that?"

"We?" He raised an eyebrow. We walked out of the apartment and down the stairs. When we turned the corner I saw Felicia sitting quietly in the passenger seat. Her head was down so she hadn't spotted us yet. "We?" Holly said again.

I held up the bandaged arm. The pitching arm. "No reason to save it."

"That ain't the only reason, nigga."

"Nope, but it's the only one we gonna talk about. Now, how do we get him?"

"Guess."

It didn't take much to put it together. "Cynthia, his son's mother?"

"Who else?"

"How you doing that?"

"Don't worry 'bout the details. It's being handled."

"You ain't forcing her into nothing."

"What the fuck kind of question is that? That's Smokey's style, putting his hands on women. That's the reason this shit is so easy."

"She's willing to give him up just like that?"

"Wouldn't you?"

I shrugged. "Why would this time be any different? She's put up with it this long."

"So what's different now?" He finished my sentence. "Another nigga. She met somebody else, and she can't shake Smokey."

"So you're playing Cupid?"

He laughed. "Something like that. I gave her a little cash—a lot of cash—to get in the cut with the baby."

"You're paying her off."

"You saw Cissy. I'd give up all my money if I had to."

"I hear ya. So what's the word? When does it go down?"

"You just be ready to ride."

"I already told you I was ready."

He looked at me for signs of weakness. "You need a gun."

I didn't flinch, but I did remember the gun I'd left on his walkway. "I lost the one I had."

He looked at me with a challenging smile. "I can get you another one. You ready to ride?"

I hesitated, then I caught sight of Felicia. Alixe was already gone, Billy was dead, Cissy was hurt, and I wanted it all to end. I stood there at the line, probably as Holly had before he started selling drugs, probably as Smokey, Clarence, Emmet, and Malcolm once had. I stood at the line and made my choice.

My choice.

I looked down, thinking maybe the line would be visible, something tangible for me to step over. I saw nothing. Concrete. Garbage. My own feet and Holly's. He had fought my battles too long so I made my decision. Everyone had, at some point.

"I'm rolling."

Holly pulled his gun from his waistband and tossed it my way. I caught it with one hand, and it seemed to sizzle with its own life force.

I hadn't felt so alive since my time on the mound.

CHAPTER

45

Holly climbed into the backseat of the rental and squeezed Felicia's shoulder. That was all that passed between them, and I couldn't ask for anything more. Holly filled her in on his plan to lure Smokey with Cynthia's help.

"Won't he be expecting a trap?" Felicia asked. "He killed Billy, attacked Maceo, and put Cissy in the hospital. He's probably not even in town."

"You're giving Smokey too much credit."

"And you're not giving him enough. I saw him shoot Billy. I heard him laugh right after he did it. He's stupid but not that stupid. Everybody knows about you and Cynthia. She's the last person he would trust, son or not."

Holly leaned into the shadows of the backseat. "She's about to get in the cut with his son. He'll come if she calls."

Felicia remained silent, but it was obvious she didn't believe in Holly's plan.

"Can you think of something else?"

She looked out into the night. "I know how to find him." She said the words softly. "Back in the day, before Billy, I hooked up with him once."

"What do you mean, hooked up with him once?" Holly asked the question I wasn't brave enough to ask. Before Billy there was me. When had there been time for Smokey?

Felicia placed her hand on my knee and squeezed. "I met him the first week I was in Oakland. I met him out at the lake, and we hooked up once after that."

"And we never heard about it? You know how big that fool's mouth is. How come we never heard about it?" Holly leaned over the front seat.

"He met me when I was with my brothers. Reggie and Crim make a strong impression." She paused. "He wasn't gonna talk shit about me after meeting them. They made sure of that."

Plausible but there was something missing.

"Felicia." Holly's voice was hard. "Don't have us walking into bullshit you can prevent right now by telling the truth."

"I'm telling the truth." Her voice was strong and steady.

"I'll accept that," he continued, "but only if you tell *all* of the truth."

"Smokey has a big mouth. He wanted to impress me and my brothers so he told all his business. He showed me Cynthia's house and his. Not the one in Berkeley but the one up near Knowland Park."

"Knowland Park?" Holly asked.

She nodded. "Near the zoo. That's where he lives. You can run into the woods through the backyard. He bragged that he could get away by disappearing into the woods of the park if anybody ever came after him. It's a good setup. Billy looked at a place up there, but Smokey owned the best spot and the houses on either side."

"Damn!" Holly whistled softly. He sounded impressed. "He can get out through the woods, huh?"

"Yeah," she answered.

"Then we can get in the same way."

Holly called Clarence from a pay phone on East Fourteenth, and we headed to the Nickel and Dime. By the time we arrived at the bar, Clarence was there in a mob car, a nondescript black sedan, with Georgia license plates I assumed were fake. The Samoans were with him as always. All three of them were dressed down in jeans and dark T-shirts.

Felicia stepped from the car as he approached, and he stopped in his tracks. She stood there a moment trying to read his face. She knew she was safe—nothing would happen to her in the presence of Holly and myself—but she needed to know if she could trust Clarence.

The Samoans watched quietly, we all did, until another car arrived, carrying Malcolm and Emmet. They drove in between Clarence and Felicia, joking loudly in the car. Emmet stopped abruptly when he saw Felicia.

"Damn, girl." He bounced from the car and wrapped her in a tight embrace. The gesture broke the ice. "You all right? We've been worried about you. Yolanda asks me every day if anybody heard from you."

Felicia tried to pull herself away but Emmet held tight. "I'm all right."

"We didn't know if you were dead or alive. Nobody knew anything."

She finally managed to wiggle free. She put her hand on Emmet's chest to keep him at a distance. Her smile was weak, and she blinked rapidly to fight back tears. "I'm fine, I'm fine. How is Yolanda?"

"She was worried about you. You've been on her mind every day since this happened. We missed you at the funeral."

"I couldn't make it." She looked down. "I didn't know if I was safe."

Emmet raised her head up by her chin. "Look me in the eye and tell me you didn't have anything to do with Billy dying, and everybody here will make sure you stay safe."

Her voice was hoarse and husky as she answered. "I didn't have anything to do with that. I would die first before I hurt Billy."

I saw Clarence and Holly share looks of doubt but they would follow Emmet's lead. Emmet took his job as a ladies' man—a protector of women—very seriously. He fell easily into the role, perfecting it once he got married. They would have to battle him too if they decided Felicia was lying.

He held Felicia at arm's length and continued to look at her. "That's all I had to hear. You say you didn't hurt him. I believe you."

"I could never do that." Felicia turned to face Holly and Clarence. "I know you two don't believe me." Clarence relented a little under her gaze, but Holly stood firm. She addressed him directly. "Especially you, Holly. There's no love lost. I understand that. But you got to know I would never hurt Billy. I didn't pull the trigger, I didn't have anything to do with setting him up, but I can't force you to believe me."

Holly looked at me and chose his words carefully before he spoke. "Maceo needs me to cover his back. I have to make up for Billy's death, and that's what I'm going to do." He pledged his allegiance but he hadn't mentioned her as a reason.

Inside the bar I flipped on the lights and directed everyone to a center table. Both bar and restaurant had been closed tight since Cissy's attack. I took my place behind the counter and started to pour drinks for everyone.

The Samoans grabbed their drinks and clicked them together. The others followed suit while Felicia watched. There was festivity in the air, no doubt about that, and the smell of blood. They were all ready to kill to ensure that the rules stayed the same in a rapidly changing world.

"I know how to get to Smokey," Holly offered. His words brought a hush to the group. He looked at Felicia and made the decision not to betray her trust. "I found out where he stays."

"For real?" Clarence smiled.

"Yep, and I gotta admit the shit is kinda genius."

"Genius from that monkey?" Emmet pulled a cigarette from a gold carrying case and crossed his legs.

"Monkey's appropriate"—Holly laughed—" 'cause it's up by the zoo. Knowland Park. The man bought three houses side by side, and all three feed into the woods. Sweet escape route."

"Word?" Emmet blew smoke into the air. "Sounds kinda fly. Maybe I'll move in there after we bump him."

Clarence gave him a pound. "I was thinking the same thing myself."

"He said there was three." Malcolm spoke up. "I wouldn't mind being ya neighbor."

They laughed loudly at the idea of splitting up Smokey's bounty. I kept quiet and watched Felicia. She twitched nervously while the fellas talked all around her.

She wouldn't meet my gaze whenever I offered a smile. I had been locked on her for a couple of minutes when I noticed Holly watching us both.

He caught my eye and shook his head. I held my hands up in surrender.

We followed the 580 highway along the rim of hills that lined Oakland. Below us the city glittered with colored lights like the inside of an exposed transistor. The three of us—Holly, myself, and Felicia—were in the lead car as we moved toward the entrance to Knowland Park. The park was a heavily wooded area, with campgrounds, abandoned buildings, and a decrepit zoo that housed the saddest animals I'd ever seen: blind bears, scabby lions, and giraffes with limps.

The houses along the mountains were supported by metal stilts above the sloped canyons. The drop-off was steep and the area was still roamed by wildcats and coyotes. Few of the homes, million-dollar or not, had traditional backyards, and most of the residents had grown used to the sight of deer outside their windows. It was beautiful and sad at the same time, just like the rest of the city.

I pulled off the freeway and drove directly into a bank of redwoods. It would be impossible to spot the car from the road below.

Felicia led the way as we trekked through the dense valley of trees. Emmet and Malcolm stayed near the cars to serve as lookout while the rest of us made our way toward Smokey's house. We walked north up a hill with little support, using the lights of the houses as our guides.

I focused on the route, unwilling to let my mind explore the how and why of my situation. Before leaving the bar I took two painkillers from Clarence, but the aches in my body were still vivid.

"Right here." Felicia waited until everyone gathered around before she pointed. "That's the one. Right there in the center."

"How you know that?" Clarence asked. His voice was cold, and he looked from me to Holly. "We can't be keeping secrets on a mission like this."

Holly had covered for Felicia at the bar, so we all waited for him to answer. "No secrets, man. You got my word."

Clarence avoided looking at Felicia or me. "Only your word. This whole mission is riding on you, man."

"I hear ya." Clarence drew a line but Holly didn't back down. "You know everything you need to know."

Clarence looked at him for a long moment, then nodded his head. He turned to Felicia. "You got all the players in Oakland lined up to protect you. Anybody get hurt"—he paused—"I'll take the rest of 'em out just to get to you myself."

We found level ground that gave us a full view of Smokey's living room. The television played to an empty room, and three beers sat on the table.

"Where ya girl at?" Holly whispered behind me.

Before I could answer, we all saw Felicia hoist herself onto the deck that led into Smokey's house. She slipped in through a sliding glass door before any of us could call out or go after her.

"Man, what the fuck is this?" Clarence kicked a rock at his feet.

"Look." I pointed to the living room, where Smokey entered with three more beers in his hand. All the lights were on, and it felt for a moment like watching a movie. We were all mesmerized, knowing Felicia was in the house. Smokey took a seat and handed the remaining beers to people we couldn't see.

"We got to go up there." I started forward but Holly held me back.

"She ain't following the rules. She on her own, man."

I saw Felicia's shadow before the others. She was in the hallway behind Smokey with her gun leading the way. She put her finger to her lips to hush Smokey's guests and then placed the barrel on his neck.

He didn't have time to turn before a flash of light erupted from the gun and ripped the back of his head off.

CHAPTER

46

I stepped into the brightly lit room just as Felicia shot five more bullets into Smokey's twitching body. Holly, Clarence, and the Samoans came in right behind me, guns drawn and directed at the other people in the room. We all stopped short, surprised. Then Felicia turned the gun on Smokey's guests.

"I got one more. Just for you, Reggie." There was no love in her face as she gazed at her brother. There was nothing recognizable about her.

"Flea." Reggie moved toward her with his hands in the air. He shot a worried glance at the five of us. "Flea, you gotta come home with us. We need to get up out of here tonight."

She shook her head, but Reggie kept talking. "We can't stay in Oakland, shit is a mess, and we can't protect you. If we back in Los—"

"Why you do it, Reggie?" Her voice was dead, mechanical, like it had never been used.

Reggie was startled by her question, just as I was. "Flea, let's get the fuck out of here," he said.

She held the gun steady. Pain crept onto her face. "I loved him, Reggie."

"W-w-what you t-t-talking about?" Crim looked frantically from his sister to his brother.

"Tell him, Reggie. Tell him. I want to hear you say it out loud."

"Flea." Reggie looked around the room for help. There was none, just a collective silence. Slowly the meaning of the family drama registered with us all.

"Tell him, Reggie. Now."

"W-w-what she talking about, Reggie?" Crim was frantic. The truth hadn't registered with him yet. I was sick to my stomach. I knew in Fresno that Felicia was holding something back, and now it was clear.

"Who was with Smokey, Reggie, when he shot Billy? Who was with him?"

"Flea, you don't understand."

"What's to understand?" Tears rolled down her face. "I know I loved him."

Reggie's anger came to the surface in one quick flash. "He wadn't family. How you gonna choose him over me?"

Crim stood up while Reggie spoke. His mouth dropped open in disbelief.

"Why'd you do it, Reggie?" Felicia asked again.

" 'Cause. He was trying to push me out. I set that shit up with the Mexicans! I opened up L.A. to him, and then he tried to pull a move like I didn't matter. Who was he? Who the fuck was he to put me down like some bitch?"

"You blew that deal yourself, Reggie. Then you decided Billy had to die because you were a fuckup. Tell me why I'm suppose to choose you after that. Explain that to me."

" 'Cause we blood."

Felicia snorted. "What does that mean? Daddy didn't care about blood, so why should I? You didn't care about blood, so why should I? You put yourself over me when you killed him. All you had to lose was a business deal. Just business, Reggie, but you took everything from me like it wasn't nothing."

"Flea, man, you know I wouldn't do you like that, but he disrespected me. You know the rules. I can't let shit like that slide. He called the shot, and I played it out."

"Did you think about me when you killed him?" Felicia's shirt was wet with tears that ran freely.

Reggie couldn't answer, and it deflated her. The realization that the center of her world, her own peace of mind, meant nothing to her brother made her crumble in on herself.

Reggie raced on with his nowhere explanations. "I set that up! That money, that deal was mine, and this motherfucker comes from nowhere trying to call a shot. He acted like he didn't know who I was!"

"You ain't shit, Reggie." Her voice rose; then she took steady aim at her brother. Crim moved toward Reggie but stopped when he saw Felicia's eyes flick his way.

"What the fuck is wrong with you, Flea? How the fuck you gonna aim a gun at me!"

She pulled back the hammer as Reggie began to hop nervously from foot to foot. My heart was in my throat as I watched Felicia's revenge unfold. Somehow I'd known from the beginning that all debts owed by Felicia, and even myself, could only be paid with the blood of kin.

Reggie turned desperately to Crim.

"He can't help you. Look at me. Turn back and look at me," Felicia directed coldly.

Reggie seemed to shrink before the gun and his sister's withering anger. His mouth moved, soundless, as he gasped for words, air, or meaning. All three abandoned him.

"You killed him. You took him from me, Reggie." I saw a single tear slide down her cheek but she flicked it away with a quick whip of her head.

"You can't love a nigga that hard, Flea. Not over family."

"You killed him." Each letter in her sentence dragged the temperature down around us. There was no going back. Reggie knew he had finally met his fate. Bravado escaped him. While he bounced and looked desperately around for help, Felicia's anger crystalized into a hard tangible entity. Crim's silence was deafening as he watched his brother and sister.

"He wadn't yo' blood. We blood." He placed his hand where his heart should have been. "We blood, Flea." Felicia nodded once, to let him know she understood, and fired right through his hand, plastering it to his chest as he fell backward.

Crim rushed forward as Felicia fell to her knees. "F-f-f-felicia." Crim sounded desperate. Maybe he hadn't expected her to actually shoot Reggie.

I had.

"He took Billy from me. I had to, Crim. I had to."

She crawled over to Reggie and placed his head in her lap. His blood poured out onto her clothes as his eyes stared at nothing. "Oh, Reggie, Reggie." She cradled his head and rocked him.

Crim pulled Reggie's body away from her and held his brother in his arms. "You killed your brother, Flea, just like Daddy killed Mama. You just like Daddy, Flea. You just like Daddy." Crim said the words as if there was nothing worse in the world. Reggie's reign of terror, the devastation he brought to his sister's life and to his many victims, meant nothing in light of their father's crime.

He stood up and looked at her with horror. She reached out to him but he backed away. Felicia dripped with Reggie's blood while all of us stood around, silently.

"He killed Billy, Crim."

"That's your brother, Flea, that's your *brother*."

He continued backing up until he reached the hallway. I saw panic in her eyes. Since we'd left Fresno, revenge had flowed in her veins and kept her alive. I don't think she'd seen past the moment of Reggie's death. But, now, faced with the same exile her father knew, she looked desperate.

"Crim!"

He shook his head. "I'll keep your secret till I die, Flea, but we ain't family no more." I saw that his face was damp with tears. Tears for both his brother and his sister. "We cain't never be blood after this." He looked at Reggie. "That all ran out in the ground." His words flowed steady and clear.

"Don't leave me here. Where you going? Crim!" He turned on her and aimed his own gun at her face. She kept moving toward him anyway. Despite the evidence all around her, throughout her life, she didn't believe her brother would kill her.

I did.

"G-g-git back." He backed his way to the front door.

"Crim." She kept moving. "Crim, don't leave me here." Her wail split my heart in two.

"Get away from me, Felicia." He pulled back the hammer of his gun. A red dot danced on her forehead.

"Drop it, motherfucker, drop the gun." Clarence sounded nervous. He raised his own gun to center on Crim's forehead. The red of the lasers made a cross beam in the middle of the room.

Felicia continued to move toward Crim with her arms

outstretched. "You gonna kill me?" Tears streaked her face. "Do it. I'm ready to go."

"Felicia!" I called out again, but I couldn't penetrate the drama that coursed through the veins of brother and sister. "Flea, baby."

The sound of Reggie's name for her made her turn and smile at me. For just a second she was the old Flea, the one on campus, the one I loved. My heart knew in that second that if I didn't do something I would never see her again.

I stepped out, thinking I could save her, hoping for redemption. I was guilty too, and I was finally waking up to the fact. "Maceo," Holly hissed.

Crim kept his gun steady. I saw a second red dot, then a third and a fourth appear on his face. Behind me Holly, Clarence, and the Samoans had their guns trained on him.

"Felicia. Come on, baby." I reached for her, but she pulled away. "Let's get out of here. We have to get out of here."

"Crim, please."

He backed out of the door, we heard footsteps, then he was gone. Felicia dropped to the ground and howled in grief. She landed in a pool of blood and when she realized what she'd done she started to scream. She screamed in a way that made me realize that for all purposes she was dead now too.

"We got to get her out of here," I yelled.

Holly came up beside me as I lifted her up. I left the rest of them to deal with Reggie's and Smokey's bodies. I had to get Felicia away.

"Maceo," Holly called to me.

"I got to get her out of here."

Felicia was the only woman I would choose over him. We both knew that. I tried to ignore the guilt but it dogged me as I pulled her back through the wooded path. There wasn't a woman alive, not even Cissy, that Holly would put above me. The knowledge didn't make me feel like less of a man, it just clarified who I was.

We made it to the car just as Emmet and Malcolm's car sped off down the hill. They must have heard the gun-shots and made a choice. I hustled a dazed Felicia into the car and headed back into the flatlands.

We were back safely on 580, miles away from Smokey's house, when I heard her moan at my side. "Oh, Billy." The words were clear.

I wasn't sure she was coherent, but the sound of Billy's name brought him into the car. It also brought my shame along with him. I realized that I had chosen a woman over my best friend, the only brother I would ever have, and she made me understand with one word that I would never even be number two in her eyes. It was Billy, Billy, and then Billy again.

I kept driving. She had to understand, I told myself, that I loved her just as much as Billy ever had. I glanced in the rearview mirror, and for a second I swear I saw his face. He wore a look of pity, directed right at me. What does it take, his expression seemed to ask, to make you understand that even with me gone it will never be you?

CHAPTER

47

I had to wash away the blood.

That was my primary thought as I guided Felicia through the front door of the cottage. We made it inside without being noticed by anyone in the front house. Upstairs Felicia remained motionless, vacant, as I stripped the wet clothes from her body. I tried to still my thoughts as I cleaned her up. I had to remain focused and not let my mind wander to the divide I had crossed so easily in one night. I couldn't acknowledge it yet, not while she was still in my care. But it was there. There in my shallow breathing, the clammy sweat that covered my body.

I turned on the shower and pushed Felicia inside. The smell of iron was strong, the wet, rusty metallic scent that would blister in my nostrils for the rest of my life.

I tossed my clothes in the corner and climbed in under the spray of water. Felicia was slumped against the wall as far from the onslaught as she could manage. I reached out and grabbed my toothbrush from the sink. I ran the tip across a bar of soap and picked up her hand. I worked the bristles gently beneath her nails, scrubbing intently to wipe away all traces of her crimes. She collapsed against my body. I put my arms around her and remembered her saying that my arms never felt safe. I wanted to make up for that. I loved Felicia beyond reason so I held her there, under the steady stream of water, until we were both washed clean. We stayed that way until the water ran cold.

In my bedroom I pulled back the sheets and motioned for her to climb inside. Not until then, not until she moved her feet to climb inside, did I notice the anklet, my anklet that I'd given to Billy to return to her, dangling from her leg.

It broke my heart.

I'd bought it as a gift for her before I even asked her out. The second week of school, after sitting next to her only four times in class, hearing her laugh only once, I bought it. When she sat down next to me that first day and slipped the gum on my desk I knew. I knew the way

Daddy Al said he knew when he saw Gra'mère for the first time at a bus stop in Louisiana. I knew the way Midnight Blue did when he saw Desiree in that New Orleans alley. I knew the same way Felicia did when she saw Billy in Crowning Glory.

I knew so much that I ran out and spent a month's salary on jewelry that represented who I thought she was: a butterfly, something light and pretty, something that you could barely feel if you held it in your hand. That wasn't her at all. It was the way I might describe her love for me, but not who she was as a person. Felicia was pretty, there was no question about that, but there was nothing light about her. Despite her flirting and laughter there was a heaviness at her center, and it was the heaviness that bound us together. I recognized it; it felt familiar. We never shared it, but maybe for a while my presence allowed her to put hers aside. I wanted to believe that.

I watched her as she turned away to face the wall. After a while her shoulders rose and fell with her breathing, and I relaxed, relaxed enough to think past the moment I'd just reached.

In the bathroom I gathered up all the clothes and towels and anything else with traces of blood. Outside, I went around the main house to a brick barbecue pit Daddy Al built years ago. It had a chimney that stretched up and over the cottage. I threw all the items inside and doused them with lighter fluid. I struck a match and waited until the flames caught on my discarded jeans, crept to my rugby shirt, and spread to Felicia's clothes. I closed the door and watched the smoke snake up into the sky.

The sun was up but the streets were still quiet. The air was thick, indicating yet another scorcher of a day.

I went to the car, grabbed my duffel bag from the

trunk, and took Felicia's clothes from the backseat. My bare feet sank into the pebbles of the driveway as I made my way back to the house.

"Maceo." Daddy Al stepped onto the back porch of the main house. He wore his pajamas and looked every minute of his seventy-one years. "You're not in Louisiana." He said it as if he had never quite expected me to go there in the first place. He also didn't seem surprised to find me in my underwear with black smoke billowing from a rarely used barbecue. We both tried to ignore the smoke and the acrid smell that enveloped the backyard.

"No, sir. I'm not in Louisiana."

"That's your bag?"

"Yeah." I held up the duffel.

"Then you're not leaving today?" His voice cracked with unmistakable age. I shook my head, but he wouldn't accept that. "You lost your voice or something?"

"No."

"I asked you a question."

"No, I'm not leaving."

"I see."

"How's Cissy?"

"I don't see where that's your concern." His hands trembled. I could see how tightly he gripped the doorknob. "I didn't see a lot of things for a while, but it's clear now." He paused. "Well, you got one bag, you might as well go 'head and pack the rest."

Right then I heard Alixe's voice. She had told me I would lose more than her, and the warning had come true.

"This don't mean nothing but what it means, Maceo. I'm still your granddaddy. I'll never turn you away. I'll never stop loving you." He meant what he said, but it had been the first time since I was a little boy that he referred to himself as granddaddy and not father.

"I'll start packing up as soon as I can," I answered.

He nodded and turned to go back in the house. I understood his decision. I had made the choice for him when I crossed the line. My journey to this place was filled with zigzags as I danced around my destiny, crossed back and forth, from black to white, and finally gray. With each turn, with each choice, another part of me died and became harder. I was shocked by Billy's death, less so when I heard about Jorge and Sera's, numb when Reggie and Smokey died before my eyes, cold as granite when I held my own gun. A part of me was gone, had been gone for a long time, but it took the death of a friend and the disappearance of the woman I loved to understand that I'd only been fooling myself.

Maybe Holly had always known it was just a matter of time for me. Maybe Daddy Al knew it too. I was the only one who had ignored the obvious. Without an anchor, I was no different from any other boy seduced by the game. I had willingly stepped onto the dying ground.

Inside the house I dropped down beside Felicia to fall asleep. I didn't dream in colors or pictures, but as I drifted off I heard sound, bright vivid sound. I heard the wail of car horns from Billy's funeral, the anguish in Regina's voice as she sang, and the call of the wild: "Hustla down!" That marked the end of youth for me. I heard it all, but I saw not a single picture to go with it.

When I woke up the space beside me was empty. The sheets were cold and no longer held the promise of another body. I knew right then but I still hoped. I hadn't lost that. I hadn't lost the ability to hope in the face of the obvious.

The house was quiet, the sky outside the window pitch black, and she was gone. As I walked down the stairs into a dark living room, a familiar image projected onto the mirror across from the television. It was Reggie, on screen, leaning into Billy's casket.

I'd forgotten about the tape in my bag, but she had found it. It all came clear. Those were the sounds I had heard in my sleep: the replaying of Billy's funeral. I walked toward the TV to turn it off and saw Felicia's anklet hanging from the knob. As I pulled it off I knew with complete certainty that I would never see her again.

Not even in my dreams.

That was my sacrifice. That was the price Daddy Al spoke of, that Alixe warned me about, and it stung to my core. The rules of the game would forever divide us. The drug culture bred a dying ground that expected a sacrifice of whatever you held most sacred.

I had given in abundance.

But you know what killed me the most?

I knew at that moment, with all the ashes scattered around me, that I would do it again even if I reached the same destination each time. I would travel the same road a hundred times, because at the beginning of each journey I would have the hope that somehow, one way or another, it would turn out differently.

I could hope each time that she would be mine.

ACKNOWLEDGMENTS

I have many people to thank for their contributions to The Dying Ground; I never, not even for a second, believed this was a solo journey.

First and foremost my four pillars of strength, The Tramble Women, Judy, Nichole, Michelle, my mother—it's so easy to battle the winds of life, but given the chances that I do, with your love as my shield, I have been truly blessed by each and every one of you.

Daniele Spellman and my six-month tenure at Spellman Artists Colony—complete with meals and generosity of spirit. That is a gift I can never repay.

Charles A. Murray, founding member of the BKH social club; your inspiration could never be measured.

ACKNOWLEDGMENTS

I have many people to thank for their contributions to *The Dying Ground*. I never, not even for a second, believed this was a solo journey.

First and foremost, my four pillars of strength, the Tramble Women: Judy, Nicole, Nichelin, and Nichelia. It's so easy to battle the winds of life, and take the chances that I do, with your love as my shield. I have been truly blessed by each and every one of you.

Daniele Spellman and my six-month tenure at Spellman Artists Colony—complete with meals and generosity of spirit. That is a gift I can never repay.

My agent at ICM, Richard Abate, to whom I am forever thankful for his enthusiasm, honesty, advice, and dedication. Richard, your input was an integral part of this process.

My editor at Villard Books, Melody Guy. Melody, what a bonus you are. I thank you for making the transition as smooth as possible.

Charles A. Murray, founding member of the IHOP social club; your inspiration could never be measured.

Jonathan Mosley, the closest thing to a brother I've ever had. Lets face it, we are bona fide family now and I couldn't love you more.

Barbara Skelton, for creating such a loving environment, then allowing me to call it home. Kobe and I thank you from the bottom of our hearts.

The girlfriends, my beautiful and colorful tribe of Warrior Women, sassy and true to the core: Dioni Perez, Angela Scott, Lori Buster, Stacy Green, Christine Marino, Julie Larson. I adore each of you without restraint. It's just not possible to have better friends.

Nolan Coleman, Sr., my sweet granddaddy, and the real life inspiration for Daddy Al—I love you. Eliza Willie White Coleman, who still cheers me on the loudest—I can hear you. And my beautiful grandmother, Versie, who gives meaning to quiet grace—you're my heart.

Malcolm Spellman, your life and love are all over these pages. I've lost the key that unlocks the two of us.

The following contributed in unmeasured ways to this book: Keith Adkins, Manie Barron, Karen Rupert, Eve LaDue, Valerie Joyner, James M. Marshall, Tamar Love, Chastity Whitaker, Maurice Newburn, the staff of the Albany Library, Tessa Loehwing, Marjorie Weingrow, Anne Healy, Dave Miller, Anita and Jorge Otano, Peter Fredman, Peter Crooks, Grace Lee, Jim Kravitz, Beth Waldman, Lisa Lamoureaux, Anne Reid, Emy Mendoza, Kathleen Dodge, Megan Gaynor, and Kobe, my funny little muse. Thank you all.

Lastly, I am grateful to all my angels, whether they are known to me or not.

Nichelle D. Tramble
New York, New York

A SPECIAL NOTE FROM
THE AUTHOR, NICHELLE D. TRAMBLE

I've always been curious about the roads people take to adulthood. What does it take to get them there? What do they sacrifice along the way? What do they gain? These were all questions I tried to answer when writing *The Dying Ground*. I allowed my main character, Maceo Redfield, to pause at the lines of demarcation, to ponder the result, but still continue to go further and further away from his own center of gravity.

What was a challenge to me as a writer was first trying to understand how a person could willingly travel into a world of crime. The second challenge was to keep Maceo a sympathetic character while he made that journey. I didn't want to write about the traditional bad guy with a hard-knock life. I wasn't interested at all in writing a character who was forced into a life of crime by circumstance. My goal was to present a young man with a background most people would envy. His family, the Redfields, are almost too good to be true, but that's still not enough. Neither is his enrollment at a prestigious university, or his incredible athletic talent. All that pales considerably to the seductive world of drug dealers, and Oakland's dope game in the late eighties, and that was an interesting dilemma for me.

I read something by Grace Paley once in which she urged writers to "write what they don't know about what they know." That was just the most amazing, straightforward advice I ever heard, and that's what I've tried to do here. There was so much I didn't know about the history of Oakland, the drug culture, and the male point of view, but I tried to infuse it with enough of my own knowledge to make it believable and real.

The sky above the Bay Bridge was a gunmetal gray, and in the distance I could hear the low rumble of freight trains that ran along the Eastshore Highway. I loved the sound, and hadn't realized how much I missed it until it echoed down the early morning streets. The wheels on the tracks, the whistle of the train, the foghorns on the Bay were all part of the soundtrack of my life in Oakland; sounds, like smells, that gave me definition.

It wasn't just the streets and people that claimed me, but the city itself. As I took it all in I realized just how much I was stamped by the place that I'd fled after Billy's murder in 1989. I was only hours back—a newborn—having rolled in with the mist off the Bay, quiet, and under the cover of night. I hadn't planned to come back, but an ominous phone call triggered my speedy return. During my travels I found that the open road suited me so I stayed away as long as I could. I grew accustomed to living a nomad's existence, and I found kinship rather than family with men and women who were not at all interested in who I claimed to be.

I liked being a person without a name; I relished the

blank looks I got when I introduced myself as Maceo Albert Bouchaund Redfield. At home any one of those names would have elicited some sort of response, but on the road it hadn't meant shit. Not a single thing. So I convinced myself that the disinterest translated into freedom.

The delusion worked until a single phone call from my aunt Cissy shattered the fragile sense of peace I'd built for myself. The plea on the other end of the phone line was riddled with urgency—*Holly's in trouble, Maceo*—and it meant my days of wandering were done.

It was time to make amends.

After two years of drifting I finally knew there was only one place that could offer me a shot at peace, and that was my hometown. The city was my crossroads, the crooked man with the slanted grin, my temptation, and I wanted to beat it. I wanted to win, and yet I still had expectations, because when the Oakland skyline came into focus, a part of me expected to see grave dust hanging above the city, or a mourner's shroud of black clouds, to acknowledge all that had been lost with Billy's death.

Yet the world hadn't stopped, neither had I, and I'd learned the truest, if not the hardest, lesson of my friend's murder.

Life goes on.

The wind was high as the sun broke over the bay, bending trees and fences and moving the chilly fog of early January out into the Bay. Nature had conspired to give her wayward son a fitting welcome-home party, and the theatrics matched my dark mood.

Looking for a reprieve I turned up the heater in my car, then scanned the boulevard until my eyes landed on a Flight Athletic billboard towering over the intersection. During my travels from South Texas through New Mexico and finally California, my way had been shadowed by billboards that featured Cotton, and now a new one loomed above me, barely visible in the mist that blanketed San Pablo Avenue. It featured a bare-chested Cotton, hawking his gray-and-white basketball shoes with his full name—Cornelius Knox—written above his head. His matching Anaheim Vanguards shorts were pulled down low enough to reveal the elastic band of his underwear and the stitching that read: LET ME FLY. The shoes were christened Fort Knox in his honor, with the famous taglines GUARD 'EM WITH YOUR LIFE and WORTH THEIR WEIGHT IN GOLD scattered along the edge.

He looked like a king, and I wasn't the only one who thought so. In pure Oakland style, a fan had climbed the scaffolding to add what they thought was missing from the picture. The tagger had used black spray paint to draw a crown above Cotton's head, then red to give him a long, flowing robe. Beneath the additions in bold, block letters the piece was finished with the rallying cry from *Scarface*: THE WORLD IS MINE.

I had to smile. It made me proud. I understood the fan worship and I knew where it came from. Cotton was a warrior-king to the brigade of lost boys who littered the Oakland streets. The raw aggression he used on the court was an emotion they recognized, and they loved him for that. Loved him because he hadn't been spit-shined into respectability or polished to the point of forgetting who he was, and more important, forgetting who they were.

The friends of his youth remained his friends, and Vanguard games were often filled with guests of the superstar who had rap sheets longer than his stats for college and pro combined. He'd said more than once that he didn't consider the other players to be a part of his family. His teammates were coworkers. The only family he had was in Oakland.

The management's frustration with Cotton's stance

was obvious in their vaguely coded public comments about "synergy" and "team dynamics," but they couldn't fault his play. He might not smile and clown for the camera or refer to his coach as a "second father," but he delivered on the court by averaging twenty-nine points a game and making the All-Star team three years in a row. At the end of the day it didn't matter that he was quick with his fists or barely contained his contempt for authority, because he filled seats, which filled the pockets of the people in the front office. The phrase role model was never used to describe him, but he was featured in three different commercials promoting a soft drink, his athletic shoes, and a sporting-goods chain.

I was proud of Cotton's triumphs, and I cheered his success from the sidelines, but I also knew that the campaign was a façade, and now, because of recent events, so did the rest of the world. While the advertisement celebrated all that was golden in the ballplayer's life, the discarded USA Today on my car seat exposed the darker side to his tale. The newspaper also filled in the details Cissy left out, and more simply, it clarified the reasons for my return.

Shooting Guard Questioned in Murder Investigation

San Francisco (AP)—Jan. 14, 1992—A woman was found bludgeoned to death in a San Francisco hotel room registered to Anaheim Vanguard star Cornelius "Cotton" Knox. The former Oakland resident missed Tuesday's game against the Sacramento Kings in Anaheim after he was detained by the San Francisco District Attorney's Office for questioning. Police are seeking information about an unidentified man seen fleeing the hotel room on the night of the murder.

Cotton.

A dead body.

An unidentified man.

The words flashed at me like Morse code.

Since the first year Cotton had entered the league, he'd spent every NBA All-Pro weekend with his boys from Oakland, a gangsta's ball in whichever city hosted the game; Houston, Philly, Denver, and finally Oakland in 1992. Sometimes his guest list for the All-Pro included as many as twenty people, expanding and deflating from year to year to allow for arrests, marriages, illnesses, and murders. But no matter how many people came and went, there was always one name that never changed.

Holly.